Praise for *Biggest Flirts*,
the first book in the Superlatives trilogy

"Teen romance fans on the hunt
for a flirty fix will find plenty to enjoy
in this sexy, fun beach read."
—*Kirkus Reviews*

"Entertaining and engaging."
—*School Library Journal*

Also by Jennifer Echols

the superlatives

most likely to Succeed

JENNIFER ECHOLS

Simon Pulse

New York   London   Toronto   Sydney   New Delhi

SIMON PULSE
An imprint of Simon & Schuster Children's Publishing Division
1230 Avenue of the Americas, New York, NY 10020
This Simon Pulse edition August 2015
Text copyright © 2015 by Jennifer Echols
Cover photographs copyright © 2014 (back) and 2015 (front and spine) by Michael Frost
All rights reserved, including the right of reproduction
in whole or in part in any form.
SIMON PULSE and colophon are registered trademarks of Simon & Schuster, Inc.
For information about special discounts for bulk purchases, please contact
Simon & Schuster Special Sales at 1-866-506-1949 or business@simonandschuster.com.
The Simon & Schuster Speakers Bureau can bring authors to your live event. For more information
or to book an event contact the Simon & Schuster Speakers Bureau at 1-866-248-3049
or visit our website at www.simonspeakers.com.
Cover design by Regina Flath
Interior design by Mike Rosamilia
The text of this book was set in Adobe Caslon Pro.
Manufactured in the United States of America
2 4 6 8 10 9 7 5 3 1
The Library of Congress has cataloged the paperback edition as follows:
Echols, Jennifer.
Most likely to succeed / by Jennifer Echols. — First Simon Pulse paperback edition.
p. cm. — (The Superlatives)
[1. Dating (Social customs)—Fiction. 2. Love—Fiction. 3. High schools—Fiction.
4. Schools—Fiction.] I. Title.
PZ7.E1967Mo 2015
[Fic]—dc23
2014029505
ISBN 978-1-4424-7452-9 (hc)
ISBN 978-1-4424-7451-2 (pbk)
ISBN 978-1-4424-7453-6 (eBook)

For readers of
Biggest Flirts *and* Perfect Couple
who told me you couldn't wait for
Kaye and Sawyer's book. I appreciate you.

1

I LEFT CALCULUS A MINUTE BEFORE THE BELL so I'd be the first to arrive at the student council meeting. Our advisor, Ms. Yates, would sit at the back of the classroom, observing, and I wanted her vacated desk at the front of the room. At our last meeting, Aidan had taken her desk in a show of presidential authority. But as vice president, I was the one who needed room for paperwork. A better boyfriend than Aidan would have let me sit at the desk.

A better girlfriend than me would have let *him* have it.

And that pretty much summed up our three years of dating.

The bell rang just as I reached the room. I stood outside the door, waiting for Ms. Yates to make her coffee run to the teachers' lounge and for her freshman science class to flood past me. A few of them glanced at me, their eyes widening as if I were a celebrity. I remembered this feeling from when I was an underclassman, looking up to my brother and his friends. It was strange to be on the receiving end.

As the last of the ninth graders escaped down the hall, I stepped into the room, which should have been empty.

Instead, Sawyer De Luca sat behind Ms. Yates's desk. He must have left his last class *two* minutes before the bell to beat me here.

Sensing my presence, he turned in the chair, flashing deep blue eyes at me, the color of the September sky out the window behind him. When Sawyer's hair was combed—which I'd seen happen once or twice in the couple of years I'd known him—it looked platinum blond. Today, as usual, it was a mess, with the nearly white, sun-streaked layers sticking up on top, and the dark blond layers peeking out underneath. He had on his favorite shirt, which he wore at least two times a week, the madras short-sleeved button-down with blue stripes that made his eyes stand out even more. His khaki shorts were rumpled. I couldn't see his feet beneath the desk, but I knew he wore his beat-up flip-flops. In short, if you'd never met Sawyer before, you'd assume he was a hot but harmless teenage beach bum.

I knew better.

I closed the door behind me so nobody would witness

the argument we were about to have. I wanted that desk. I suspected he understood this, which was why he'd sat there. But long experience with Sawyer told me flouncing in and complaining wouldn't do me any good. That's what he expected me to do.

So I walked in with a bigger grin on my face than I'd ever given Sawyer. "Hi!"

He smiled serenely back at me. "Hello, Kaye. You look beautiful in yellow."

His sweet remark shot me through the heart. My friend Harper had just altered this dress to fit me. I didn't need her beautifully homemade hand-me-downs, but I was glad to take them—especially this sixties A-line throwback as vivid as the Florida sunshine. After a rocky couple of weeks for romance with Aidan, I'd dressed carefully this morning, craving praise from him. *He* hadn't said a word.

Leave it to Sawyer to catch me off guard. He'd done the same thing last Saturday night. After two years of teasing and taunting me, out of the blue he'd told me he loved my new hairstyle. I always had a ready response for his insults, but these compliments threw me off.

"Thanks," I managed, setting my books down on the edge of the desk, along with my tablet and my loose-leaf binder for student council projects. Then I said brightly, "So,

Mr. Parliamentarian, what's *modus operandi* for letting the vice president have the desk? I need to spread out."

"*I* need to spread out." He patted the stack of library books in front of him: an ancient tome that explained procedure for meetings, called *Robert's Rules of Order*, plus a couple of modern discussions of how the rules worked. For once Sawyer had done his homework.

"Taking the parliamentarian job seriously, are we?" This was my fourth year in student council. We'd always elected a parliamentarian without fully understanding what the title meant. Ms. Yates said the parliamentarian was the rule police, but we'd never needed policing with a charismatic president at the helm and Ms. Yates lurking in the back. Nobody ran for parliamentarian during officer elections in the spring. Ms. Yates waited until school started in the fall, then pointed out that "student council parliamentarian" would look great on college applications. One study hall representative volunteered, got approved, and never lifted a finger during meetings.

Until now. "I have to be able to see everything and look stuff up quickly." Sawyer swept his hand across his books and a legal pad inscribed with tiny cryptic notes. "Last meeting, Aidan didn't follow parliamentary procedure at *all*. But I'll share the desk with you." He stood and headed for the back of the room, where a cart was stacked with extra folding chairs for the meeting.

Normally I would have told him not to bother retrieving a chair for me. His suggestion that we share a desk was the best way to make me drop the subject and sit down elsewhere. He knew I wouldn't want Aidan to think we were flirting.

But this week wasn't normal. Aidan had hurt my feelings last Saturday by dissing my hair. We'd made up by Sunday—at least, I'd told him I forgave him—but I wasn't quite over the insult. The idea of him walking into the room and seeing Sawyer and me at Ms. Yates's desk together was incredibly appealing.

Sawyer held the folding chair high above his head as he made his way toward me. He unfolded the chair behind the desk. I started to sit down in it.

"No, that's for me. I meant for you to have the comfy chair." He rolled Ms. Yates's chair over, waited for me to sit, and pushed me a few inches toward the desk, like my dad seating my mother in a restaurant. He plopped down in the folding chair. "Will you marry me?"

Now *this* was something I'd expected him to ask. In fact, it was the first thing he'd ever said to me when he moved to town two years ago. Back then I'd uttered an outraged "No!"

He'd wanted to know why—he wasn't good enough for me? Who did I think I was, a bank president's daughter?

After a while, though, I'd gotten wise to Sawyer's game. Every girl in school knew he wasn't exclusive and meant nothing by his flirtations. That didn't stop any of us from having a soft spot for this hard-living boy. And it didn't stop me from feeling special every time he paid me attention.

Something had changed this school year when he started practicing with us cheerleaders in his pelican costume as school mascot. He stood right behind me on the football field, imitating my every step, even after I whirled around and slapped him on his foam beak. When we danced the Wobble, he moved the wrong way on purpose, running into me. With no warning he often rushed up, lifted me high, and gave me full-body, full-feathered hugs. Because he was in costume, everybody, including Aidan, knew it was a joke.

Only I took it seriously. I enjoyed it too much and wished he'd do the same things to me with the costume off.

My crush on him was hopeless. He was toying with me, like he toyed with everyone. Plus, I was committed to Aidan. Lately this was hard to remember.

"Yes, of course I'll marry you," I told Sawyer, making sure I sounded sarcastic.

The door opened, letting in the noise from the hall. "Hey," Will said, lilting that one syllable in his Minnesota accent. Lucky for him, derision about the way he talked had waned over the first five weeks of school. He'd started dating my friend Tia, who gave people the stink eye when they bad-mouthed him. And he'd made friends with Sawyer—a smart move on Will's part. Sawyer could be a strong ally or a powerful enemy.

Sawyer waited for a couple more classroom representatives to follow Will toward the back of the room. Then he turned to me again. "Would you go to the prom with me?"

"Yes." This was the game. He asked me a series of questions, starting with the outlandish ones. I said yes to those. Eventually he asked me something that wasn't as crazy, forcing me to give him the obvious answer: I had a boyfriend.

Here it came. "Will you sit with me in the van to the game tonight?"

A spark of excitement shot through me. A few weeks ago, Sawyer had passed out from the heat on the football field in his heavy mascot costume. Ever since, he'd ditched the suit during cheerleading practice and worked out with the football team instead, claiming he needed to get in better shape to withstand entire games dressed up as a pelican.

I missed him at cheerleading. I'd assumed he would ride with the football players to our first away game, but I wished he would ride in the cheerleader van. Now my wish was coming true.

Careful not to sound too eager, I said, "I didn't know you were riding with us. You've been more football player than cheerleader lately."

"I'm a pelican without a country," he said. "Some unfortunate things may have gotten superglued to other things in the locker room after football practice yesterday. The guys went to the coach and said they don't want me to ride on the bus with them because they're scared of what I'll do. The coach *agreed*. Can you believe that? I'm not even innocent until proven guilty."

"*Are* you guilty?" Knowing Sawyer, I didn't blame the team for accusing him.

"Yes," he admitted, "but they didn't know that for sure." He settled his elbow on the desk and his chin in his hand, watching me. "You, on the other hand, understand I never mean any harm. You'll sit with me in the van, right?"

I wanted to. My face burned with desire—desire for a *seat*, of all things. Next to a boy who was nothing but trouble.

And I knew my line. "We can't sit together, Sawyer. Aidan wouldn't like it."

Sawyer's usual response would be to imitate me in a sneering voice: *Aidan wouldn't like it!*

Instead, he grabbed Ms. Yates's chair and rolled me closer to him. Keeping his hands very near my bare knees, he looked straight into my eyes and asked softly, "Why do you stay with Aidan when he bosses you around? You don't let anyone else do that."

Tia and my friend Harper grilled me at every opportunity about why I stayed with Aidan, too, but they didn't bring up the subject while representatives for the entire school could hear. My eyes flicked over to the student council members, who were filling the desks and noisily dragging extra chairs off the cart, and Ms. Yates, who was making her way toward the back of the room with her coffee. Aidan himself would be here any second.

I told Sawyer quietly but firmly, "*You* would boss me around just as much as Aidan does. What's the difference?"

"That's not true." Sawyer moved even closer. I watched his lips as he said, "I wouldn't ask for much. What I wanted, you would give me willingly."

Time stopped. The bustle around us went silent. The classroom disappeared. All that was left was Sawyer's mouth forming words that weren't *necessarily* dirty, yet promised a dark night alone in the cab of his truck. My face flushed hot, my breasts tightened underneath my cute yellow bodice, and electricity shot straight to my crotch.

The many nights I'd pulled Tia away from Sawyer at parties over the past two years, she'd drunkenly explained that he had a way of talking her panties off. I'd heard this from other girls too. And he'd flirted with me millions of times, making me feel special, but never quite *this* special. Now I understood what Tia and those other girls had meant.

Abruptly, I sat up and rolled my chair back.

He straightened more slowly, smirking. He knew exactly what effect he'd had on me.

Bewildered, I breathed, "How did you do that?"

"It's a gift."

His cavalier tone ticked me off, and I regained my own voice. "That's what I would worry about. During study hall, you give me the 'gift'"—I made finger quotes—"but you've moved on to the next girl by lunch. No thanks."

His face fell. "No, I—"

Aidan sashayed in, greeting the crowd as he came, already starting the meeting.

Sawyer lowered his voice but kept whispering to me as

if nothing else were going on and Aidan weren't there. He said, "I wouldn't do that to you. I wouldn't cheat on you, ever."

Aidan turned around in front of the desk and gave us an outraged look for talking while he was making a speech. Sawyer didn't see it, but I did. I faced forward and opened my student council binder, cheeks still burning.

Sawyer had complimented me, part of a strange new trend.

He'd dropped the playful teasing and blatantly come on to me, a brand-new pleasure.

And he'd gotten upset at my tart response, like he actually cared.

I leaned ever so slightly toward him to give the electricity an easier time jumping the arc from my shoulder to his. His face was tinged pink, unusual for Sawyer, who was difficult to embarrass. I was dying to know whether he felt the buzz too.

Apparently not. I jumped in my chair, startled, as he banged the gavel on the block that Ms. Yates had placed on her desk for Aidan. "Point of order, Mr. President," Sawyer said. "Have you officially started the meeting? You haven't asked the secretary to read the minutes."

"We don't have time," Aidan said. Dismissing Sawyer,

he turned back to the forty representatives crowding the room. He hadn't argued with us about who got Ms. Yates's desk, after all. He didn't need to. Instead of presiding over the council from here, he simply reasserted his authority by running the meeting while standing up. Sawyer and I looked like his secretarial pool.

"We have a lot to cover," Aidan explained to the reps, and I got lost in following him with my eyes and listening to him, fascinated as ever. About this time of year in ninth grade, he'd captured my attention. Previously he'd been just another dork I'd known since kindergarten. I'd preferred older guys, even if they didn't prefer *me*.

But that year, Aidan had come back from summer break taller than before, and more self-assured than any other boy I knew. That's why I'd fallen for him. Confidence was sexy. That's also why, until recently, I'd felt a rush of familiarity and belonging and pride whenever I glimpsed him across a room.

After years with him, however, I was finally coming to understand he wasn't as sure of himself as he wanted people to believe. He was so quick to anger. He couldn't take being challenged. But as I watched him work the room like a pro, with the freshman reps timidly returning his broad smile, I remembered exactly what I'd seen in him back then.

Sawyer looked bored already.

"We're entering the busiest season for the council," Aidan was saying, "and we desperately need volunteers to make these projects happen. Our vice president, Ms. Gordon, will now report on the homecoming court elections coming up a week from Monday, and the float for the court in the homecoming parade."

"And the dance," I called.

"There's not going to be a homecoming dance," he told me over his shoulder. "I'll explain later. Go ahead and fill them in about the homecoming court—"

Several reps gasped, "What?" while others murmured, "What did he say?" I spoke for everyone by uttering an outraged "What do you mean, there's not going to be a dance?"

"Ms. Yates"—he nodded to where she sat in the back of the room, and she nodded in turn—"informed me before the meeting that the school is closing the gym for repairs. The storm last week damaged the roof. It's not safe for occupancy. That's bad news for us, but of course it's even worse news for the basketball teams. The school needs time to repair the gym before their season starts."

Will raised his hand.

Ignoring Will, Aidan kept talking. "All of us need to get

out there in the halls and reassure the basketball teams and their fans that our school is behind them."

I frowned at the back of Aidan's head. He used this bait-and-switch method all the time, getting out of a sticky argument by distracting people (including me) with a different argument altogether. Basketball season was six weeks away. The homecoming dance didn't have to die so easily. But hosting the event would be harder now, and Aidan didn't want to bother.

I did.

"Help," I pleaded with Sawyer under my breath.

Aidan had already moved on, introducing my talk about the election committee.

Out in the crowd Will called, "Excuse me." An interruption like this hadn't happened in any council meeting I'd attended, ever. "Wait a minute. My class wants the dance."

I couldn't see Aidan's face from this angle, but he drew his shoulders back and stood up straighter. He was about to give Will a snarky put-down.

Sawyer watched me, blond brows knitted. He didn't understand what I wanted.

"Complain about something in the book again," I whispered, nodding at *Robert's Rules of Order*. "Ms. Yates hasn't stopped Aidan from railroading the meeting. She obviously doesn't want the dance either, but they can't fight the book."

Everyone jumped as Sawyer banged the gavel. "The council recognizes Mr. Matthews, senior from Mr. Frank's class. Stand up, sir."

We'd never had reps rise to speak before. I was pretty sure the rules of order didn't say anything about this. But it was a good move on Sawyer's part. At Will's full height he had a few inches on Aidan, and when he crossed his muscular arms on his chest, his body practically shouted that nobody better try to budge him.

Before Aidan could protest, Will said in his strangely rounded accent, "I haven't lived here long, but I get the impression that the homecoming dance is a huge deal at this school. Everyone in Mr. Frank's class has been talking about it and looking forward to it. We can't simply cancel at the first sign of trouble."

"We just did," Aidan snapped. "Now sit down while I'm talking."

Sawyer banged the gavel. I should have gotten used to it by now, but I jumped in my seat again.

Aidan visibly flinched. He turned on Sawyer and snatched the gavel away. Holding it up, he seethed, "Don't do that again, De Luca. You're not in charge here. I'm the president."

"Then act like it," I said.

Aidan turned his angry gaze on me. I stared right back at him, determined not to chicken out. Will and Sawyer and I were right about this. Aidan was wrong.

As I watched, Aidan's expression changed from fury to something different: disappointment. I'd betrayed him. We'd had a long talk last week about why we couldn't get along lately. He understood I disagreed with him sometimes, but he wanted us to settle our differences in private, presenting a united front to the school as the president and his vice president.

Now I'd broken his rule. No matter what the council decided, he wouldn't forgive me for defying him in public.

And I didn't care. Keeping the peace wasn't worth letting him act like a dictator.

"We don't have *time* to debate this in a half-hour meeting," he repeated. "There's nothing to debate. The decision has been made. The school already canceled the dance because we don't have a location for it."

"We'll move it," I said.

"It's only two weeks away," he said.

I shrugged. "You put me in charge of the dance committee. It's our job to give it a shot."

Aidan's voice rose. He'd forgotten we'd agreed not to argue in public. "You're only pitching a fit about this because you're still mad about—"

"Give me that," Sawyer interrupted, holding out his hand for the gavel.

"No," Aidan said, moving the gavel above his head.

"Mr. President," Sawyer said in a lower, reasonable tone, like talking to a hysterical child, "you're not allowed to debate the issue."

"Of course I am. I'm the president!"

"Exactly. *Robert's Rules of Order* states that your responsibilities are to run the meeting and give everyone the opportunity to speak. If you want to express your opinion, you need to vacate the chair."

"I'm not *in* the chair," Aidan snapped. "*You're* in the chair."

"I mean," Sawyer said, rolling his eyes, "you need to step down as president while we discuss this matter, and let Kaye preside over the meeting."

"I'm not stepping down."

"Then you need to shut up."

"Sawyer," Ms. Yates said sharply. I couldn't see her behind Will, who was still standing, but her thin voice cut like a knife through the grumbling and shushing in the classroom. "You're being disruptive."

"On the contrary, Ms. Yates," Sawyer called back, "the president is being disruptive, trying to bend the entire council to his will. Ms. Patel's study hall elected me to represent them. The student council approved me as parliamentarian. It's my duty to make sure we follow the procedure set down in the council bylaws. Otherwise, a student could sue the school for a violation of rights and due process."

The room fell silent, waiting for Ms. Yates's response. Horrible visions flashed through my mind of what would happen next. Ms. Yates might complain to Ms. Chen that Sawyer was disrespectful. They could remove him from student council or, worse, from his position as school mascot. All because he'd helped me when I asked.

Underneath the desk, I put my hand on his knee.

"Sawyer," Ms. Yates finally said, "you may continue, but don't tell anybody else to shut up."

"So noted." Sawyer pretended to scribble this reminder to himself. Actually he drew a smiley face in *Robert's Rules of Order*. "Aidan, if you're really running the meeting, let Will bring up the idea of saving the dance, then put it to a vote."

Aidan glared at Sawyer. Suddenly he whacked the

gavel so hard on the block on Ms. Yates's desk that even Sawyer jumped.

Sawyer didn't take that kind of challenge sitting down. I gripped his knee harder, signaling him to stay in his seat. If he could swallow this last insult from Aidan, he and I had won.

2

THE REMAINING TWENTY MINUTES OF THE meeting seemed to take forever. But Aidan followed procedure— at least I figured he did, because Sawyer didn't speak up again. By the time the bell rang to send us to lunch, the council had agreed that as head of the dance committee, I would now be in charge of relocating the event instead of canceling it.

On top of leading the committee in charge of homecoming court elections.

And leading the committee in charge of the parade float. I didn't understand why Aidan opposed the council taking on more projects when he simply passed all the work to me.

As everyone crowded Ms. Yates's door, Sawyer stood and stretched. Then he leaned over and said in my ear, "We make a good team. Maybe you and I got off on the wrong foot."

"For two years?" I asked.

He opened his mouth to respond but stopped. Aidan brushed past the desk on his way out the door. He didn't say a word to me.

Will was the last rep remaining in the empty room. He paused in front of the desk. "Thanks, you guys, for taking my side."

"Thanks for taking ours," I said, standing up and gathering my stuff, which was tangled with Sawyer's stuff. One side of my open binder had gotten caught beneath his books.

"For me, this wasn't just about the dance," Will said. "People have been talking about it, and Tia told me what fun it was last year. Of course . . ." He glanced sidelong at Sawyer.

I knew what that look meant. Sawyer and Tia used to fool around periodically, up until she and Will started dating a few weeks ago. The homecoming dance last year had been no different. Too late, Will realized what he'd brought up.

"It *was* fun," I interjected before Sawyer could make a snide comment that everyone would regret. "Come on." I ushered them both toward the door.

"I was student council president back in Duluth." Will followed us into the hall and closed Ms. Yates's door behind us. Down at the end of the freshman corridor, a teacher frowned at us. Will lowered his voice as he said, "That is,

I was *supposed* to be president this year, before my family moved. I know what the president is supposed to do, and Aidan's not *doon* it. Sometimes you have to stand up and tell somebody, 'You're not *doon* it right.'"

I thought Sawyer would make fun of Will's Norse *doon*. He might have stopped insulting Will behind his back, but he wouldn't be able to resist a comment to his face. Yet he didn't say a word about Will's accent.

Instead, Sawyer grumbled, "If the storm had destroyed the gym completely, the business community would rally around us, give us money, and solve the problem for us. They'd get lots of publicity for hosting our homecoming dance. Nobody's going to help us just because our roof leaks."

"Leaking isn't good PR," Will agreed. "I signed up for the dance committee and I want to help, but I'm the worst person to think of ideas for where else to hold an event. I still don't know this town very well."

"Doesn't the Crab Lab also own the event space down the block?" I asked Sawyer. "One of my mother's assistants had her wedding reception there. Could you sweet-talk the owner into letting us use it for cheap? Better yet, for free?"

"It's booked that night," he said.

"That's two weeks from now," I pointed out. "You've memorized the schedule for the event space down the block?"

"A fortieth class reunion is meeting there after the homecoming game," he said. "The owner asked me to wait tables. I said no because of the dance. I have an excellent memory for turning down money."

Sawyer waited tables a lot. While a good portion of our class was at the beach, he often went missing because he was working. Even though he'd helped me in the meeting, I was a little surprised the dance was important enough to him personally that he would take the night off.

And, irrationally, I was jealous. As we stopped in the hall and waited for Will to swing open the door of the lunchroom, I asked Sawyer, "Who are you taking to homecoming?"

He gaped at me. "You!" he exclaimed, like this was the most obvious answer in the world and I had a lot of nerve to joke about it. He stomped into the lunchroom.

Will was left holding the door open for me and blinking at us. He didn't understand the strange social customs of Florida.

"It would help if you could brainstorm over the weekend," I told Will, pretending my episode with Sawyer hadn't happened. "Ask around at lunch and on the band bus tonight. See if you can scare up ideas. Maybe we'll think of something by the next meeting."

"Sounds good," he called after me as I headed across the lunchroom to the teacher section.

Aidan, Ms. Yates, and I had eaten at one end of a faculty table after the last council meeting, discussing projects like the dance. Possibly the one thing worse than spending lunch with Aidan while he was mad at me was spending lunch with Aidan and Ms. Yates, who, judging from the expression on her face, hadn't liked how the meeting had gone down. But I was the vice president, so I straightened my shoulders and walked over.

They were deep in conversation. Trying not to interrupt them, I looped the strap of my book bag over the back of the chair beside Aidan. They both looked up anyway. I said, "Sorry. I didn't know we were meeting, or I would have gotten here sooner. I'll just grab a salad and be right with y—"

Ms. Yates interrupted me. "This is a private talk."

"Oh" was all I could think of to say. My face tingled with embarrassment as I slipped my bag off the chair and beat a retreat across the lunchroom to the safety of Tia, Harper, and the rest of my friends. By the time I finally sat down with my salad, they were spitting out and shooting down ideas for where to have the dance—led by Will, who repeated how angry he was at Aidan for what he'd been *doon* in the meeting.

I listened and waited for them to come up with something brilliant. For once I stayed silent. I still smarted from Ms. Yates telling me I didn't belong at the adult table anymore. And I wondered whether I deserved it. Lately I got so *furious* at Aidan, but I was probably going through an immature phase, like cold feet before a wedding. We'd known almost since we started dating that we were destined for each other. All summer we'd been planning to apply to Columbia University together. Whenever Aidan annoyed me, I needed to take a deep breath before I spoke—as my mother reminded me each time I mouthed off to her—and make sure the problem was really with him, not me.

And I knew in my heart that the problem was mine. Since the school year started, I'd been creeping toward a crush on Sawyer like peering cautiously down from a great height. The Superlatives mix-up had put me over the edge.

On the first day of school, the student council had run Superlatives elections for the senior class. We *thought* Harper and our school's star quarterback, Brody, had been voted Perfect Couple That Never Was. If I'd been in charge of the elections, as in years past, that mistake wouldn't have been made. Even though I was still the chair of the elections committee, Ms. Yates wouldn't let me count the votes. Since I was a senior this year, I had a conflict of interest.

But without me to watch over them, the wayward juniors had screwed up the whole election. They said I'd been chosen Most Likely to Succeed with Aidan. That sounded right. He was president. I was vice president.

Here's what didn't make sense: In reality I'd been elected Perfect Couple That Never Was with Sawyer.

When I realized the juniors' mistake, Ms. Yates had made me tell Brody and Harper they didn't really win the title, since they'd started dating because of it. But I wasn't allowed to divulge the truth to anyone else. Each person in the class could get a maximum of one Superlatives position, so the single error had created a snowball effect. Almost every title was incorrect. And since Harper had already taken the pictures and sent them to the yearbook printer, Ms. Yates wanted to leave well enough alone. Not even Sawyer was in on this secret.

Definitely not Aidan.

I was thankful Harper and Brody had been able to work through their problems and keep dating after I told them the truth. They were adorable together, even if part of what made them fun was the fact that they were so obviously mismatched.

Now I was cycling through the same feelings Harper had when she believed she'd been paired with Brody. She'd seen Brody with new eyes and longed for a relationship with him because she'd mistakenly thought someone else had told her it could work. The only difference was, this time there was no mistake. I was *not* Most Likely to Succeed along with Aidan.

The senior class said Sawyer and I should be together.

I'd started to think so too.

Which was dumb, because the election was just a stupid vote for yearbook pictures. Aidan and I would attend Columbia together, take a while to establish our banking careers in New York, and then get married. After three years of knowing that was my plan, letting a class election change my mind didn't say much about my decision-making skills.

Neither did obsessing about Sawyer. On the far end of my table, he attacked his huge salad with the appetite of a seventeen-year-old, half-starved vegan. When he looked up and saw me staring, he tapped his watch, then splayed his hand, wiggling all five fingers. He meant he would meet me at the cheerleading van at five o'clock this afternoon, and we would ride to the game together, exactly as I'd promised (not).

I couldn't wait.

I didn't see Aidan again. Usually he waited in his car for me after cheerleading practice let out at the end of school. Today when I crossed the parking lot, his car was already gone. Angry as I was with him, his conspicuous absence left me feeling empty. I stepped into the heat of my own car and headed home.

As I drove, I decided I should have expected Aidan wouldn't check in with me after school. The first couple of years we'd dated, he'd met me at every chance, even if we had only a few minutes together—before school, between classes. But lately he waited for me less and less. And on the rare occasions when he offered me a ride to school, I told him I'd rather take my car in case I decided to go somewhere afterward. I didn't have specific plans, but riding with him would take some of my power away.

We never stood each other up, though, so I knew I would see him after the game, like we'd said. Normally we might "watch TV" at my house, since my parents were good about leaving us alone. But late tonight they were driving to the airport to pick up my brother, Barrett, who was coming home from college for the weekend. They were likely to return at the wrong time, tromping through the middle of my make-out session with Aidan. So instead, I was spending the night with Harper, and en route, Aidan was taking me to her granddad's strip of beach to "watch the ocean" for half an hour before dropping me off at her house.

Thinking about Aidan, I pulled my car to a halt at a

stop sign. Enormous water oaks, dripping Spanish moss, extended their arms overhead. The houses along this section of the main road through town were ugly 1970s split-levels facing a parallel street, as if turning their backs on the history of the place. Aidan lived in the house to my right. The yard was a neat, flat expanse of grass, unbroken by a single tree except the ancient oaks lining the edge. Every time I'd passed his house since he got his license in tenth grade, I'd glanced at his driveway to see if his car was home.

This time it wasn't.

But I would be in that car with him tonight, driving in the other direction down this road, toward the beach. On three occasions at the beach before, we'd gone all the way. Each time I'd fantasized about the next time, dreaming of how it would be better. He would suddenly become a caring lover. He would make sure I enjoyed it as much as he did. We wouldn't get into a snarky argument afterward about whether I really deserved an A two points higher than his on our last English paper.

I wasn't fantasizing about that now. With sudden clarity I saw our half hour together tonight. We would fool around. I would feel like a failure, not heady with love like girls were supposed to feel after they went so far with their committed boyfriends of three years.

A wave of nausea broke over me, and I knew why.

I put my forehead against the steering wheel. "Damn it, Sawyer," I whispered. It was hard to cast Aidan as my hero after finding out the senior class had chosen Sawyer as my perfect guy. And especially after he'd whispered to me in the student council meeting. The setting hadn't been sexy, yet he'd set my body on fire. I could only imagine what he would talk me into if he ever got me alone.

The car behind me honked.

I drove on.

As I pulled in to my driveway, I saw Aidan was there ahead of me. In fact, he'd taken my parking space. I continued around to the extra pad near the front door, like a guest. After I stopped, I checked my phone to see if he'd sent me a message. Nothing.

Wary, I climbed the steps to the wide front porch and opened the door. The scent of fresh-baked peanut butter cookies wafted out—my mother's specialty and Barrett's favorite. I walked through the marble foyer and the formal living room, into the kitchen.

Aidan sat at the kitchen bar with a plate of the cookies and a glass of milk. "Hello," he called with no enthusiasm.

"Hi there," I said with an equal lack of emotion. I rounded the bar to the kitchen side and stopped in front of him. "What'cha doing?"

He nodded toward the door to my mother's office. "I've asked you a couple of times to check on your mom's recommendation letter for me. You keep forgetting. But you told me she was taking this afternoon off since Barrett's coming home, and I figured I could catch her. Sometimes when you want something done right, you have to do it yourself."

I heard the accusation in his voice. He was angry with me about the student council meeting. I didn't understand what I hadn't done right, though. *He* was the one who'd gotten parliamentary procedure wrong.

I didn't pursue it. I was more interested in what he was really doing here. "The deadline for early admission to Columbia is a month and a half away," I pointed out.

"I didn't want to wait until the last minute. I'm way more responsible than that."

Again, I knew he was accusing me of something. I just wasn't sure what. Saving the homecoming dance made me *more* responsible than him, not less.

I slid my book bag onto the counter to remind him this was my house.

It worked. He sat back on the stool and seemed to really look at me for the first time. "It's just that I don't have a ticket to Columbia without this letter." His tone had changed. Usually he spoke with the bravado of a politician, even when we were alone. But occasionally he dropped the act and let me see the boy underneath.

"I know," I said quietly, my automatic reaction to Aidan's half apologies.

"Your ticket to Columbia is living right here in the house with you," he said. "It makes me nervous that I don't have a letter in hand."

I nodded. That I could understand. When I had an English paper due, I didn't even leave it in my locker in case that part of the school caught on fire. I carted the paper around with me until I handed it in. Academic paranoia was one of the many things that had bonded Aidan and me over the years.

And now that I'd half-accepted his half apology, his attitude was back. He popped a last bite of cookie into his mouth and wiped his fingers on a napkin. "Want to go upstairs to your room?"

The last thing I wanted right now was to make out with him. His apology hadn't been *that* convincing.

He raised his eyebrows, confident I'd say yes, only impatient for my answer. His calm assurance was exactly what I'd fallen so hard for in ninth grade. Now it grated on my nerves.

But I figured I was only shell shocked from the council meeting, and Ms. Yates's dismissal of me in the lunchroom, and the false closeness I felt with Sawyer. I would get over my negative feelings about Aidan soon enough. I didn't want to make things worse between us by telling him the truth.

So I gave him a very good excuse for not taking him upstairs to my bedroom. I looked pointedly at my mother's office door, then back at him. "Are you crazy?"

"She's busy."

"My dad's probably upstairs."

"He'll leave us alone. Your parents love me." He leaned over the counter and whispered, "I have a condom."

My jaw dropped. He wanted to have *sex*? Making out in the middle of our argument might have had some healing properties. Having sex sounded downright repugnant. After all, we'd only done it three times total, on special nights, when we were getting along.

And why take the big risk with my parents home? Now, suddenly? Weird.

"No thanks." I slid a cookie from one of the cooling racks beside the oven and took a bite.

"Why not?" he asked. "You've always jumped at the chance before."

Forcing myself to match his calm, I chewed and swallowed, even though the cookie had gone dry in my mouth. Only then did I say, "*Jumped* at the chance? I don't *think* so."

He glared at me. "It's Sawyer, isn't it?"

My heart pounded. I would have denied it, except that I was such an awful liar.

Instead, I used Aidan's own bait-and-switch tactic, easing out of trouble. With another glance at my mother's door to make sure it was still closed, I lowered my voice and said, "You think I'm cheating on you with Sawyer, and that's the only reason he and I happened to agree with each other in the student council meeting today? No. We agreed because we and the rest of the student council were right, and you were wrong."

Aidan shook his head. "You'd be too scared to cheat on me with Sawyer. But you're taken in by his act. You're as dumb as every other girl at our school."

The door to my mother's office burst open. She wore her business suit from her morning at work. She probably hadn't taken it off while baking cookies because she planned to wear it to pick up Barrett at the airport. As she phrased it, she might be off duty sometimes, but she was always president of the bank.

And she wore a big smile, because Barrett was coming home. Or Aidan was here. Or both.

She turned to me. "Hi, sweetie." She air-kissed my forehead so her perfect plum lipstick wouldn't rub off. Then she glanced at the cookie in my hand. "For shame. Those are for

Barrett." No matter that she'd served Aidan the same cookies herself.

She turned back to Aidan. "I think you'll be happy with this, and so will Columbia." She slid an envelope printed with her Columbia alumni club logo in front of him.

Aidan swiped the letter off the counter so fast that it never stopped moving. He raked back his barstool and stood. "Thank you, Mrs. Gordon."

I cringed. My mother hadn't changed her name to Gordon when she married my dad. She was still Sylvia Beale, BA, MBA, President and CEO. I'd heard her chew out people who insisted on calling her Mrs. Gordon as if women had no choice in naming themselves. But Aidan called her Mrs. Gordon, no matter how many times I warned him.

And she always gave him a pass. Her grin didn't falter as he walked toward the back door.

At the last second he remembered me. "See you after the game, Kaye," he threw over his shoulder.

"Yep, see ya," I said, already turning to toss the rest of my cookie in the trash. I'd lost my appetite. I heard the door close behind him.

When I straightened, my mother was watching me with her hands on her hips. "What's wrong between you two?" she demanded.

I sighed, and kept sighing, like I'd been holding my breath since study hall. "The gym roof got damaged by the storm. Aidan decided to cancel the homecoming dance instead of relocating it, without consulting the rest of the student council. I wanted to move it. So did everybody else. We nearly had a mutiny in the meeting. The upshot is, I have to figure out how to fix the dance now, and he's furious with me for speaking up."

"I would be too," my mother said. "You led a *mutiny?*"

"He wasn't following parliamentary procedure." I felt sheepish for the first time.

My mother closed her eyes and shook her head. "Parliamentary procedure! It's high school, Katherine. It's a high school dance. Your job is to get *out* of high school, holding your student council office in front of you like a key that opens the door to Columbia. Nobody cares what you actually *do* as vice president."

"I care," I protested. "The parliamentarian cares."

She narrowed her eyes. "Who's the parliamentarian?"

"Sawyer," I mumbled.

"The blond boy who works as a waiter at the Crab Lab?" my mother asked. "The one whose father went to prison?"

Now I really regretted piping up at the dinner table on the first day of tenth grade and gleefully dishing to my mother about the school's new bad boy who'd already managed to get suspended. I shifted gears. "Will cares—Tia's boyfriend. Practically everybody at the meeting was on my side."

"What about Ms. Yates?"

"She sided with Aidan because she doesn't want to get off her butt."

"It's hard to hide attitude," my mother said. "Yours won't earn you much of a teacher recommendation, which was supposedly the reason you ran for vice president in the first place." She crossed the kitchen, took down a plastic container, and started transferring the cookies from the cooling racks so I couldn't eat any more. "You may care about the dance today. The real test is, who will care in twenty years, or five years, or even a year from now whether you held this one dance in high school? The answer is, nobody."

A year from now I would be a college freshman in New York. That *did* make a Florida high school homecoming dance sound insignificant. Trouble was, I couldn't picture what I'd be doing on a Friday afternoon in mid-September on the campus of Columbia. But I could picture the dark dance I was supposed to have two weeks from tonight in the high school gym, with a boy's hand creeping down my hip. And in my mind, my dance partner wasn't Aidan anymore.

My mother was still talking. "You need to be smarter

about picking your battles. This dance isn't worth the trouble. When we agreed you should increase your extracurriculars for college admissions, I never intended for you to get involved in a time-consuming activity that would distract you from your studies. Cheerleading is bad enough. If, on top of that, you're taking on the responsibility of moving an entire dance, I can only imagine what's going to happen to your AP English grade, and there goes valedictorian. Don't you have a paper to write on *Crime and Punishment* this weekend?"

These last words I heard as an echo down the hall. I'd left the kitchen while her back was turned. I tiptoed up the stairs and through the master bedroom to the smaller front porch on the second story, which we referred to as Dad's "office." Most days he wrote his books and articles here, where he could see his dock through the palm trees, and his sailboat, and the lagoon that served as his escape route to the Gulf of Mexico.

"Hey, my Kaye," he said without looking up from his laptop. He sat in his cushioned lounge chair, sunglasses on, iced tea beside him. Barefoot, he wore board shorts and a holey Columbia T-shirt that he might have owned since college. He would still be wearing this when my parents left for the airport tonight. My mother would look him up and down with distaste and tell him to change. In response, he would put on flip-flops.

"Hi," I huffed, plopping into the other chair.

He examined me over the top of his sunglasses. "Why so glum?"

I told him in a rush how Aidan had canceled the dance and my mother had told me I should have shut up and let Aidan run over me.

As soon as I said "Mom," Dad started making a noise— *rrrrrrrrrrrrrnnnnnnt*—like I was a big loser on a game show. "You know I don't like that kind of talk between my ladies," he said.

"You asked," I said bitterly.

He stuck out his bottom lip in sympathy. "Come on now. Your mom just wants to make sure you don't bite off more than you can chew."

"Oh, ha!" I sneered. "Funny you should say that. She won't let me eat Barrett's cookies, either."

He rubbed his temple like I was giving him a very familiar headache. "Kaye. Your mom sees her baby only once every few months. She couldn't sleep last night because she was so excited to see him today. She misses him desperately. And she'll miss you desperately too. When you go off to Columbia and come home again, she'll bake *you* cookies and get mad at *me* for eating them. Promise."

I doubted it.

"And as for Aidan," Dad went on, "I know you're spending tonight over at Harper's, but you're making some time for Aidan in there somewhere, huh?" He gave me a cocky grin.

"Yeah," I grumbled.

"The two of you are a little high strung, we could say. You might have let Most Likely to Succeed go to your heads a bit. You need some space for a few hours. But when you see him again tonight, I'll bet you both feel completely different about each other."

I didn't know then how right he was.

3

AN HOUR AND A HALF LATER, I DROVE SLOWLY across the school parking lot, pretending I was concerned about traffic safety, but actually looking hard for Sawyer's dented old pickup truck among the cars near the boys' locker room and the school buses. He wasn't here yet.

Unless he'd ridden with someone else. I'd heard rumors about him being with other girls—usually fooling around with them at parties, not dating them—but honestly, I didn't know much about his love life. If he was dating someone else, Tia would know, but she might not tell *me*, because I acted like I didn't care.

And I didn't. That's what I told myself as I accelerated toward my ride, the cheerleader van. But as I parked, I was still gazing across the vast lot. I watched under the HOME OF

THE PELICANS sign for Sawyer's beater truck to appear.

"Loser," I said to myself as I got out of the car. After I stepped up into the van, a quick glance around told me 1) Sawyer wasn't on it, and 2) Grace and Cathy were early, which was bizarre. They hadn't used their extra time to bring our cooler and twenty pompons out of the girls' locker room, though. Rather than disturb them, force them to look up from their cell phones, and listen to their excuses for why they were physically fit to cheer tonight but not to carry pompons sixty feet, I started making trips myself.

And watching for Sawyer's truck as I walked.

By my fourth trek, some juniors had arrived to help me. They were a lot more responsible than the other senior cheerleaders I'd been saddled with. When we had the van loaded, I chose an empty seat toward the back. Ellen tried to sit with me. I got along fine with Ellen, Cathy, and Grace most of the time. That was the head cheerleader's job, and the student council vice president's job: to make friends with everyone. But if I was Snow White, their dwarf names were Shut Up, Hapless, and Drunken. I really could not deal with Ellen's conversation halfway to Orlando.

I told her I was saving the seat for Harper, which was true. She was the yearbook photographer. She'd planned to snap shots on the marching band's freshman bus during the drive to the game, since the yearbook didn't have enough freshman shots, and on the cheerleader van during the drive back. I didn't mention to Ellen that Harper wouldn't be occupying the seat until later. If Ellen sat with me now and complained to me about how her remedial math class was so haaaaaaard, that wouldn't leave the space open for Sawyer.

I stashed my bag beneath the seat, settled against the window, and scanned the parking lot again for a certain undesirable pickup. *There* he was, finally, making a beeline for us, driving right over curbs like he was in a Humvee. That might explain why his truck sounded the way it did. He parked beside my car, got out, and looked up at the van.

I looked away.

A few seconds later the van door rolled open. My stomach fluttered with butterflies. I would not look. I couldn't let him know how I was beginning to feel about him. He teased me constantly, which must be why our class had voted that we should get together. But his teasing came with a side of mean, as surely as the fries he served with shrimp at the Crab Lab. He might turn on me if he knew he had the upper hand.

I wished I could switch my fantasies off.

"Hello, ladies." He stood in the open doorway, waving with two hands like he'd been crowned homecoming king and was surveying his royal subjects during the parade.

Girls cheered him: "Sawyeeeeeerrrrr!" We were cheer-leaders, after all. But some of us were more interested in Sawyer than others. The ones who had a taste for danger.

And then there was me.

He locked eyes with me right away. His eyes were clear and blue and made my heart race.

He moved toward me, then past me, into the back of the van with a huge canvas bag—probably containing his bulky pelican costume. Well, fine. If he wanted to ignore me for once, I could ignore him, too. Or pretend to.

That ended when Grace squealed, "Sawyer, damn it!" because he'd tickled her as he passed or bumped her with his bag. Her voice cut through me, my usual reaction to girls squealing when Sawyer bothered them. It hurt to be reminded one more time that Sawyer flirted with me *exactly* like he flirted with every other girl at school. I meant noth-ing to him, and if I ever thought we had the kind of electric connection I'd felt during the meeting today, that was my mistake.

At the same time, I felt the completely illogical tempta-tion to *do something* to pull his attention back to me, before it was too late.

And then, having dumped his bag on top of the pompons—I

heard the swish of the plastic strands—he came back up the aisle and collapsed in the seat beside me.

I felt like I'd won the lottery. Seeing Sawyer from across a football field or a classroom or the van made my heart race. Having him right next to me gave me a sensation like I'd stuck my finger in a light socket. But I needed to calm down. The school convoy would stay parked another fifteen minutes, waiting for stragglers. Maybe he was paying me a brief visit before settling with a girl he liked better for the trip.

"Give me some more room here. I'm hanging in the aisle." He bumped me to make me scoot toward the window. "What's the matter?"

"You, being rude."

"No, what's *really* the matter?" He gave me his special expression, an intense stare with one eyebrow raised like an evil genius, which cracked me up if I wasn't careful. "Is Aidan still mad at you?"

"Yes." I didn't want to discuss Aidan with Sawyer, though. "And my mother's mad at me for expending too much energy on extracurriculars, when she's the one who wanted me to join more stuff in the first place."

He kept giving me the nutty look. "That is *so weird*."

"What is?"

"Parents who give a shit what their kids are up to."

I felt guilty, suddenly, for complaining about my problems. According to rumor and the more reliable account I'd heard from Tia, Sawyer had *actual* problems at home. His mom up in Georgia had kicked him out two years ago, and he'd come to live with his dad, who'd just been let out of prison. His older brother ran the bar at the Crab Lab and had gotten Sawyer a job as a waiter, but there was no love lost between them. Tia had said their fights in the Crab Lab kitchen were legendary.

In short, Sawyer had been taking care of himself for a while. And he'd schooled me for complaining.

The next second, though, he relaxed and moved closer with his elbow on his knee and his chin in his hand. The late afternoon sunlight streamed through the window and into his eyes, making him squint, but he didn't back away. "Seriously, why is your mom on you about that?"

I shrugged. "My brother is coming home from college for the weekend."

"Already?" Sawyer asked. "Didn't their school year just start?"

"He was there all summer," I explained. "Currently he's flunking out of Brown."

"*Barrett?* Is *flunking?* He was the valedictorian here."

"Well, I guess technically he's not *flunking*," I admitted. "He's getting Bs and Cs. To hear my mother tell it, that's flunking. She made him repeat those classes over the summer and bring his GPA up."

"I see." Sawyer's tone made it clear he didn't see at all.

"She was already disappointed that he didn't get into Harvard and had to settle for Brown. His high school GPA was perfect and his test scores were phenomenal, but he didn't have the extracurriculars to look well rounded. That's when she got on me about adding some. But I tried out for cheerleader, and she told me that's not what she had in mind. She's like, 'What career will that help you with, professional cheerleader?' And I was already on student council, but she pushed me to run for office. Now that I'm in charge, she's like, 'Why are you expending effort on something other than school?' It's frustrating."

"I can tell," he said. "Maybe you should concentrate on another kind of extracurricular activity." He put his arm around me, with his hand in my hair.

Here we went again. He came after me because something about me screamed *target* to him. I knew he was only making fun of me, like he made fun of everybody, and I should stay away from him.

Especially since I had a boyfriend.

My deep, dark secret was this: Lately when Sawyer touched me, my palms got sweaty. And I liked it. My make-out sessions with Aidan weren't as frequent or intense as they'd been when we first started dating three years ago, but we *did* still have them. And of course, there were the few times we'd gone all the way. But nothing we'd done affected me like Sawyer getting a laugh at my expense.

So I would put up with Sawyer exactly to the point that my ironic patience might start to seem suspicious to onlookers, and they figured out I had a crush on him.

Or, worse: *He* did.

Sawyer stroking my hair definitely was something I wouldn't tolerate if I didn't like him. I tried to dodge away from his hand, which hurt because he'd already wound a curl around his finger.

"Ow!" Collecting myself, I informed him drily, as if he wasn't holding me captive by a thread, "I don't like it when people touch my hair."

He raised his brows. "That's a completely different statement from 'Stop touching my hair, Sawyer.'"

It certainly was. And now that he'd pointed this out, I was afraid he *did* suspect the truth. Overdoing my reaction now, protesting too much, would just draw attention to the fact that my crush on him was getting more serious. I gave him my best withering look—I was good at these, if I did say so myself—and grumbled, "I'm sensitive about my hair, Sawyer. I just had a huge fight with Aidan about this." In fact, that's where my recent trouble with Aidan had started.

I'd never straightened my hair, but I hadn't been bold enough to let it pouf twice the size of my head, either. I'd worn it tamed in twists or braids until two weeks ago. Natural hair had been gaining popularity—not so much around small-town Florida, but in the parts of America that mattered, like New York and California and TV. I wanted to try it.

I'd finally found the courage to spend a long Saturday unbinding my hair and nudging my curls to life. My mother had been supportive and helpful at first, working with the twists I couldn't see in back. Halfway through she'd started complaining that she made enough money to pay someone else to do this.

When we had finished, I liked the way it looked. I couldn't wait to show Aidan when we went out that night. He'd told me it looked like an Afro. Logically I knew I shouldn't have taken this as an insult, but he'd *meant* it as an insult. I was wearing my hair the way it grew on its own, more or less, and he told me it was ugly. Or dated. Or at least not what he wanted or expected in girlfriend hair.

"Judging from the part of your fight that I overheard at

the Crab Lab," Sawyer said, "I think you came down too hard on Aidan about that." I couldn't see what he was doing, but it felt like he was looping a bit of my hair around and around his finger, then carefully pulling his finger out, curling iron–style, seeing if my hair would stay that way. It would.

"*You?*" I exclaimed. "Are taking up for *Aidan?*" Sawyer made fun of everybody indiscriminately, but later you'd see him having a halfway normal conversation with most people. Not with Aidan. He definitely had it in for Aidan. Probably because Aidan's life was so put together, and Sawyer's wasn't.

"I'm definitely not taking up for him," Sawyer said, tugging at a curl, eyes on my hair rather than my face. "It would be fine by me if you hated him now, but you'd hate him for the wrong reasons. At the Crab Lab, it seemed like you were dancing around the edge of calling him a racist. I don't think that's what he meant. None of the girls at school are doing their hair like yours. It makes a statement. Aidan doesn't want his girlfriend to make a statement."

Sawyer was just running his mouth, saying anything he could think of to get a rise out of me. This time it was working.

"That's not true," I said. "Aidan *wanted* me to run for vice president of the student council. I make statements in that job constantly."

"Correction: Aidan doesn't want his girlfriend to make a statement he hasn't preapproved. You can't make a move in student council without him okaying it. If you did, he'd force you to undo it. He'd make you backtrack even if your idea was good, just for spite. That was really clear in the meeting today." Sawyer paused. His eyes flicked to mine. "I can tell from the look on your face he's done that to you plenty of times before."

I glared at him, neither confirming nor denying. The problem with Sawyer was that he moved through the halls of the school with a scorched-earth policy, insulting everyone in his path, but he actually was perceptive about what made people tick. Including me. That's why his insults were so effective. He understood what buttons to push.

His lips were very near my cheek as he said, "Here's my theory. You've been angry with Aidan for a long time. You knew how he'd react to your hair. That's exactly why you did it."

Sawyer had gotten a rise out of me before. But this time he'd taken antagonizing me to a whole new level. I felt my face burning, and it seemed like the space between us was hot with energy. He'd correctly guessed something incredibly personal about me that I'd only half acknowledged myself.

And he acted like he'd only dropped another insult, or made a comment about our team's chances at the game tonight. "God, your hair is *so cool*," he said. "None of the curls are the same diameter. It's like the track of nuclear particles during fission. It's a shame you waited so long to wear it this way."

"It's hard to maintain," I said weakly. "It gets dry. It gets squashed when I sleep. Boys mess with my curl pattern. You act like natural hair is this strange, exotic thrill. It's patronizing."

Finally (regrettably) he pulled his hand away and looked at me. "Would I patronize you?"

"No, but you also would never be nice to me, even if you were faking."

"That is correct." He bent his head toward me. The lighter top layers of his hair fell forward, revealing the darker blond underneath. "Go ahead, touch my hair. It's this strange, exotic thrill. Get your revenge."

Any second he would decide he'd proven his point and sit up. I could be patient. But while I waited, my eyes fell on his nape, where his thick hair became light and fine. I couldn't help wondering what it felt like.

He repeated, "Touch it," which I now realized was going to attract some unwanted attention from the other girls in the van if they couldn't see what we were really doing. He groped in my lap for my hand. This was dangerous. My cheerleading skirt rode up so high when I sat down that my boy shorts underneath almost showed. His palm brushed across the top of one of my thighs, then the other. He found my hand and placed it on the back of his neck.

My fingers sank into his hair. I needed to pull them out. But as I did, they stroked his hair. It felt different from my own wiry hair or the coarse strands of Aidan's. Sawyer's was like warm water against my skin.

Over the sounds of girls laughing and the van's air conditioner blasting, I heard a muffled beeping. The ringtone wasn't mine.

"Excuse me, won't you, darling?" Sawyer said in a British accent like a debonair spy. He pulled his phone out of his pocket, touched the screen, only glanced at it, and put the phone back.

"You don't answer your phone?" I asked.

"I don't answer *her*."

I felt a pang that he was having a quarrel with another girl.

Then he eased the tension, moving his head into my personal space and shaking it so that his hair fell into his eyes. "You can touch it some more. You know you want to."

I fingered a white-blond lock curving around his ear. "You have such a baby face. Do you even shave?"

He gave me a sideways glare.

"The guys on the football team make fun of you," I ventured. Tentatively I traced my fingertip down the hard line of his jaw. He *did* have stubble, just golden and nearly invisible in the sunlight glinting across his face.

"Right," he said, "I don't need to shave. Let me show you." He grabbed me, one hand cradling the back of my head and the other bracing my shoulder so I couldn't duck away. He rubbed his chin across my neck.

"Ow, ow, ow, rug burn." Normally I would have squealed, but I didn't want him to let me go.

He stopped, eye to eye with me. Our faces had never been so close. This time I knew he felt the electricity buzzing between us as strongly as I did. His lips parted. His breath stroked across my cheek.

We couldn't stay like this. The cheerleaders carried on around us like what we were doing was normal. It wouldn't be long, though, before these gossip-hungry girls took notice.

He was thinking the same thing. Holding my gaze, he whispered, "If you were so mad at Aidan, why'd you run back to him?"

My friends had asked me this so often in the past few months, my answer came automatically. "I was looking at the long term. We're applying for early admission to Columbia."

I wanted to get off the subject of Aidan as quickly as possible, though. "Are you applying anywhere?"

"No," he said.

"What are you going to do, live in a box underneath the interstate?"

Sawyer raised his head and backed away. There was no expression in his blue eyes. Sawyer *always* had an expression, easy to read. He poked fun at me. He laughed at me. He enjoyed the fact that he made me uncomfortable. That's why I ribbed him right back. But this time his face was blank.

Without warning, he stood and moved up the aisle.

"Where are you going?" I called. The other cheerleaders turned to me in question. Too late I realized I sounded like I wanted him to stay.

He stopped in the open doorway and threw over his shoulder at me, "Back to my box." He jogged down the steps.

I watched for him out the window. In a moment he crossed behind the van and headed for one of the football team's buses. He disappeared up the steps. A few seconds later he came reeling down to the pavement again like they'd thrown him.

He walked over to one of the four band buses next. The door was closed. He knocked. The door folded inward. I recognized Tia's long auburn hair as she reached down and held out her hand to him. He let her pull him up the stairs.

The door shut.

I stared at that bus until the cheerleading coach, Ms. Howard, finally guided our van into motion, leading the school caravan across central Florida. Maybe Sawyer had planned to ride with the band all along, and he'd only been visiting me. Yet he'd dumped his pelican costume into the back like he planned to stay. I couldn't help thinking I'd actually offended him with my comment about the box. But that wasn't possible, when Sawyer acted like he didn't have any real feelings.

At least, not for me.

4

I SPENT MOST OF THE DRIVE WITH MY FORE-head pressed to the window, staring at the orange groves flashing by beside the interstate, mulling over the homecoming dance. I was *trying* to brainstorm for an alternate place to hold it, but I kept getting sidetracked by my anger at my mother, and Ms. Yates, and Aidan, and a mass of confused feelings about Sawyer. Anger at him, too, for storming off without explanation, guilt that I'd really hurt him somehow, lust as I remembered his hand in my hair.

As soon as the van pulled to a halt in the opposing school's parking lot, Sawyer climbed back up the stairs. He hardly glanced at me as he moved down the aisle. I peered nonchalantly over my shoulder, as if I were just curious about the view out the back windows. He was sitting beside the pompons on the bench, stripped down to his gym shorts, pulling the bird suit up to his knees.

Sawyer had never had an ounce of fat on him, as far as I could tell. But the last time I'd seen him with his shirt off, after the Labor Day race, he'd looked drawn and sinewy, like he could kick anybody's ass more through sheer force of will than bodily strength. In the two and a half weeks since then, he'd been working out with the football team, and I could tell. He'd gained muscle. Most guys going down that path would have gained confidence, too. Sawyer didn't need any.

Grace grinned at him from the nearest seat. "Want me to zip you up?"

"Yeah," Sawyer said with none of the teasing tone he usually took with Grace. After putting his arms into the feathered suit and flexing his bird gloves, he stood. Grace rose beside him and put her hands at the base of his spine, her fingertips probably brushing across his bare back. She moved the zipper all the way up to his neck. I wondered if he shivered at her touch.

Next she bent, flashing everybody her full butt in her boy shorts underneath her cheerleader skirt, and fumbled with his costume bag. She came up holding the huge pelican head. "Here, Sawyer," she said, "I'm giving you head."

Cathy and Ellen squealed with laughter. Sawyer, who

normally would have shot her a sly grin and said something even dirtier in response, only turned bright red and looked straight at me.

Suddenly I realized I'd been staring at him the whole time, and he'd noticed.

"Aw, he's blushing!" Cathy exclaimed.

"Sawyer, blushing?" Ellen echoed. "Grace and Sawyer, sitting in a tree."

Ugh. I faced the front and dove under the seat for my bag.

A huge white shape filled my peripheral vision. The pelican stood beside me in the aisle, holding out his gloved hand. He carried my pompons in the crook of his other wing. I took his hand, and he pulled me up like a feathered gentleman.

The rush I'd felt when he singled me out and paid me romantic attention—bird suit or not—was doubled when he escorted me into the stadium, already loud with crowd noise and brightly lit even though the sun wouldn't set for another hour. My mother might tell me being head cheerleader was the *opposite* of Most Likely to Succeed, but cheering at football games was the most fun I'd had in high school so far.

Thirty minutes later our team kicked off. The stadium was crazy with excitement. The opposing team had beat us last year, but this season Brody had led us to wins in our first three games. If he and the team could pull off a difficult victory tonight, our chances were good of making it all the way to the playoffs. Knowing this, our fans packed the smaller guest side of the stadium and overflowed into the home side. All the football parents and marching band parents were here, and every cheerleader's parents except mine.

Most of the students from our school were here too. Aidan had driven to the game with a couple of other guys: our friend Quinn, whose boyfriend, Noah, was on the football team, and Kennedy Glass, the yearbook editor, who was self-important enough to think someone cared whether he attended the game or not. Come to think of it, Aidan had driven here for the same reason. He didn't understand football, but he felt it was his duty to show up since he was student council president. That's the way he'd explained the trip to me, anyway. He hadn't said anything about wanting to support me personally or see me cheer.

So I didn't scour the stands to spot him and wave. I just cheered. My fellow cheerleaders might annoy me with their weekend drinking and nonstop whining, but they were terrific athletes. We made pyramids—I was lightest, so I was on top—and I knew I wouldn't fall, because they would hold me. We led the crowd in chants, and the students were great about playing along. We hadn't come in third in the state cheer championships last winter for nothing.

For short stints I turned around with my hands on my hips and my back to the crowd, watching for Brody's big plays. Dad loved football. I'd spent many weekends curled up on the couch with him while he explained the rules to me. Now, even from field level, I could watch our formations and warn the other cheerleaders that we needed to get ready to make some noise.

In short, I felt like a successful head cheerleader—way more of a success than I was as student council vice president. If only my mother thought this counted.

But my favorite parts of the night were the dances we'd choreographed. Whenever the opposing team had the ball and it looked like our team would slog through the next several plays without much movement, I pointed at Tia, who was drum captain, up in the sea of band uniforms in the stands. She consulted with Will about what jam to play next, then gave me a hand signal to tell me which one. I passed this along to the cheerleaders. The next thing we knew, we were dancing to a groove. I felt high. Little kids held on to the chain link fence separating the crowd from the field, shaking their bottoms, dreaming about being cheerleaders themselves one day.

And for the whole game, Sawyer acted like he always did with me on the field. He could flirt all he wanted and Aidan would never say a thing as long as Sawyer was in costume, because it was a big joke. He danced right behind me and missed the turns, bumping into me on purpose. Several times I slapped him away when he tried to look up my skirt (which wouldn't have mattered anyway with my boy shorts underneath, but it was the principle of the thing). During halftime he always disappeared to take his suit off in the locker room and pour cold water over his head, but this time he returned a few minutes early. He sat beside me on the players' bench, slipped his feathered arm around my waist, and watched the end of the opposing marching band's show.

Sawyer might be angry with me in real life, but the pelican always loved me.

After the game, exhilarated from our big win, I dumped my pompons in the van and snatched Sawyer's bag for his costume. I wanted an excuse to wait outside the locker room for him. I needed to know whether he was still mad, or the drive back would kill me.

I stood to one side as the football players filed out of the locker room. Brody gave me a high five. Noah shook his freshly shampooed head very close to me, spraying me with water. Then Sawyer emerged in his gym shorts only, carrying the huge foam bird head in one hand, with the rest of the costume draped over his other arm like something dead.

"I brought your bag," I called.

His eyebrows shot up in surprise, but he walked over. "Hold this." He handed me his costume and his head, trading for the bag. He fished a Pelicans T-shirt out of the bag and dove into it, biceps flexing as he pulled it over his head. I was sorry to see his bare chest go. Strangely silent, he took the costume from me and stuffed it into the bag.

I ventured, "You could come back to the cheerleader van for the ride home. I'm sitting with Harper, but we could all three move to the back." As if we were all close friends, and this was the most normal suggestion in the world.

He slung the strap of the bag over his shoulder and eyed me. "That's okay. I'll ride with the team."

"No, you won't," a football player called as he passed.

"The fuck you will," another voice agreed.

Sawyer's eyes never left my face. He said more quietly, "I'll ride with the band. Thanks, though."

"All right." I stood there uncertainly. He shifted his bag from one shoulder to the other, looking past me at the football players and marching band members milling around the parking lot, not quite ready to board the buses for another long drive. Finally I burst out, "We need to talk."

"Or, *you* need to talk," he said, "obviously."

I crossed my arms. "That's exactly what we need to talk about: this attitude of yours."

"Oh, my *attitude*," he said bitterly.

"You're in the costume and you're nice to me. You . . ." I glanced at the football players limping by and lowered my voice. "You come on to me."

"You like that, do you?" he sneered. "When I'm dressed up like a giant bird? That is completely illegal in the state of Florida."

I held my hands out flat. He was proving my point for me. "Then you get out of the suit, and you're an asshole, like now. I don't want to do this dance with you anymore. If this is how you feel about me, stay away from me and keep your hands off me, suit or no suit." I turned my back on him and stomped toward the van.

As I went, my head was swimming with what had just happened. I wasn't even sure where my sudden anger had come from. It was just *so frustrating* for Sawyer to embrace me like I was his favorite—and the instant I tried to show him I felt the same way, he lashed out at me. I wasn't going to do it anymore.

And I wasn't going to stop and peer back at him, either, because that would show him how much I cared—*again*.

Five steps later, I couldn't help it. I looked over my shoulder.

He stood where I'd left him, gazing down at his shoes like he was trying to figure out one of Ms. Reynolds's calculus equations.

And now I was caught between *Good, I've hurt him* and *Oh, no, I've hurt him.*

Disgusted with myself, I trudged up the steps of the van, only to see that some strange girl had taken the seat next to mine. It took me a split second to recognize Harper.

She was like a hand-knitted scarf. Breaking up with Kennedy and dating Brody over the past month had unraveled her, but she was made of gorgeous yarn. Now she was knitting herself back together in a new pattern. This meant I did a double take sometimes when I saw her, because she wasn't always wearing her signature glasses with a retro dress. Without them, she was a pretty, dark-haired girl I'd never met.

Tonight her long hair was pulled into a high ponytail. She wore a simple tank top and a few crazy necklaces with olive cargo pants. She looked as beautiful as ever, only with a lot of the effort taken out—as if she was finally more concerned with her photography projects and her sweet boyfriend than her own self-image. I envied her.

The first thing out of her mouth was "Where's Sawyer?" She stood up to let me into the seat.

Flopping down next to her, I grumbled, "On the band bus, I guess. Why?"

"Brody told me the football team kicked him off their bus, and Sawyer said he was going to hitch a ride with the cheerleaders. That's the main reason I wanted to ride back with y'all. I thought I could get some candids for the yearbook before we leave, while the lights are still on. Sawyer is a walking, talking photo op."

"He was going to ride with us to the game," I said, "but he rode on the senior band bus."

She gave me a skeptical look. "But he was all over you during the game."

"That's because he loves me with his costume on, and he hates me when he takes it off."

"I don't think he hates you when he takes his costume off," she said.

I shrugged through the first part of her sentence and talked through the rest. "I don't care anymore." As the van's engine rumbled to life and the overhead lights blinked out, I turned to the window and watched the distance grow between us and all our school buses. I had no idea which one Sawyer was on, or whether he was staring out his own window as our van pulled away into the dark.

I turned back to Harper. "How are things with Brody?"

She eyed me. In her pause, I realized I'd jumped from complaining about my relationship with Sawyer to asking her about her relationship with her boyfriend. Basically, I'd admitted I liked Sawyer way more than I should.

If Harper read my mind, though, she kept it to herself, as usual. She said enthusiastically, "Things are *good* with Brody."

"Have you . . ." I winked at her.

She looked around us—with good reason. Half the girls on this van had dated Brody in the past. Satisfied that they were involved in their own confabs, she said quietly, "Not yet. I did get on the pill, like I told you, but I still don't think I'm ready."

"That's okay," I assured her. Harper had never dated anyone for long. Suddenly becoming the steady girlfriend of one of the most popular guys in school must have been a shock to the system.

"But we've . . ." She bit her lip and looked guilty.

"You've *what?*" I insisted.

"Done stuff I can't tell you about on the cheerleader van." She raised her eyebrows knowingly.

"Sounds serious."

"I guess we're pretty serious. But *serious* makes it sound like we're under pressure, when we're the opposite. My dates with other guys have been ex-cru-ci-a-ting. So awkward.

Now"—she shrugged—"I'm just making out with my cool new friend. And really enjoying it."

"Have you thought about what you're doing after graduation?" I asked. "Will you try to stay together?"

"We're both applying in state, mostly. Oh!" She gripped my arm. "A scout from the University of Florida came to the game tonight to see Brody and Noah play."

"That's fantastic!" Brody was the best quarterback our school had scored in years. Noah was the right guard who kept him from getting sacked—or tried to. The opposing team tonight had been tough. Despite Noah's efforts, Brody had landed on his ass a couple of times. "What did the scout think?"

"He told Coach he's impressed. What if Brody got to play for the Gators? And I'm sending Florida my portfolio. They have a killer journalism department. Maybe I'll get a scholarship out of it." She held up her hands. "It might not work out, but we're trying to go with whatever happens. It's not a definite plan, like you and Aidan applying to Columbia together."

"Right." After all my pining after Sawyer tonight, I still needed to make up with Aidan. The thought made me a little ill.

"I hear you and Aidan had a problem in the student council meeting today," she said. "Good thing you're sleeping over with me. We'll talk through what happened. Or help you forget about him, whichever."

"Yeah." I did look forward to spending the night at Harper's tiny cottage where she lived with her mom, behind their huge Victorian bed-and-breakfast. Harper and Tia and I didn't have much time left together. We'd be going to different colleges next August. And if Tia and Will both got into drum corps like they wanted, we wouldn't see much of her past June.

But tonight I would get to hear about Tia's night in marching band with Will, her polar opposite. I would hear more about the mysterious experiments Harper and Brody had been performing on each other. If I couldn't pry the details out of Harper, Tia would. And they would ask about Aidan and me, kissing and making up and then exploding again in the student council drama . . . but they would be reserved with their questions. I could tell their enthusiasm about my relationship with Aidan had waned over the years. Kind of like Aidan's own enthusiasm, and mine.

That was normal when two people had been dating for all of high school. Aidan and I had something good together and, moreover, long term and stable. Hardly anybody else in our school could say that. It didn't make sense for us to break up just because we'd been dating forever and there might be someone better around the corner—like Sawyer, of all people. That kind of search would drive a person crazy.

Harper leaned toward me to whisper, "There will be a surprise waiting for you when you come over."

"Oooh, what is it?" I couldn't imagine. Her parents' divorce was finally going forward, which she said was good. But her mom had a hard time keeping the B and B afloat. There was definitely not any redecorating going on.

Harper looked around the van again before she said, "Sawyer."

I felt the blood rush to my face and goose bumps break out on my arms in the air-conditioned van. "What do you mean, Sawyer?"

"You know," Harper said, "he and his dad have been living in a rental house on the same street as my granddad."

"No, I didn't know." It made sense that Sawyer lived near our little downtown, which enabled him to get drunk outside the Crab Lab, then walk to our friends' parties and then home without getting behind the wheel and killing anyone. But I'd never given a lot of thought to where home was for him. He just appeared.

"He had a big fight with his dad a few nights ago," she

said, "and he left. He stayed with my granddad at first. They know each other because Sawyer cuts my granddad's grass. Anyway—"

"How could Sawyer *leave*?" I'd had some huge fights with my mother before, but it had never crossed my mind to sleep at someone else's house because of it.

"He and his dad don't get along, apparently, and this was the last straw. Unfortunately for Sawyer, my granddad has finally rejoined society and gotten a girlfriend. I told you about Chantel. My granddad says Sawyer is cramping his style. Granddad talked to my mom about it, because they're actually speaking again. It just so happens that my mom has been looking for someone to help with breakfast at the B and B, since I refuse to do it anymore."

"I'm so proud of you for standing up for yourself." Harper was introverted. Serving breakfast and associating with her mom's guests at the B and B—different ones every week— had been a special kind of torture for her, like a cat in a room full of toddlers.

"Me too. But I've felt awful that it left my mom in the lurch. Along comes Sawyer, who's willing to work just a couple of hours a day as long as it doesn't interfere with his evenings waiting tables at the Crab Lab. And he needs a place to stay."

"Sawyer is serving breakfast at your B and B?" I asked incredulously.

Harper nodded. "He does a great job, much better than I ever did. After he's fed everybody, he actually sits down and talks to them if he has time before school, whereas I made up any excuse to hide in the kitchen. He can be very charming to the elderly and people he doesn't know. You'd be shocked."

"Wait a minute." The full meaning of what she was saying finally hit me. "Sawyer is *living* at your B and B?"

She laughed nervously. "Actually, no. We don't have an empty room. It's too soon after Labor Day. But one of the rooms will be empty Monday, and he'll move over there. Mom says he can stay through hurricane season, until business picks up again around Christmas. Right now he's staying at our house."

I gaped at her. "The house where you *live*?" Harper's place was a two-bedroom. When she and Tia and I had sleepovers there, one of us had to take the couch in the living room.

"Yeah."

She'd told me all of this so calmly that I sensed I was protesting too much again. I asked logically and rationally, "Doesn't that weird you out?"

"Not really. He basically comes in, grumbles, and wanders away again. He's a lot like my granddad."

"But your whole reason for telling your mom you didn't want to help at the B and B anymore was that you're not a people person," I reminded her. "You need your personal space. You invite friends over occasionally, sure, but people hanging out too long drives you nuts."

"I don't have to entertain him," Harper explained. "He doesn't say much. It's like he's not there." She looked past me out the dark window, searching for a reason that would make better sense to me. Finally she settled on "I feel safer while he's over."

"Safer from whom? Your dad? I thought the divorce was finally going through. You think he'll come back?"

"Probably not," she said vaguely. "I just don't mind Sawyer being there."

"Doesn't Brody mind?" Brody didn't strike me as the jealous type. He was way too confident for that. But bad boy Sawyer living with Brody's girlfriend? That was different.

"Sawyer called Brody to tell him," she said. "And anyway, it's only for a few more nights. Next week he'll move over to the B and B, and it'll be like we're neighbors, that's all. We were neighbors before."

"Now you'll be neighbors who eat breakfast together every morning," I pointed out.

"Yeah, I've thought about that, but Sawyer put it best.

He said a lot of people in the same class at school might feel uncomfortable moving in together, so to speak, but he and I have gotten all that out of the way and have nothing left to feel uncomfortable about, because he's already slipped me the tongue." She laughed.

She stopped laughing when she saw the way I was looking at her. "I told you about that," she reminded me. "Two weeks ago, when I thought Brody was getting back together with Grace. Sawyer was doing me a favor."

"He sure was." Brody and Harper's relationship had worked out now, but they'd had a rocky start, complete with Harper and Sawyer trying to make Brody jealous—and succeeding. When I'd heard about this, I'd burned with jealousy myself. Sawyer never offered himself up when Aidan and I had trouble—which, lately, was all the time.

"Why didn't you tell me before now that Sawyer moved in?" I complained. These were big changes in Harper's home life, and they'd been going on for half a week. I couldn't imagine why I'd been left out of the best friends call tree.

"Because." Harper lowered her voice and bent toward me again for privacy from the cheerleading van, a.k.a. the school's rumor mill. "Ever since you figured out that you and Sawyer were really the ones elected Perfect Couple That Never Was, you've acted strange about him."

Before I could protest—*Strange, how?*—she went on. "I didn't want this to be a big deal. It's *not* a big deal. He'll just be there when you come over. Of course Tia won't care, since the two of them are such good friends. I figured you wouldn't mind either, now that you know why he's there. And I wouldn't want to give him the impression he's not welcome, when he doesn't have anywhere else to go."

Harper wasn't one to throw her weight around or scold, but I was almost sure she was giving me a warning look.

The next second I grabbed her shoulder to keep her from tumbling into the aisle as the van hit the on-ramp for the interstate too fast and we lurched around the curve. My stomach spun with the van. I'd just realized Harper's warning not to kick Sawyer when he was down had come too late.

As the van straightened and Harper was no longer in danger of sailing across it, I took my hands off her and slapped them over my mouth. I opened them to tell her, "Sawyer got mad at me and went to ride on the band bus because I told him he didn't have any plans after graduation and he'd be living in a box under the interstate."

Harper gaped at me. "Kaye!" When even *she* acted outraged, I knew I was in trouble. "Why did you say that?"

"I didn't know he was *actually* homeless! It seemed like a clever reaction to . . . He was . . ." I tried to remember exactly what he'd been doing to me when I insulted him. My most distinct impression was of him running his fingers through my hair, whispering in my ear, and making chills rush down my arms. That's what I'd pushed him away for.

"He teases you and bugs you," Harper said gently. "But he's a real person."

"I know that," I said, careful not to snap at Harper, who never deserved it.

It was a night of firsts. As soon as we arrived at school, I would have to tell Sawyer I was sorry.

The senior band bus beat us back. Watching out my window as we pulled to a stop, I saw Sawyer open the door of his truck and heft the bag with his costume into the passenger side. I was afraid I wouldn't be able to apologize at Harper's house later with Harper and especially Tia there—at least, not the way I wanted.

"See ya soon." I jumped over Harper into the aisle with my bag and pompons in tow, raced down the steps, and galloped over to Sawyer's truck just as he was glancing over his shoulder to back out. When he saw me, he gave me that cold, emotionless look again, but he cranked down the window.

"Can I have a minute?" I asked.

He bit his lip and gazed at me like he wasn't at all sure

I deserved a whole minute. Finally he turned off the engine and raised his eyebrows at me.

"I had no idea you'd moved out until Harper told me in the van," I said in a rush. "When I mentioned the box, I wasn't trying to insult you."

He watched me silently for a moment. "You *were* trying to insult me. Just not about *that*. You were insulting me for not being good enough to get into Columbia."

"Saw-yer!" A shrill majorette, decked out in skimpy sequins, pushed past me to lean through his window. This was a freshman who didn't view the head cheerleader and student council vice president with the proper awe. She was young enough to be rude. "I didn't drop my baton even *once* during halftime. You can't make fun of me anymore!"

"Oh, I can always make fun of you," he assured her.

To put as much of herself as possible through his window, she stood on her tiptoes in her knee-high majorette boots, with her sequined ass in the air. I stood there staring at it, feeling like a bellboy lugging my bag and pompons around. Without ceremony I walked one parking place over, unlocked my trunk, and dumped my stuff inside. I didn't want to interrupt Sawyer when he was busy coming on to his new girlfriend for this particular half hour.

"Kaye," Aidan said beside me.

I whirled around. "Hey!" I was halfway between guilt that he'd almost caught me talking to Sawyer, and satisfaction that Sawyer could peek in his rearview mirror and see me talking to *Aidan*. Maybe *Sawyer* could find out what jealousy felt like, for once. I hadn't been so glad to see Aidan in months.

"Do you want to follow me back to my house so I can drop off my car?" I asked. "Or we could go to the beach now. I brought my bag for Harper's, and I'm sure my car would be safe here overnight." As I heard my own words, I pictured making out at the beach with Aidan, as we'd planned.

And I didn't want to.

He shocked me by saying, "I don't think we should go."

"Okay," I said a little too cheerfully. "Why not?"

"I talked to Ms. Yates."

I nodded. "Again? At the game?" Maybe they'd realized they'd been wrong to protest saving the homecoming dance.

No such luck. "I mean, I talked to her in the lunchroom today," he said. "She told me about the screwup with the Superlatives elections."

"Oh." I felt fresh sweat break out along my hairline. Ms. Yates must have decided Aidan, as student council president, needed to know about the Superlatives problem after all. I wished I'd told him first. I *should* have told him, even if he'd had to keep it a secret from Ms. Yates that he knew.

And now that I'd spent the whole game cuddling with Sawyer, I felt like I'd been caught.

"Being elected Perfect Couple with Sawyer doesn't mean anything," I said quickly. "I'm sure it was just a joke. Sawyer probably organized people to vote for him and me, just to make me mad." I did think this was possible—though if it was true, that was *some* joke, and Sawyer had done more than try to make me mad. He'd tried to get my attention.

"That doesn't matter," Aidan said. "The idea of him going after you is so ridiculous anyway. I mean, it's *Sawyer*." He wrinkled his nose as he said Sawyer's name. "I'm more offended that you lied to me about being elected Most Likely to Succeed with me. But that doesn't matter either. What matters is that you screwed up the election."

His words hit me like a slap in the face. "*I* didn't screw up the election," I protested. "I had nothing to do with it. Ms. Yates wouldn't let me work on the election staff because I'm part of the senior class. That's exactly *why* the election got screwed up, if you ask me."

"But you were still in charge," Aidan said. "You were supposed to tell the staff what to do, and somehow they didn't get the message. When that happens in business, someone at the top resigns so confidence in the organization can be restored."

"You're resigning?" I was astonished. Aidan was way too proud of his position to let go so easily.

"No," he said. "Not me."

"Me?" I squealed. "You're asking me to resign?"

"Yes."

This made no sense. I was counting on entering "student council vice president" on my college applications, and Aidan knew it.

"I don't understand this," I said. "Maybe you're taking this too far because I'm your girlfriend, and you don't want to be seen as soft on me. But Aidan, there's something to be said for that sometimes. We're *not* in a corporation. We're in high school, and I *am* your girlfriend. You seem to be forgetting that a lot lately."

"Then maybe you shouldn't be my girlfriend." At the shocked look on my face, he blinked and said, "We need to take a break and find out."

I'd been wrapped up in what he was saying to me, trying to maneuver out of his anger. But as he uttered these words, suddenly I became aware again of a good portion of the student body moving all around us. Football players streamed out of the team buses, lugging bags of equipment into the locker room. Members of the marching band wearing bright tank tops and their uniform pants, or plaid shorts and their military-style uniform coats, honked obnoxiously on their instruments as they walked to the band room. Sawyer's majorette followed them, swinging her sequined butt.

But Sawyer hadn't left yet. He might be able to hear what Aidan and I were saying. He could certainly see Aidan scowling down at me like an outraged teacher.

I asked carefully, "You want us to take a break because you're mad about the election? It was a mistake, Aidan."

"Not just because of that. I've been thinking about this for a while. We've been partners for a long time. I'm not convinced we're such a good match, in our personal lives or in student council."

Oh, now I understood. I managed to mumble, "So, when I fucked up the Superlatives election, that was the last straw."

He winced at my curse word, but he said firmly, "Yes."

"Which you found out about from Ms. Yates at lunch."

"Right," he said more uncertainly.

"That's why you came to my house this afternoon." My voice was rising, and Aidan was glancing around to see who was listening, but I didn't care anymore. "You'd already decided you would tell me tonight that you wanted to 'take a break'"—I made finger quotes—"but you wanted to get your recommendation letter for Columbia from my mother first. And you wanted to screw me one last time!"

He reached out for me. I never knew what he intended to do—hug me, hit me. Most likely he meant to slap a hand over my mouth to silence me. But he looked so angry that adrenaline rushed through my veins. Necessary or not, I jumped backward, out of his reach.

He crossed his arms and glowered at me. Nothing made him madder than *me* getting angry with *him*. "This is exactly why you need to resign. Using that language and talking about your sex life in the school parking lot!"

"*My* sex life!" I exclaimed. "Weren't you there?"

He looked up at the dark blue sky, gathering self-control. Then he said, "Don't try to argue your way out of this. I'm not changing my mind."

"*Your* mind?" I asked. "Since when does a student council president get to decide that other elected officials should resign?"

"That's what's best for the school," he said.

"I'm not resigning." Even if I wanted to, I couldn't. What would my mother say?

"We'll see, after I talk to Ms. Yates again," Aidan sneered.

"And after I talk to the parliamentarian," I shot back. "There are rules for trying to make your girlfriend resign just because you've broken up with her."

"Oh." Aidan rolled his eyes and shot me the bird.

Speechless for the first time, I stared at him, trying to get my head around the fact that my longtime boyfriend, the one I'd thought I would marry, had broken up with me and was now shooting me the bird. If *that's* how mature he wanted this breakup to be, I wished I had my mother's entire container of homemade cookies to throw at him one by one.

Finally I said, "Thanks for confirming that I've wasted the last three years with you."

He stalked away. A few band members who'd stopped to witness our fight were watching me and talking behind their hands.

I wondered if Sawyer was listening. I wouldn't give him the satisfaction of turning to look.

No, I took the only possible course of action in this situation. Blinking back tears, I went off in search of Harper and Tia.

5

WAY ACROSS THE PARKING LOT, WILL STOOD
beside one of the band buses. He wore his uniform pants but
had already ditched his coat. He pulled his T-shirt off over
his head, wadded the cotton into a ball, and reached upward
with it.

Tia stuck her head out of the bus window and laughed
with him, then accepted the T-shirt and lobbed another
out the window at him. At the last second before the shirt
fell to the pavement, he snagged it from midair with one of
his drumsticks. He shook it out and pulled it over his head.
Then he reached up to the window again.

Tia put her hand out the window. They held hands for
a few moments while she smiled down at him and told him
something. I was still half a football field away from them

and couldn't hear anything they said, but I knew they were stalling, milking another minute of excitement out of seeing each other before he walked away to make sure all the instruments safely traveled the distance from the truck to the band room. He and Tia would be separated for only fifteen minutes. They were ridiculous, acting like they wouldn't see each other for a month.

That's how Aidan and I had felt about each other when we were fourteen.

Now Aidan had told me he wasn't sure I was good enough for him because I hadn't upheld his high standards of running an election correctly—even though I hadn't been allowed in the room when the votes were counted.

It had finally happened. My mother had told me a million times that because I was a woman, I had to work twice as hard as a man for the same amount of respect. And I was black, so I had to work four times as hard. To get twice as much respect, I had to work eight times as hard, and that's what she expected of me.

But she'd been wrong. I worked as hard as I could, eight times harder than most people, probably fifty times harder than Tia, who didn't work at all, and Tia was still acing the tests and ruining the curve in calculus. My mother might want me to have twice the respect of other people, but she gave me none. She demanded perfection. I wasn't perfect. I would have to work sixteen times as hard, and I just couldn't do it anymore.

My tears blinded me. I didn't notice Will had come across the parking lot to meet me until he filled my blurry field of vision. "Kaye," he said, "what's wrong?"

"Math," I sobbed.

"Um . . . Come over here." He grabbed my hand and tugged me toward the band instrument truck. "Watch out," he warned, settling his other hand at my waist and guiding me through the half-dressed band members kneeling over black cases laid out across the asphalt. He slid onto the back bumper of the truck and sat me down beside him.

"Now," he said, "what's wrong besides math?"

"I hate it here," I grumbled to the silhouettes of the palm trees that dotted the parking lot.

"Really?" he asked. "I love it here. I just wish it wasn't so hot."

I sniffled. "It's Florida, Will."

"They keep telling me that." He eyed me. "Tia will be out in a sec. She's looking for some stuff she lost on the band bus."

"Uh-oh," I managed to say calmly, my voice gravelly. "What'd she lose this time?"

"Her phone, one of her drumsticks, one of her shoes, and her bra."

"Her *bra*?" I repeated. "You might have had something to do with her losing her bra."

"She said it was uncomfortable on the long drive. I was helping."

A shadow fell over us as the lights overhead were blocked. We both looked up to see Sawyer standing in front of us, his gloved hands on his padded hips. The white pelican suit glowed like it was some mutant creature born of a nuclear accident in a B movie.

"Why are you in costume again?" Will asked.

Sawyer reached out and swatted Will to one side.

Will slid off the bumper and nearly fell. "Hey!" he yelled.

Sawyer settled next to me, then scooted back into the truck to give his padded butt more room. He put his arm around my waist where Will's had been. With his other hand he turned my chin so I had to look at him. His white-gloved thumb erased the tracks of tears on one of my cheekbones, then the other.

I didn't want to admit how touched I was by this gesture. "You're getting mascara on your glove," I said.

He held his glove up in front of his foam head, appearing to look at it. He wiped it on my bare knee.

Out in the field of instrument cases, Will and Tia were talking. He must have told her I was upset. She ran toward me, hurdling rows of cases as she came. "What's the matter?" she called when she was still surrounded by discarded drums.

"Aidan told me he wanted to take a break," I said shakily. Sawyer squeezed my shoulder.

Tia reached us and stomped her foot. "What the fuck for? Was it because of the shit in student council today?"

I sighed. "That probably had something to do with it, but he's mad at me for other stuff too. I don't meet his standards. He wants me to resign as vice president."

"Wait until I find him," Tia said. "I'll take every one of his standards and shove them up his— *What?*" Exasperated, she turned to Will, who was poking her in the side.

"That's not helpful right now," he said.

"It's helpful to *me!*" she exclaimed.

"Come on." He started to pull out the ramp attached to the underside of the truck where we were sitting, but Sawyer's costume overflowed into its path. "Tia and I have to get into the truck. Scoot over, bird," Will said, kicking Sawyer's cushioned butt.

Sawyer rose, pulling me up with him. But he didn't let me go. The soft padding and feathers of his costume enveloped me. Rather than fighting him, I let him hug me.

Will and Tia tromped up the ramp and maneuvered a huge xylophone on rollers onto it. Steadying the lower end, Will walked carefully backward. "Oh, wait," Tia called, "I don't have it. Oh, ack!" The xylophone slid down the last foot of the ramp, knocking Will in the gut. "Are you okay?" she called.

"We didn't really need that lower octave, anyway," he groaned.

Sawyer put his hands over my ears.

Taking the hint, I inhaled deeply and shut my eyes, letting myself melt into his softness. I could still hear Will and Tia flirting as they coaxed instruments down the ramp and other band members laughing as they passed. But their voices were muffled and smoothed over, just as Sawyer's downy but firm hug was soothing.

For those few seconds in Sawyer's arms, I tried to live in the moment and remember what I loved about high school: my friends, our sports events, and our fun gatherings like the homecoming dance, which I was more determined than ever to save. It wasn't until rare interludes like this, when I felt the weight lifted from my shoulders for a short time, that I realized how much pressure I was under, and how that anxiety turned my whole world dark.

Through my closed eyelids I sensed a flash. Blinking, I

pulled away from Sawyer just as Harper snapped a picture of us with her fancy camera.

"I'm so sorry," she said. "You two hugging with Kaye in her cheerleader outfit and Sawyer in his pelican costume struck me as a symbolic photo for our school. It's also one of the weirdest things I've ever seen." She turned to me. "I hear Aidan wants a *break*?" She held her camera out of the way with one hand while she embraced me with the other.

"Tia told you already?" I asked into Harper's shoulder. Tia wasn't good at keeping news on the down-low.

"Tia isn't happy with Aidan," Harper said as she let me go.

And then—granted, the lights in the parking lot were bright, the shadows strange, and I was feeling out of sorts after my cry—but I could have sworn Harper gave Sawyer a knowing look, like they were hiding something from me.

Which was ridiculous. I spent way more time with Sawyer while he was in costume than Harper did, and I still didn't know which part of his bird head he saw from.

She stuck out her bottom lip at me in sympathy. "Are you okay to drive?"

"Oh, sure. I'll see you in a few." I turned to Sawyer. "Did you put your costume back on just so you could hug me, even though you're still mad at me? Because that's kind of sweet, and kind of twisted."

He shrugged.

"Well, go take it off. I know you're hot."

He nodded, nearly poking me in the eye with his foam beak, and curled his arm to show me his bird biceps.

I actually managed a laugh. "Yes, *that* kind of hot. You are one sexy waterfowl."

He swaggered toward his truck, lifting his huge feet high and wagging his feathery bottom.

Suddenly the instrument truck, the cheerleader van, and all the buses around me were moving, like curtains rising and sets changing behind an actress onstage. Everyone in the parking lot drove away at one time, making the windblown palm trees seem stark and lonely. Only Sawyer remained, out of his costume again and unable to get over his anger at me, yet waiting for me behind the wheel of his truck.

I got in my car, and he followed me to Harper's.

It was impossible to stay depressed in Harper's tiny house with the five of us pushing past each other and laughing about it: me, sweet Harper, hilarious Tia, Harper's hippie mom, and of course Sawyer. Just as Harper had said, he didn't draw a lot of attention to himself or make much noise. It was almost like he was trying to blend in so Harper's mom wouldn't kick him out. He kept his clothes in a backpack stuffed under a side table. I knew this because he drew some out right after we arrived, then disappeared to take a shower.

Harper's mom made us cookies from store-bought frozen dough. They didn't taste nearly as good as my mother's homemade, but I appreciated them more because they were made specifically for me. I was stuffing the fourth in my mouth when Sawyer stepped out of the bathroom in a cloud of steam, wearing his Pelicans T-shirt and threadbare sweatpants that hung low around his waist.

He looked like a different person with his blond hair wet and dark. But the defiant lift of his chin was the same as always when he saw me holding my bundle of pajamas. He motioned with his head toward the bathroom door.

I jumped up, eager to ditch my sweaty cheerleading duds. As I passed him, our bare arms brushed. I asked, "Did you use all the hot water?"

He said quietly, "I wouldn't do that to you."

I locked myself in the bathroom and set my clothes on the counter. Even though I'd had no idea when I packed my overnight bag that Sawyer would be here, luckily I'd brought a cute tank and pajama pants, sexy without being indecent. I wasn't worried about how I would look to him. It was the feel of his breath in my ear as he'd passed me that still sent shivers up and down my arms—and now the idea that I was stepping into the shower where he'd just been. (Naked.)

Harper might think this sleepover was innocent. She was wrong.

I hurried through showering and brushing my teeth so I didn't miss anything. When I exited the bathroom, the living room was empty. Harper's mom's door was closed like she'd gone to sleep. Laughter pealed from the opposite direction. I padded down the hall and found Harper in her room, which was wallpapered with photos and art and fashion shoots she'd torn from magazines. She shared her desk chair with Tia as they scrolled through Harper's yearbook photos on her computer. Sawyer lay on his stomach crossways on Harper's bed with his chin propped on his hands, looking over their shoulders. I stopped in the doorway. He turned around to glance at me and patted the bed beside him.

Any other night we'd found ourselves thrown together like this, I would have flounced across the room to drag Harper's beanbag chair closer to the computer. I *never* would have accepted Sawyer's invitation to lie next to him. But Aidan and I were on a break. I was a free woman who could do what I wanted.

And though I wasn't at all sure where I stood with Sawyer, we'd definitely moved into new territory for us. What I *wanted* was to lie down beside him.

"Oh my God, is that Xavier Pilkington?" I exclaimed, keeping my eyes focused on Xavier's photo filling the computer screen as I crawled onto the bed beside Sawyer. There was a moment when I had to decide whether to settle a few inches from Sawyer or lie right alongside him with our arms and hips and legs touching. I chose to touch him. If he was still so angry with me that he found me distasteful, this would serve him right. Cooties.

"Doesn't Xavier look great?" Harper asked, grinning at me over her shoulder. She did a double take when she saw how close Sawyer and I were lying, but she smiled right through it and turned back to the computer.

"Like a 1940s movie star," Tia agreed, "especially with the grease in his hair. How do you make people look so good, Harper? If you really want to expand your business to wedding photos, you should post what Xavier normally looks like as the 'before,' and this picture as the 'after.'"

"Two-part secret to good pictures." Harper held up one finger. "Lighting." She held up a second finger. "Lots of frames. Let me pull up the rest of my shots for Most Academic, and you'll see why." She opened another folder and expanded a photo of blond Angelica, primly perfect as usual, next to Xavier, who looked like Harper had caught him mid-sneeze.

"Ah, there's our Romeo," I said.

Sawyer laughed. For someone with a great—even if snarky—sense of humor, he didn't laugh a lot. The sound warmed me up.

"Speaking of Angelica," Tia said, turning to me.

"Don't tell her," Harper muttered.

"She needs to know!" Tia defended herself. "Kaye, I swear to God, not ten minutes after Aidan told you he wanted to take a break, I saw him talking to the majorettes and, specifically, hitting on old Angelica."

"You don't know that he was hitting on her," Harper reasoned. "She's dating Xavier."

"Oh, and you think Aidan couldn't steal a girl from Xavier Pilkington?" Tia challenged her. "Xavier's mom still cuts the crusts off his sandwiches."

"I'm not saying he *couldn't*," Harper clarified. "I'm saying I saw Aidan having that conversation with Angelica too, but that didn't automatically signal he was making a move in *my* mind."

"You're right," Tia said. "Most likely they were discussing the Higgs boson and the standard model of particle physics. It only *looked* like he was hitting on her."

Tia was what my mother referred to as "highly excitable." She had a reputation for stirring up trouble. Aidan might have been passing pertinent information along to Angelica about the student council's upcoming doughnut sale or something. He wasn't the type to hit on girls. But what did I know? He'd never had the chance before. Maybe he would become our school's playboy now that he'd decided our relationship was temporarily over.

And his choice of Angelica struck me. In the student council's incorrect tally of the Superlatives votes, Angelica had won Most Academic along with Xavier. In the newer, correct tally Ms. Yates had *claimed* we weren't letting out of the bag, Angelica had won Most Likely to Succeed with Aidan. Maybe he wanted to date the girl whom the school had paired him with. He obviously had no use for *me* now that he knew I hadn't really won the title. And now that he had my mother's recommendation letter.

I said, "I guess we won't be on a break after all, then. We've broken up permanently, because there's no way I can out-nerd that girl."

"You got that right," Harper said at the same time Tia said, *"Es la verdad."*

As I uttered this realization, I honestly expected Sawyer to smooth his fingertips across my back. Maybe I would poke him in the ribs in retaliation. Maybe not. But he'd embraced me in a full-bird hug when Aidan handed down his initial decree. Seemed like my letting Aidan go deserved at least *some* touch from Sawyer. He didn't move, though. He kept staring at the computer screen.

"Now *that's* a handsome bloke," he said. The photo was of him in the pelican costume—actually, it could have been *anyone* in the pelican costume, but I assumed it was Sawyer—looking very studious and contrite as he sat in Principal Chen's office with his legs crossed at the knees, reading *Crime and Punishment*. Perfect.

Suddenly I felt a flash of panic that I hadn't started my Dostoyevsky paper, which was due to Mr. Frank on Monday. My mother had reminded me this afternoon that the title of valedictorian probably hinged on everyone's AP English grade because Mr. Frank was a stickler. But getting up from Harper's bed to make a few outline notes when I was trying desperately to flirt with the class criminal was something Angelica would do, *not* something I would do.

Not anymore.

I called, "Are you really using that picture for Most Likely to Go to Jail?"

"Yes," Harper said. "Kennedy complained. He said I hadn't really taken Sawyer's photo for his title in the yearbook if his face wasn't showing. But we were on deadline. Kennedy had to let it through. And we're not using this next one for Most Likely to Succeed, but we're putting it in one of the front collages." She clicked to a picture of Aidan and me grinning behind Ms. Chen's desk—we'd fought over who would sit in the chair that day too, and finally pushed it out of the way—with Sawyer behind us, only one huge cartoon eye of the pelican popping up over Aidan's shoulder. Sawyer had photobombed us on purpose.

"That's classic," Tia cackled.

"You were in the *way*," I said quietly, actually poking Sawyer in the ribs this time. I turned toward him.

When he faced me, we were already so close that I could feel his breath across my lips. His deep blue eyes were serious.

And then he turned forward again without touching me or flirting back at all, like I was some freshman majorette he found more annoying than sexy.

I took the hint. We stayed on Harper's bed for another half hour as she led us through an overview of the senior class. I laughed with Harper and Tia. Sawyer laughed with Harper and Tia. Sawyer and I didn't laugh together.

"Enough," Harper finally said. "Even *I* get tired of photography after eighteen hours." She turned off the computer and led the way out of her bedroom, through the narrow hall to the living room.

We filed behind her. I was the last one out, behind

Sawyer. It wasn't often that I was this close to him when we were standing up and he wasn't dressed as a pelican. I was eye level with his shoulder blades. I got a great view of the white-blond, baby-fine hairs at his nape. And I was disappointed he didn't take this opportunity to turn around and grab me playfully. Maybe it was all in my head, but I got the impression he was dissing me by doing nothing.

When we emerged from the hallway, Tia was rummaging through the kitchen, insisting she was hungry again, and Harper was trying to help her find the right junk food. Sawyer put a hand on the armrest of a wing chair and the other on the armrest of the sofa and hopped over both, then plopped onto one end of the sofa, as if he did this four times a day and that was his *place*. My first instinct was to join him on the sofa. The night had been squeaky clean so far, and it would stay that way if we weren't sitting next to each other.

But I wouldn't give him the satisfaction of chasing him around. I chose the wing chair and didn't look at him.

Tia was the one who claimed the other end of the sofa, collapsing her entire five-foot-nine frame onto it while clutching a bag of chips. She looked and sounded like a tree falling in the forest. Harper took the other side chair and clicked the remote so the TV turned on to our usual viewing, a bridal gown reality show.

Actually, I didn't know whether this show was *their* usual viewing. Maybe they only watched it with me whenever we had a sleepover, because it was *my* usual viewing. I'd been planning my wedding to Aidan ever since we started dating. Perhaps a little before. Harper would have a Florida wedding, barefoot on the beach. Tia, if she changed her mind and got married someday, would probably elope. But my wedding would be in New York where I would live and work, and the gown would be the centerpiece. In an old city that embodied intellect and effort and the collective culture of the entire world, my dress would stand out, a white work of art against the somber gray stonework of a church, or a monument, or a bank, wherever Aidan and I decided to hold the ceremony.

This had been my dream for years, more consistent than my fantasy that our next sex together would finally blow my mind. I had recited the slowly evolving details of my dream wedding to Tia and Harper. Suddenly the entire scenario seemed hopelessly naive, an invention of sixth grade instead of ninth.

Now I was in twelfth, and I was hoping against hope that Harper and Tia wouldn't bring up my obsession in front of Sawyer.

"There's . . . ," Harper began as a bride swept across the screen in a classic gown with a slim silhouette. She was about to say the dress was perfect for me. It was exactly the kind of gown I would have called dibs on the other hundred times we'd watched this show.

Behind the retro glasses she'd settled across her nose when she took out her contacts, her eyes flicked to Sawyer. "...a dress that should not be accessorized with pink cowboy boots," she finished as the bride pulled up the hem and showed off her special brand of quirky.

"That's a Kaye dress," Tia said, typically missing our hints at subtlety and restraint. "If you wore that with pink cowboy boots, your mama would shit twice."

Luckily, the next dress was exquisitely sewn with hundreds of delicate fabric flowers, a Harper dress. Following that was a cleavage-baring number with sheer panels down to the navel in front and the butt crack in back—definitely a dress for Tia, who couldn't tell sexy from raunchy. The conversation moved far enough from the topic of *me* that I worked up the courage to steal a glance at Sawyer.

He was asleep. His elbow was draped over the armrest, cradling his chin. His eyes were closed, his blond eyelashes casting long shadows down his cheeks.

"Hey," Tia said, shoving his shoulder. Without opening his eyes, he let out a groan.

"Come on," Tia said, pulling his arm until he stretched

out across the sofa with his head on her thigh. He never opened his eyes, and the whole process was so seamless that it looked like he'd slept in her lap a million times. Maybe he had. The two of them had been off and on forever. They made my attempts at flirting with him look like something out of kindergarten.

In deference to him, she turned off the lamp on the table next to her. The only light remaining came from the TV hung over the fireplace, and a faint glow from the streetlights outside through the gauzy curtains on the big front window. Now Sawyer and Tia looked like a boyfriend and girlfriend getting cozy.

Watching them with a ball of resentment burning in my stomach, I realized I didn't have a chance with Sawyer, even if I wanted one. We both pretended I was too good for him. But realistically, why would *he* want a stick-in-the-mud like me? Life-of-the-party girls like Tia were more his speed. Staring at them owning the sofa together, with Tia's hand lying on his chest, was a great way to finally drive that fact home to my beleaguered, lovelorn brain.

That's when Tia piped up. "So, Kaye, tell us more about this break you're taking with Aidan."

6

"NO!" I WHISPERED HOARSELY AND A LITTLE desperately, nodding toward Sawyer in Tia's lap.

"He's asleep," Tia said in her normal tone.

"If he is, you're going to wake him up." I was still whispering.

"Nothing wakes him up," Harper offered. "He sleeps like a log."

"So it's okay to discuss my personal business in front of him? I don't *think* so. Any second he's going to jump up and startle us. 'Ha-ha, I've been listening to you the whole time.'"

Tia shook her head. "He's always worked such long hours at the Crab Lab, and now the mascot job takes a lot out of him. It's harder than you'd think, so physical, bouncing around in the heat with that heavy costume on."

"I *know*," I said haughtily, offended that Tia would imply she understood more about Sawyer's mascot job than I did. *I* was the one who stood next to him at games.

"Anyway," Harper spoke up, "I don't think he'd tell anybody your personal business."

"I think he would," I said flatly.

"What exactly is your problem with him?" Tia asked, sounding miffed. "You act like he's a criminal."

"He did get voted Most Likely to Go to Jail," I reminded her.

In the dusky room I saw Harper raise her eyebrows at me. She and I knew he hadn't actually won this title, since he'd won Perfect Couple with me. The real winner of Most Likely to Go to Jail was our school pothead, Jason Price.

"Sawyer and I are pretty good friends," Tia said, which was the understatement of the century, "and I can tell he's dead serious about cleaning up his act. He's always been black and white, all or nothing. When he went vegan last spring, that was it. He never looked back. So if he's saying no alcohol and pot now, I can guarantee he hasn't fallen off the wagon. You haven't seen anything to think he has, have you?"

The fact that she asked this question made me think she wasn't quite as sure about Sawyer as she claimed. "I haven't,"

I admitted. "But Tia, you talk like he's been clean for years. He passed out at school only *three weeks* ago. And I just . . ."

"You just what?" Tia insisted.

Her usually bright face drew into frown lines. She shifted, moving her arm down Sawyer's body as if protecting him. He didn't move, didn't even stir or flutter his eyelids, as far as I could tell in the near dark. I couldn't see Harper's eyes because her glasses reflected the bridal gowns on TV, but she sat up cross-legged in her chair, attentive to my answer.

Without anyone coming out and saying it, I knew we weren't really talking about Sawyer's reform. They wanted to know why I didn't go after him, now that Aidan was—temporarily, at least—out of the picture.

"Sawyer's never been serious with girls," I said. "But he's been *with* a *lot* of them. He's got this whole secret underlife. Cheerleaders tell stories about him fooling around with girls I never even knew he'd gone out with."

"Why are they doing that?" Tia asked. "They're assholes."

"But what if the stories are true?"

"So? He's not in a steady relationship with anybody. He's not cheating. Why does fooling around with a lot of girls detract from his moral character?" Now she was talking about herself. We were back to the argument we'd had a million times, in which I expressed concern that she wasn't being very picky about whom she slept with, and she told me to stuff it.

I shouldn't have done it, but I took the bait. "When's the last time *you* had sex with him?" I asked. "It probably hasn't been a month."

"Do we want to go here?" Harper asked. "I do not want to go here."

Tia's mouth set in a hard line. "Define sex," she said.

Damn Tia. Now I was thinking about all the ways Tia and Sawyer might have played around with each other in the past few years. They'd probably done things that I'd never tried in three years with Aidan, and that Aidan would have said were too dirty anyway.

"There's no fighting during girls' sleepover night," Harper declared.

"Seriously," Tia kept on anyway, "because there's different kinds of sex."

"Now you're baiting her," Harper scolded Tia. "Just tell her what she wants to know."

Tia scowled at me, then opened her free hand. "Okay. The last time I did *anything* with him was about a month ago, before Will and I got together."

"Well, after you and Will had been *together*," I corrected her, "but before you actually went on a date." I happened to have heard about some of the things she'd been seen doing with Sawyer one weekend *after* she'd already made out with Will.

Tia grimaced and rubbed her brow like I was giving her a headache. "The past is past. I don't see why this matters."

I couldn't believe I was doing it, but I laid my biggest fear down flat on the table for them to peer at. "Because if Sawyer slept around before, he'll do it again."

"People change, Kaye," Tia said solemnly. "I've changed."

I frowned at her. "You're not wearing a bra."

She looked guilty, then pulled out the neck of her T-shirt and peered inside. "I couldn't find it on the band bus. Nine times out of ten, I've changed. I definitely would not run back to Sawyer or to *anybody* when I've made a promise to Will. Will is too fucking awesome."

Sawyer finally stirred—whether because she'd said his name again or she'd said the *F*-word with such gusto, I didn't know. He rolled onto his side, shifting his head on her thigh. Now that he might be awake-ish, I was even more alarmed at what she said next: "As long as you're on a break with Aidan anyway, why not experiment, so you won't spend your entire life since you were fourteen with one guy? I'm sure Sawyer would be glad for you to use him."

I cut my hand back and forth violently across my throat,

hoping the horrified look on my face told her how serious I was about her shutting up. Even Harper shook her head.

Ignoring Harper, Tia gave me her best *Who, me?* face and put her hands up like she couldn't imagine what she'd done wrong.

I already felt vulnerable because Aidan had broken up with me and Sawyer seemed to have rejected me. If Sawyer was playing possum and heard this discussion, I would die of embarrassment. Desperate to keep her from saying anything else, I found a notepad printed with the B and B logo, plucked a pen out of the side-table drawer, and wrote her an angry note. "Sawyer wld not b 'glad 4 me 2 use him,' WTF. And if I did, Aidan wld never go out w me again." I tore it off the pad—silently—and reached across the coffee table with it. Harper half stood to grab it, then delivered it to Tia. Harper read it over her shoulder.

Tia snapped her fingers, meaning she wanted my pen. I winced at the noise but handed the pen to Harper, who delivered it. Tia scribbled an answer below my note. This took so long, and I was so afraid of what she'd say, that I had half a mind to look over her shoulder while she was still writing. I was afraid this might rouse Sawyer—with my panicked breathing or the sound of my heart palpitations. Finally she gave the paper to Harper, who read it with a perplexed expression, then handed it to me.

"Aidan wld b <u>more</u> likely 2 go out w u again bc he wld see ur not waiting around 4 him & his Higgs boson BULLshit. In the meantime u cld experiment w Sawyer. Tell me u don't want 2 & ur lying like a dog." Under this she'd drawn a dog stick figure with its tongue hanging out, lying on what appeared to be several yards of shag.

"Shhh," Harper said, even though nobody had said anything for several minutes. I listened, though. Underneath the drone of TV brides, I recognized Will's voice and Brody's laugh on the other side of the front door.

"We'd better go out there before they ring the doorbell and wake up my mom," Harper said more quietly than we'd been speaking before, as if my written exchange with Tia had caused a pall to descend over the night.

"They won't," Tia said as loudly as ever. "Brody wouldn't risk her wrath. They're plotting something."

"Then we'd better go out there before they execute their plot and get me in enormous trouble," Harper said.

"I'm curious what they'll do," Tia said. "Wait."

We waited. The only lights were still the flickering color from the TV and the soft glow from the streetlights through the window curtains. The only sound was the whisper of televised voices. Then Will's voice again, hushed, and Brody's.

JENNIFER ECHOLS

Suddenly the fireplace seemed to explode, making me squeal and Tia jump. Sawyer grunted and rolled all the way over on Tia's thigh with his back to the room.

Harper peered into the fireplace. She rummaged in the ash and brought out a tennis ball.

"Brilliant," Tia said. "You're right, Harper, we have to stop the rogue teens before they cause more harm." She half rose. Sawyer threw both arms over his head to block out sound and light.

"Kaye, come over here right now." Tia said it with such authority, and I was so surprised at this, that I obeyed, edging between the sofa and the coffee table. She rolled out from under Sawyer and held his upper body suspended until I sat down where she'd been. She laid Sawyer's head in my lap.

And then . . . I'm not sure what I'd expected to happen next, but it wasn't this: Tia and Harper left the room as fast as they could go, closing the front door carefully behind them.

Warmth washed over me, followed by a case of the shivers. I couldn't believe, after all the teasing I'd suffered at Sawyer's hands for the past two years, he was in my lap. The night had suddenly come way closer to a wild fantasy I'd only half acknowledged: that we would end up together.

But he *was* asleep. I was convinced now that I felt his

deep, even breaths against my hand. An Oscar-winning actor couldn't fake it this well. And when Tia had ordered me over, it almost seemed she was calling on me to protect his rest, not to wake him or flirt with him or make Aidan jealous.

In front of the house, somewhere just beyond the door, Harper talked in a low voice. "I'm surprised you're still up. You got hit pretty hard in the third quarter."

"Yeah," Brody responded. "I don't feel that kind of thing until the next day. You have about eight hours left to use me."

"Oh, *really*. Use you how?" Harper's tone was knowing and provocative—like Tia's was all the time. I'd never heard Harper speak this way before. I recalled what she'd hinted to me in the van about Brody and her exploring each other.

I'd lost my virginity with Aidan not long after Tia had lost hers with Sawyer. Harper hadn't had sex even now. But suddenly I felt like the naive one, because Harper and Brody were in love, and my time with Aidan hadn't meant what I thought.

Their voices faded as they wisely walked away from the house, where Harper's mother wouldn't overhear. I was left with only the TV wedding preparations and Sawyer's warmth in my lap.

He rolled farther forward and slipped his hand between my legs, propping himself in that position, like my thigh was a pillow. I suspected at first he was awake after all—but he never snickered, and if he'd meant to take liberties with me, his hand would have been six inches higher.

I put my hand in his hair, lightly so as not to rouse him, and fingered those baby-fine strands all over again, while I watched all my past goals play out on television like the most mindless reality show.

I lay stretched out on the sofa, with an actual pillow underneath my head, and covered in Harper's psychedelic first attempt at quilting. The TV was off and the room was black, but I knew where I was because of the big window on one side of the chimney, glowing faintly. My arm hung down, touching something warm—and when I peered in that direction, it took me a few moments to recognize Sawyer on the floor right next to the sofa, with his back against it, in a sleeping bag that Harper had owned since at least third grade. My hand was on his shoulder.

Harper and Tia must have bedded us down when they came back inside. They sure hadn't woken me up when they moved me. But they must have woken Sawyer, or he would have landed pretty hard on the floor. And after he'd given me his place on the sofa, he'd stayed as close to me as possible.

I took a satisfied breath, for once wholeheartedly enjoying the tingles in my fingers and the feeling of doing something slightly wrong, and went back to sleep.

The window was pink with sunrise. A tinny alarm sounded quietly.

"It's mine," Sawyer whispered, fumbling with his watch. "Lie back down."

I was bone tired and sore from my night of cheering. I never complained because I would sound silly compared with football players like Brody getting sacked, and because my mother might use my whining as an excuse to suggest I quit. This morning Sawyer's order to sleep more was almost as delicious as my light touch on him had been the night before. Gratefully I collapsed on the sofa again and curled into a ball, warming myself in the chilly air conditioning.

Covers rustled. A cozy weight fell across me as he draped the sleeping bag over my quilt.

"Thanks," I muttered, snuggling lower.

A shadow descended over me. I felt his lips brush my forehead.

I listened as he crossed the room, opened the front door, locked it from the inside, and quietly shut it behind him.

*   *   *

"Breakfast!" Harper's mom sang. "If you don't get it while Sawyer's cooking it, you don't get it." Before I even saw her, she'd walked out the front door, headed for the B and B.

I sat straight up into bright morning sunlight with a horrible realization, which must have been growing in my subconscious while I slept: I'd lost my back-and-forth note with Tia.

I jumped up and shook out the quilt, then the sleeping bag, then my pillow, then Sawyer's pillow, which he'd tossed into a chair. No note. I looked under the furniture and behind the sofa. Next I scanned the tables. My note could have gotten stuffed into any one of these art books.

"Morning!" Harper said brightly, coming around the corner and blinking behind her glasses. Tia stumbled after her. Tia was not a morning person.

"Do y'all know what happened to that note we were passing around last night?" I asked, trying my best not to sound hysterical.

"No," Harper said, turning upside down to peer under the furniture herself. Her glasses fell off with a clatter. "Maybe it got thrown away."

"Didn't I have it last?" I asked Tia, who stared back at me like she was still in REM sleep and someone had glued her eyelids open.

"Never mind," I told Harper. "But if you find it, burn it."

"Okay." Harper laughed like it wasn't a big deal. We all washed up and changed into clothes that wouldn't scare the guests at the B and B. But my mind was racing. Harper was probably right. I could tell by looking around that she'd cleaned up the mess of Tia's midnight snacks. Her mom might have been through too, tidying up while I was still asleep. One of them had thrown the note away like trash.

Or Sawyer had found it.

And the last thing he'd done before leaving was to kiss me. If he'd read our note about me having a fling with him, the kiss was his way of saying yes.

Over in the B and B, we sat down to a full breakfast with Harper's mom and her eight guests at the biggest dining room table I'd ever seen, all dark scrolls like the rest of the towering Victorian. That is, Harper and Tia and I sat down. Sawyer kept getting up to check food in the kitchen or pass around a fresh basket of orange rolls.

He used his best waiter persona. He was polite and conversational to the elderly people at the table, offering them ideas for tourist attractions and the best roads to get them there. He was mature like a maître d' in a three-piece suit at a fine hotel, except that he was still wearing his Pelicans T-shirt and sweatpants. I actually *had* seen him in gentlemanly waiter mode before, when Barrett and I ate at the Crab Lab with my parents.

Several of the guests went off to start their day. Harper's mom was deep in conversation with the last two couples. Harper nodded toward the kitchen door, meaning it was safe to make our escape. We took our dishes with us so Sawyer wouldn't have to bus them. He was methodically working through a huge pile of plates, dumping food in the garbage, rinsing the dishes, and setting them in the dishwasher or dropping them to soak in an industrial-size sink. He was doing the work of probably six people at the Crab Lab.

He looked up when we walked in. "Sorry I flaked out on y'all last night," he said.

"What's the last thing you remember hearing?" Tia asked playfully. She winked at me.

Oh God.

Sawyer said without missing a beat, "The girl who had her heart set on a strapless dress, but her mama said she looked like a harlot." If he'd really been awake when we started talking about Aidan—and him—he hid it well.

Harper grabbed the first pan out of the drying rack and toweled it off. "You don't have to do that," Sawyer told her. She ignored him, talking to Tia about our walk to the beach in a few minutes. She turned to him only to ask if he could go with us.

"Thanks," Sawyer said with a quick glance at me, "but I'm working a double shift at the Crab Lab. I need to make up the hours I'm missing on Friday nights."

My heart went out to him. I would spend the morning relaxing by the ocean and trying to recharge for more school on Monday. He would be working and apparently needed the cash rather desperately. It didn't seem right that we both had gotten to play hard at the game last night, but he had to pay for that now, and I didn't.

"I'll dry," I told Harper, "and you put away, since you know where everything goes." She wasn't really paying me any attention, but she moved when I pushed her and dragged the dish towel out of her hands. I took her place. Now I stood beside Sawyer.

"So, you're going to stay at Harper's house until a room opens up here?" I asked him.

"Yeah," he said absently, concentrating on scrubbing something sticky out of the bottom of a pan.

"What are you going to do when you can't have the room here anymore? Harper said that will happen in December." I hoped I sounded like a concerned friend, not the girl in the van last night who'd made the comment about the box. I felt like I'd aged a year since then.

Tia chose this moment to wake up and pay attention. "I

want him to move in with us at my house," she interrupted. "We should have the whole main floor done by December, so we'll have plenty of room. I just have to . . ." She glanced at Sawyer. "It's complicated."

"Complicated how?" I asked.

Sawyer looked up from the sink and gave me a warning glance. He didn't want to talk about it.

But Tia didn't understand warning looks, and there was pretty much nothing on the planet she wouldn't talk about. "I have to convince everybody," she said. "The main problem is Will. He says"—she broke into an incredibly bad imitation of a Minnesota accent—"'I trust you, and I trust Sawyer, but I don't trust you and Sawyer. He's quit drinking, and you've cut down, but what if you both fall off the wagon and something happens?'"

Sawyer glanced over his shoulder at her and wagged his eyebrows.

She laughed. "Will worries about these things. I'm like, 'But I am totally devoted to your body, and your accent is so sexy.'"

I should have been glad her family might give Sawyer a place to live. I *was* glad. But my jealousy wouldn't let go. I knew how Will felt.

"The main problem is my sister," Tia went on.

"Which sister?" Harper asked.

"Violet. You know, she's moved back in, and she doesn't want a guy moving in too, because she's sworn off guys for the next five minutes. But the main problem is my other sister."

"Which other sister?" Harper asked.

"Izzy," Tia said.

"Do you realize there are three main problems?" I spoke up, trying not to sound as irritated as I felt.

Tia looked at me. "What?"

"You've said 'The main problem is . . .' three times."

"Yeah," she said. "That's what I'm trying to get across here. It's an uphill battle. So the main problem is Izzy."

"She doesn't even live with you anymore," Harper pointed out.

"That's what *I* say," Tia said, "but she's working on my dad. She's like, 'I got pregnant at seventeen. Tia's going to college. Trust me, you need to protect her from boys. The last thing you want to do is invite one to stay in your house.' Of course, this whole conversation is going on in Spanish, which I'm not as fluent in as they are, and the word for 'pregnant' sounds like 'embarrassed,' so I misunderstood what she was saying at first. I'm all like, 'I don't need to be protected, and I'm not embarrassed to have a boyfriend! Why should I be embarrassed just because *you* got pregnant?' The discussion kind of devolved from that point. I'll spare you the details."

Sawyer didn't speak through any of this. He left the sink to pull yet another fresh batch of orange rolls from the oven. Passing behind Tia with the basket, headed toward the dining room, he tugged on one of her braids. She responded by patting his shoulder.

"Let's get going," Harper said. "I love the beach in the morning."

I didn't have an excuse to hang around the kitchen until Sawyer came back. We left for Harper's cottage without me exchanging another word with him, or a glance, or gaining any more insight into whether he'd really found our note, or what the kiss was for.

At Harper's granddad's private strip of beach, just across the road and a block down from her house, I grilled her and Tia on ideas for where we could hold the homecoming dance. Tia predictably opted out because she didn't like being told to think too hard. Harper, who was good at thinking outside the box because that's where she lived pretty much all the time, couldn't come up with a single idea when I really needed her.

Finally I gave up and played in the water with them, floated in the ocean, and soaked up vitamin D on the beach to try to feel better about my life spinning out of control. I took deeper breaths, telling myself to *relax or die*, when I thought about going home to lunch with my mother.

I'd gotten a pass for the morning because Barrett and Dad were out on the sailboat. But my mother was making a big lunch with all Barrett's favorites—this was a little strange to me, because she cooked so seldom lately that I doubted she knew what *my* favorites even were—and I was required to be there.

Sure enough, the family lunch was everything I'd feared it would be, and more. My mother riddled Barrett with questions about college, ending each one in a barb about why he didn't make better grades. Barrett said as little as possible. Dad gently encouraged my mother to back off.

At some point my mother noticed I was there and asked, without much enthusiasm, "How was your game last night?"

"Pretty bad," I said. "Aidan broke up with me." I took another bite of salad.

My mother's jaw dropped. "I warned you about your mutiny. I hope it was worth it."

"Sylvia, wrong thing to say," Dad scolded her in an even tone, which was the only tone Dad had. But I was already pushing back my chair.

"No, ma'am," my mother called sharply. "You are not excused."

I stomped out of the dining room, down the hallway, and halfway up the stairs. At that point I realized the stomping was childish. I wasn't going to sit there at the table while my mother insulted me, but I wasn't going to give her the satisfaction of seeing me throw a tantrum, either. She would use that as ammunition later when I asked permission to do something.

I walked more softly up the rest of the stairs and into my room, not even slamming my door. In my bathroom I spit my mouthful of salad into the toilet and flushed.

Then I sat down in my reading chair, crossed my legs, and waited for my mother to send Dad up to talk to me. In the meantime I struggled not to cry. I couldn't look like I'd been crying when they made me come back downstairs, and I couldn't let them hear me sobbing.

But I wanted to. I struggled for every breath as I squeezed my eyes shut and thought about how unfair my life had become. This was not what high school was supposed to be like. I felt like an elephant was sitting on my chest, exactly as I had when I'd run the Labor Day 5K keeping pace with Cathy, who had longer legs than mine.

By the time Dad predictably knocked on my door and let himself in half an hour later, I was more or less calmly looking out at the neighbors' gardener cutting their grass behind our house. My parents' bedroom and Barrett's had the views of the lagoon out the front.

I nearly bawled and threw myself into Dad's arms when I saw him, but that's what I'd done when I was little and had an argument with my mother. So I sat quietly while he told me to make my mother happy, just this once, and come downstairs to spend time with my brother in the short space we had left together as a family.

Obediently I sat with Dad on the sofa in the family room, watching college football, which is probably what I would have done even if I hadn't been ordered to, since it gave me time with Dad. I just did it with less shouting at the TV than usual.

My mother was in her office, catching up on the work she'd missed when she left the bank early on Friday.

Barrett was up in his room, on his laptop. So much for spending family time together.

Luckily, we had another happy memory scheduled, one that would trap us all at the table together again. For dinner Barrett wanted his favorite meal, shrimp and fries at the Crab Lab.

The Crab Lab was one of the bigger restaurants downtown, with lots of waiters. Even though Sawyer was working tonight, there was no reason to think he would wait on *us*. We'd been there as a family plenty of times, and he'd never served us before. In fact, I hoped he wouldn't, after what my mother had said about him yesterday.

But I did hope I would catch a glimpse of him. Share a joke with him. I could casually repeat the joke later when I texted him to ask whether, according to parliamentary procedures, Aidan could really oust me as student council vice president. In three years I'd never tried to get close to any guy except Aidan, and I wasn't sure how it was done. I promised myself I would try with Sawyer. At least that gave me something to look forward to on this horrible weekend.

I should have been more careful what I wished for.

7

"GOOD EVENING, MS. BEALE," SAWYER SAID in a tone even brighter than the pleasing-the-elderly speeches I'd heard from him at breakfast that morning. "Hello, Mr. Gordon. I'm Sawyer, and I'll be your server this evening. Barrett." He looked down into my eyes. "Kaye. You look beautiful in blue." He set a basket of bread closest to me.

He wore his usual battered flip-flops, khaki shorts, and a Crab Lab T-shirt, with a white waiter's apron tied around his waist. His variegated blond hair looked halfway styled tonight. I approved. Even my mother had to be impressed by a neatly dressed, hardworking teen, exactly what she'd been growing up in downtown Tampa.

I should have known better when she didn't smile at being called Ms. Beale—even though, as Aidan had proven, it was quite a feat for my classmates to remember her name. Sawyer had been to my house for big parties a few times. He must have seen both surnames on our mailbox. So had everybody else, but Sawyer had *remembered*.

My mother didn't seem to care, though. When Sawyer asked for our drink orders, she just mumbled something to Dad, who opened the wine list. "What do you suggest?" he asked Sawyer.

Sawyer walked behind Dad, and they consulted the list together. Sawyer asked whether Dad was looking for a red or white, then rattled off characteristics of Riesling and sauvignon blanc brands using terminology I'd heard only on foodie TV shows. Sawyer was good at this.

"How do you know that?" my mother broke in. "Are you parroting what the restaurant has taught you about these wines, or do you know this from personal experience at age seventeen?"

I could have defended him by explaining that his brother was the bar manager, but somehow I didn't think that would impress my mother.

Sawyer straightened and appeared unsure for the first time. He said, "I don't have a good answer for that."

Dad chuckled. "*That* is a *great* answer."

I raised my hand. "Are y'all ready to order dinner? *I'm*

ready to order." I poked Barrett. "Shrimp and fries, right?" The faster we could get out of here, the better. If my mother kept on like this, Sawyer would never want to look at me again.

As soon as he'd taken our orders and moved to a different table, my mother pegged me with a stern gaze. "Is he the one who wants you to chase after the homecoming dance, even though the school canceled it?"

"A *lot* of people do," I said defensively. I pulled a slice of bread out of the basket, passed the basket to Dad, and popped some bread into my mouth. If everyone at the table had immediately started eating the Crab Lab's delicious bread, my mother would never have asked this:

"But *you* don't still want the dance, do you? Haven't you abandoned that idea now that Aidan's broken up with you? Who would you go with?"

I was tempted to blurt out Sawyer's name through a mouthful of bread, muffling the truth. I might have gotten away with it if my mother was just making conversation. But my mother never *just* made conversation. There was always a strategy, and this time she was reminding me I should have held on more tightly to Aidan, my great catch.

Besides, I got in trouble when I talked with my mouth full. "Not Florida manners," my mother would remind me. "Ivy League manners."

I chewed carefully, swallowed, and made the whole situation a million times worse by forcing my mother to wait and drawing attention to my answer. Finally I said, "I might ask Sawyer."

My mother choked midsip and put her water glass down with a *bang*, which I was pretty sure was *not* Ivy League manners. She asked sharply, "This one?" pointing with her thumb over her shoulder in the general direction of the Crab Lab's kitchen, where Sawyer had disappeared, thankfully.

"Yes," I said.

"The pelican," she said.

"Yes." I straightened in my chair, determined not to let her make me feel like shit. Or, *more* like shit.

"The one whose father robbed a bank."

"How did a pelican rob a bank?" Dad asked.

I looked over at Barrett. He'd never been very supportive in situations like this. He was good for a sympathetic eye roll, not much else. For once I could have used a comment from him, or a joke, or a subject change to distract my seething mother and befuddled dad, who was only going to make my mother angrier if he didn't stop playing dumb.

Ignoring Dad, I told my mother in a reasonable tone, "Sawyer's dad robbed a bank fifteen years ago."

"And he's out already?" my mother asked. "If he'd tried to rob *my* bank, he would be in there for life."

"He must have gotten time off for good behavior," Dad said helpfully.

"I've never understood that," my mother said. "How can anyone *not* behave well there? It's *prison*."

I took another bite of bread, since they obviously didn't need me for this conversation.

"You're not going out with that boy," my mother told me.

Again, I chewed carefully, swallowed, dabbed daintily at my lips, and returned my napkin to my lap. "Yes, I am," I said.

"You're grounded," my mother said. "Go ahead and ruin your grades trying to find a way to hold the dance, but you're not going."

I set my bread down. "I'm in charge of the parade, the homecoming court election, *and* the dance," I reminded her. "I was counting on impressing Principal Chen, whose glowing recommendation would get me into Columbia. But by all means, ground me because you don't like that I *might* ask out someone whose *father* did something wrong when I was two years old and already paid his debt to society. Because of that, I will shirk all my responsibilities and give up my Ivy League dreams."

"Sylvia," Dad said to my mother.

"I will probably move in with Sawyer after graduation," I continued, my voice getting shriller. "Maybe after a few years, I will have saved up enough money for cosmetology school."

"You lower your voice," my mother seethed.

"Why should I," I challenged her, "when I'm already grounded?"

"You're not grounded," Dad said patiently. He told my mother, "Kaye's not really going to a dance that doesn't exist with a boyfriend she doesn't have." He suggested to Barrett, "Tell us more about your classes this semester. When do you get to particle physics?"

I turned to Barrett as if I was interested in his sophomore-level physics classes too. As if *anyone* was. Dad could carry on pleasant conversation when nobody else wanted to. He'd honed his talents over a period of years in this family. The whole dinner was giving me a headache, though. I was clenching my teeth so hard I'd made my jaw hurt. I realized this and opened my mouth to relax my face, forming a hideous expression, I'm sure, just as Sawyer came around the corner balancing a tray with a wine bottle and an ice bucket.

He wasn't even looking at me, though. He set up a stand for the tray, placed the bucket on the table, then picked up the wine in a white towel. He stood there until Dad finished what he was saying to Barrett. Dad finally glanced around at

Sawyer. Then my mother glanced over her shoulder at him too. Sawyer's nervous gaze flashed between them.

"What are you waiting for?" my mother asked.

"Normally I would show the label to Mr. Gordon," Sawyer said, "since he ordered the wine. But I was waiting for some indication from you, because it seems like you might ask why I assume I should show the bottle to the man of the party."

Dad and Barrett burst into laughter. Diners at the surrounding tables looked over.

My mother saw people looking too, and bent forward over the table. "Why are you laughing? I wouldn't do that."

"You *have* done that," Dad and Barrett said at the same time. Dad added, "At that restaurant on our trip to Miami, for starters."

Sawyer kept looking from one of them to the other, with the demeanor of an accused murderer waiting to hear his verdict in court. He still didn't glance at me, which was just as well. He knew he'd gotten himself in trouble, but he had *no idea* how angry he'd just made my mother.

Or how, if we ever *did* have any chance of going out together, he'd just killed that possibility.

When Dad was finally through chuckling, he wiggled his finger, inviting Sawyer to show him the bottle. My mother scowled as Sawyer maneuvered through an impressive display of ceremonial wine pouring. First he cut the foil over the top of the bottle with a large pocketknife he produced from his waiter's apron. I wondered if he brought this thing to school every day, too, and whether that was legal. Next he brought out a corkscrew. Remembering all the comedies I'd seen in which people got hit in the eye when someone popped the cork on champagne, I gripped the edge of my seat, expecting disaster—but Sawyer opened the wine like it was nothing.

He offered the cork to Dad—who shook his head as if that wasn't necessary—placed the cork by Dad's plate, then poured a splash of wine into Dad's glass, turning the bottle carefully so it didn't drip, I supposed. Dad sipped from his glass and nodded. Sawyer filled my mother's glass half-full, then Dad's, and with one practiced movement shoved the bottle into the ice bucket, keeping the white towel wrapped around the top.

My parents always ordered wine with dinner at restaurants. I must have seen this dance performed a hundred times, but I'd never appreciated the choreography, or the performer. Funny how a crush changed everything.

Sawyer stepped back. "Is there anything else I can do for you right now?"

"You have done a *lot* already," my mother said.

This time Sawyer focused on me, his blue eyes huge, before escaping to check on the next table.

My mother shook her head at me. She didn't say a word, but her message was clear: *You are dating Sawyer De Luca over my dead body.*

At the same time Dad was asking, "What did you prove, Sylvia, attacking that child? It's not a fair fight. Let it go." He turned to Barrett. "Next time you're home, I'm hoeing the potatoes and catching the shrimp myself."

"You're making a joke out of it," my mother said, "but your daughter *just* declared she is going *out* with him."

"That's not what she declared." Dad asked me, "Is that what you declared?"

I turned away from both of them to speak to Barrett, for once. "Please, tell us more about particle physics."

That got my parents asking Barrett questions again, at least. I stayed silent and worried about what Sawyer was thinking, and whether he hated me, as he strode from table to table to the kitchen and back to another table. I saw now why he slept so soundly.

After about twenty minutes, he brought out another tray and set up a stand. He placed redfish in front of my mother, trout in front of Dad, shrimp and fries in front of Barrett (damn

Barrett and his shrimp and fries for causing all this), and the same in front of me. A couple of weeks ago when a bunch of us from school had eaten here, Sawyer had arranged my shrimp around the edge of my plate like the curls of my new hairstyle. This time the shrimp were piled humorlessly with a garnish of parsley. Judging from this, our prospects were ruined.

After he'd served us all, he drew the wine bottle out of the ice bucket, wiped it carefully with the towel, and poured my mother another glass. She looked up at him and asked, "Isn't it illegal for you to serve alcohol before you're twenty-one?"

He did that turning thing with the bottle again so it wouldn't drip as he brought it away from my mother's glass. Then he said, "The legal age to serve alcohol in Florida is eighteen, not twenty-one." He stepped behind my father and poured the rest of the wine into his glass. "But yes, I'm breaking the law. I'll be sure to tell the police chief at table six when I bring him his third Michelob." His polite waiter voice was gone. His usual snide Sawyer voice had returned.

My mother was glaring at him.

He didn't see her, though. He set the empty bottle on his tray and removed the ice bucket from the table. By that time he seemed to realize all on his own what he'd done. His lips parted. He looked at me.

Suddenly he straightened and turned very pale underneath his tan. "I'm sorry," he said to my mother. "That was uncalled for."

The table was silent. My mother's eyes had never left him, and her expression hadn't changed.

"I'm really sorry," he told Dad. "I apologize."

"It's okay, Sawyer," I heard myself telling him.

He lifted the laden tray high over his head, folded the stand, and hurried across the restaurant. He disappeared through the folding door into the kitchen.

"What did you say that for?" I hissed at my mother.

For the first time in a long time, my mother seemed taken aback. "It's illegal for him to serve us alcohol," she repeated.

"If you're so outraged, why did you let Dad order alcohol from him?"

Dad didn't jump in to defend her. He raised his eyebrows at her like he thought it was a good question.

"I didn't know it was illegal," my mother said.

"Obviously you had some idea, or you wouldn't have tried to catch him doing something wrong and embarrass him." I threw my napkin down on my plate and stood. "I am done eating with you people."

"Not again," Dad said.

"Can I have yours?" Barrett asked.

"Young lady . . . ," my mother started.

I followed Sawyer's path, winding among the tables. I had a hard time doing this without bumping anyone, and I wasn't even carrying a heavy tray and a stand like he had been. At the door to the kitchen, I hesitated, looking around to see if any of the restaurant staff was watching. As I glanced into the bar, a smaller room on one side of the restaurant, my eyes met Sawyer's dark-haired brother's.

He held my gaze, like he wasn't surprised to see me. He made no move to stop me.

I swept into the kitchen, moving fast. If anybody wanted to throw me out, they'd have to catch me first.

That was the last thing on these guys' minds, though. I'd imagined six people worked in the Crab Lab kitchen. There must have been twelve, all hustling. The equipment was new, but the walls were the original exposed brick like most of the buildings that made up downtown. The ceiling was embossed tin. Oil, steam, and Spanish floated in the air. If any cooks called to me, I didn't understand what they said. I made a beeline straight through to the back door standing open, which I assumed led to the Crab Lab's porch for employee breaks. Sawyer and Tia had experienced more escapades there than I'd really wanted to hear about.

Outside was a different world. The night, though warm, was ten degrees cooler than the kitchen, and full of the smells of cooking, not just from the Crab Lab but also from the barbecue restaurant on one side and the Indian restaurant on the other. Industrial-strength air conditioners shouted from all the buildings up and down the alley. But the Crab Lab's porch was an oasis, sheltered with an awning, furnished with picnic tables and ashtrays overflowing with cigarette butts. The railing was spun with twinkling white lights.

Sawyer stood at the edge of the wooden stairs down, arms crossed, staring at the ancient brick-paved alley. When he heard my footsteps, he turned around. "Kaye!" he exclaimed, sounding startled. "I am so sorry."

I kept coming and walked right into him, wrapping my arms around him.

He didn't move, holding his arms stiffly at his sides.

"Hug me back," I said into his shoulder. "You have to do that sometimes. We can't always run to your truck to find the pelican outfit when we need to hug."

I meant we were both in emotional turmoil. We needed a hug to calm what was going on in our heads. But as he obediently slid his hands around my waist and nestled his face in my neck with his mouth at my ear, he took a step closer. His hard thigh was between my thighs. His body heated mine through his T-shirt and my thin dress.

His arms tightened around me. I tightened mine around

him. We'd never hugged before—not when one of us wasn't dressed as a pelican, anyway. I regretted this now, because my body felt so good against his. His breath was soft in my ear. All the best parts of me started to tingle.

Without warning, he released me and took a step back. "Sit down," he said, sinking to a bench himself and patting the space beside him.

I sat very close with my knee touching his. "Will I get you in trouble for being back here?"

"Nobody gets in trouble for anything that happens on this porch. That's one reason I used to drink so much."

"Ah." That must also be the reason he and Tia had felt each other up nightly when she worked here last summer. I hadn't understood then why she put herself in that position with him over and over. I could definitely see the appeal now.

But that wasn't what I'd come here for, and I knew we didn't have much time to talk before he had to get back to work. I said, "About my mother—"

"There's no excuse for me saying that," he burst out.

"No!" I exclaimed. "*She* shouldn't have said that to *you*."

"She should be able to say anything she wants to me. Usually customers can. I don't react."

I found this hard to believe, knowing Sawyer. "Do you save it all up and release it at school?"

"Yes," he said. "But I wasn't expecting you tonight. I saw you come in, and I haven't been able to think straight since."

He was looking into my eyes and admitting that he liked me. My gaze drifted to the blond stubble on his cheeks, and then to his lips, which looked soft.

Reminding myself how little time we had, I slid my hand onto his. "My mother's powerful at her bank. According to everything I've heard, she's kind and fair to her employees. But you know the saying. A man in that position gets called the boss. A woman in that position gets called a bitch. I've been called a bitch at school just because I took charge or expressed my opinion, so I know how she feels."

Sawyer swallowed and nodded.

"And maybe she saves it all up and releases it at home," I mused. "You had no way of knowing this, but when you mentioned that she might want to see the wine label instead of my dad, you definitely hit a sore spot."

"And then your dad and your brother laughed," Sawyer said. "I know. I never meant for that to happen. I've just had female customers react that way before. I've learned to stand back and read people so I can head off anybody getting angry or embarrassed. I thought I'd gotten good at it. I *have*. I know I have." He glanced sidelong at me. "You're jamming my radar."

"Sorry," I said softly.

Pulling his hand out from under mine, he stood, paced to the porch railing, and turned to face me. "What is she going to do to me? I blurted that dumb shit about the police chief, and suddenly I saw my life flash before my eyes. She could turn me in. I could lose my job. I won't be able to get another job serving alcohol at this age, and that's where I make most of my money in tips. My brother could lose his job for convincing the owner to hire me. Hold on." He pulled his phone out of his back pocket. It hummed and vibrated in his hand. "Oh, holy fuck," he said to the screen, "really? Now?" He pocketed it again without answering it.

"What's the matter?" I asked, alarmed. "Who is it?"

"My mother." Sawyer had a way of conveying loathing in his voice, but I'd never heard him sound quite so disgusted.

"In Georgia?" I checked.

"Yes."

"You don't answer her?"

"No."

I realized something. "Did she call you last night in the van?"

He looked at the porch ceiling, remembering. "Yes."

"Does she call you a lot?"

"Yes."

"When's the last time you talked to her?"

"Two years ago, when I left Valdosta." When I gaped at him, he said, "She only wants money."

I was having a very hard time understanding Sawyer's world. "What if she's calling about something else?" I reasoned.

"She'd call my brother. I know, you're thinking, 'You should send your mom money if she needs it,' but I'm just done with her. I mean, I voluntarily came to live with my father as soon as he got out of prison. That's how bad it was with my mother."

I frowned at him. "Wait. I thought you moved in with your father because your mother couldn't handle you anymore."

He huffed an exasperated sigh. "Who told you that?"

"Several people. Tia."

He squinted at me. "I may have said that to Tia before I really knew her. My first day in town, it got around school that my dad had been to jail. Assholes were picking on me. I hit first so nobody would hit me. That seemed to work, so I started cultivating a tough-guy rep. See how great it works? Arrrrrrrg," he moaned with his head in his hands. "Fuck everybody."

I'd heard him say *that* before too, but he hadn't sounded this lost.

He looked up at me. "Everyone but you."

"Aw," I said. "That's sweet, I guess." I got up and walked over to him. He was staring at the floor again. I put my hand under his chin and lifted his head until he looked at me. "My mother's not going to turn you in, Sawyer. That was never her intention. Being critical is her way of making small talk." I was realizing this for the first time as I said it.

He removed my hand from his face and held it loosely between us, looking doubtfully at me.

"She grew up poor," I said.

Sawyer gave a short nod. He needed no further explanation.

But I wanted to give him one, to show him I wasn't completely ignorant of what this meant. "When Barrett and I were younger and she got mad at us for not working hard enough in school or refusing to eat enough dinner, she packed us in the car and drove us across town to gawk at where she grew up." Actually, *I* was the one she always got mad at, but she often made Barrett go too, in case my bad attitude had rubbed off on him.

Sawyer gave me the mad scientist face I loved, raising one eyebrow and lowering the other. "That's heavy."

"I thought so too," I said. "You got off easy." I detangled my hand from his and rubbed his arm, trying to rub some of his usual life back into him. "*I* was impressed with your waiter skills. I had no idea you were so highly trained. You never pull out all these stops when I come here without my parents."

"I'm not going to do all that shit for you guys," he muttered. "You're my friends, and I'm in a hurry to get back to another table, and y'all aren't going to tip me anyway."

"Of course we tip you!" I said, thinking back to the last time Sawyer had waited on me when I'd paid for my food myself. It was the last time I'd been here, two weeks ago exactly, and I could have sworn I'd tipped him fifteen percent.

"Not when Aidan pays, you don't."

My hand stopped on his arm as I gaped at him. "*Really?*" I was horrified. I'd had no idea Aidan was that rude to anyone but me. And Sawyer needed the money, now more than ever.

He looked away. Even in the dim blinking lights, I could tell he was blushing.

I took both his hands in mine. "You know, your parents have a legal responsibility to take care of you until you turn eighteen."

"Yeah, well, I'm about to turn eighteen."

"You don't turn eighteen until March fifteenth, Sawyer."

He raised his eyebrows. "Why do you know when my birthday is?"

"I just do." I didn't let on that I'd surprised myself with this knowledge too. I knew generally when most of my friends' birthdays were, as in, what month. I'd memorized specific days for Tia, Harper, Aidan, and Sawyer.

"That's a long time for you to go without a real place to live," I said. "Did your dad kick you out, or did you just leave?"

"I left," he said darkly.

"Why?"

"I don't want to talk about it," he said so vehemently that, nosey as I was, I didn't dare try to turn over that rock again.

Instead I said, "You should talk to someone. One of the counselors at school."

"No! Guys don't do that."

"Not the weird counselor with the muttonchop side-burns," I said quickly. "The nice one, Ms. Malone. Go in and tell her whatever you don't want to tell me. You obviously need to tell *somebody*. You're this big ball of stress." I reached up and rubbed his shoulders, kneading the soft notches next to his shoulder blades. Sure enough, the muscles there were tight with his anxiety. Even tighter than mine. "Promise me you'll go Monday."

He let out an appreciative sigh and let his head fall forward so that some strands of his hair got caught in mine. He groaned, "No."

Leaving my hands on his shoulders, I stopped rubbing. "Promise me, and there's more where this came from."

"Okay," he said instantly.

I made a few more hard circles with my fingers, then let him go. "I have something to ask you. I know we've been out here a while, though, and you need to go back to work. Our table from hell isn't your only table."

"I told another server to cover for me while I took a break," he said. "So, yeah, I need to get back, but you can ask me something. Shoot."

"It's a parliamentarian question," I said. "When Aidan broke up with me last night, he also told me to resign as vice president."

Sawyer was shaking his head.

I went on. "I told him no. He said he would go to Ms. Yates. I said I would go to you."

"Exactly." Sawyer sounded like his sarcastic self again. "There's nothing in the student council charter giving him that power. Ms. Yates knows that. After Friday's meeting, she also knows I understand the charter, and I'd make a stink. If they tried to take the position away from you, theoretically you could sue the school system for not following its own written rules. There's no way Principal Chen would let that happen."

"I shouldn't worry?" I asked. "I figured he was bluffing to see if he could make me resign."

"No," Sawyer said, "don't worry. The charter gives Aidan very little power. The only reason he has power around school is that he *says* he does, and other people believe him." He eyed me hard. By "other people" he meant me.

I would prove Sawyer wrong about this.

"Are you working tomorrow?" I asked.

"Yes."

"When?"

"All day."

I'd been afraid of this. "All night, too?"

"Yes."

"My parents are taking Barrett to the airport midafternoon. I'm going to make my escape, drive over here, explore some shops, and try to figure out where we might be able to hold the homecoming dance. Maybe I'll pop in to visit you."

"Do," he said. "I'll see you then." He didn't smile, exactly, but he looked a lot less tortured than he had when I'd come out here. I headed inside.

But as I looked back over my shoulder at him, he was staring out at the alleyway again. He ran his hand through his hair and gripped the back of his head like he wanted to pull his scalp off.

When I returned to the table, my parents were finishing their food. Barrett's plate was empty, and several of my shrimp had gone missing. Plopping down in my chair, I told my mother, "I hope you're happy. You scared the life out of Saw—"

I stopped as Sawyer himself appeared between my parents. He took my mother's plate, then Dad's. "How was everything?" he asked in his personable waiter voice.

"Delicious," Dad said. He ordered dessert.

My mother glared. Sawyer noticed and smiled at her. Oh, Sawyer.

As soon as he'd disappeared into the kitchen again, she told me, "I *meant* to scare the life out of him. I don't want that boy anywhere around you, after what I just found out about his father. Did you know—"

"Sylvia, don't," Dad said.

My mother spoke over him. "—his father grew up here in town and actually robbed a bank branch right down the road in Clearwater? That hits a little too close to home. Seth said it wasn't one of *my* branches, but—"

"Seth," I repeated. The only Seth I knew was Aidan's dad, who worked as an assistant district attorney for the county. "Did you *call Aidan's dad* right here from the restaurant so you could convince me how terrible Sawyer is? You made him look up that case on a Saturday night?"

"He didn't have to look it up," my mother said ominously. "He's the one who put that man in jail."

I could *not* believe this. Granted, Mr. De Luca sounded like a shadier and shadier character as my mother transformed his crimes from vague rumors into stark, brutal reality. But that only increased my growing respect for Sawyer.

I looked to Dad for help. He closed his eyes and took a deep breath through his nose like he was counting to ten. Barrett reached over to my plate and stole another of my shrimp. I was on my own.

I told my mother, "This is a logical fallacy, guilt by association. You damning Sawyer for what his dad did is like me damning you for what your—"

"*Kaye,*" Dad said sternly.

My mother always sounded stern. Dad never did. His use of that tone was so surprising that I was shocked out of what I was going to say.

Which was exactly what he'd intended. And it was probably for the best. Because I'd been about to point out that my mother's brother had been murdered while selling heroin in the neighborhood where they grew up. She'd been sixteen years old.

As Sawyer set a slice of chocolate cake down in front of Dad, he looked cautiously around the table at our angry faces.

"I'm sure it's delicious," Dad told Sawyer, "but I've changed my mind. Could I get this boxed up to go?"

8

THE NEXT MORNING MY MOTHER COOKED A big breakfast, and Dad congratulated me on making it all the way through the meal without flouncing away. He must have talked my mother down. She didn't say another word about Sawyer or his jailbird father. And I was in a better mood because I had something to look forward to: seeing Sawyer again.

Right after my parents left to take Barrett to the airport, I drove downtown. The Crab Lab was my first stop. I hadn't counted on running straight into their two-for-one brunch special. Sawyer grinned brilliantly at me when I came in, but so many customers flagged him down that I stood by the door for five minutes before he even made it over to me. He said he couldn't talk just then, and I understood why. I would embark on my mission by myself.

I'd strolled the brick sidewalks of our historic downtown countless times, but I saw the buildings with new eyes now that I was looking for something specific. The Crab Lab owned a restored warehouse for events. It stood to reason that, somewhere among these buildings, there was another space large enough to throw a homecoming dance. I just had to find it.

I spent hours walking into every storefront and asking the people behind the counter whether they owned such a space or knew of one. Most of them said no. Tia's sister Violet, who worked in an antiques shop, said she did have a space like that on the second floor, but we couldn't hold our dance there because it was full of dead bodies. Skeptical, I walked up the rickety stairs myself, straight into the store's antique taxidermy collection.

But Violet said the gay burlesque club might be an option. Their second story was an open dance floor practically *made* for homecoming. Dubious about my chances of convincing the owner to say yes, I walked in anyway—drawing arch looks from the men bellied up to the bar—and quickly told the bartender what I wanted.

"Well, *I'm* the owner," he said, "and of *course* you can use the second floor. In fact, I'll close down the whole place for the night so we don't have the barflies drinking among you tender innocents."

"You would do that for us?" It didn't seem real.

"I'm a graduate of your fine institution," he explained. "It's the least I can do for homecoming. Fight, Pelicans, fight!"

I drove home feeling lighter than I had since Friday. I rolled down the windows and enjoyed the hot wind scented with flowers. When I stopped at the intersection next to Aidan's house, I didn't even look to see whether he was home.

I should have stayed away from my own house a few more hours.

My parents had returned. My dad was probably upstairs on his porch, but my mother actually came out of her office to confront me.

I braced myself for another fight, but I was so, so weary.

She opened her arms.

I stiffened, resistant. Then, partly to prevent myself from crying in front of her, I walked into her embrace.

She hugged me tightly for a moment. Loosening her hold, she rubbed my back. She told me to sit down at the kitchen bar and served me two of Barrett's leftover cookies, even though they would probably spoil my dinner.

I should have known the other shoe would drop. Covering one of my hands with hers on the counter, she told me, "You can struggle, Kaye, and work, and go after your dreams. And one wrong move can ruin you forever."

I didn't retort as I had last night. I didn't have the heart. In her precisely made-up eyes, I saw real concern for me, bordering on panic. And I understood where she was coming from. She had braved terrible odds to get to college. By the time she graduated, everyone she'd loved back home was dead.

But she didn't need to worry about me. Not to this extent, anyway. My own world was nothing like hers had been. My future was not so fragile.

Was it?

"I wanted to apologize for flying off the handle a couple of times yesterday," she said.

Yep, Dad had definitely talked her down.

She said, "When I was growing up—"

And with that, she lost me. "I don't want to hear about it," I said quickly. "You grew up in a slum, surrounded by criminals and addicts. I'm sorry for what you went through, but my life is not like that."

She glowered at me for interrupting.

"Sorry," I grumbled.

"What I was going to say," she told me indignantly, "is that when I was growing up, people all around me made terrible mistakes. And those mistakes were often deadly. For that reason, it's hard for me to let people I love make mistakes. But you're right. You're not in the environment I was in. The mistakes you make won't kill you. I know that. I'll try to do better."

I shrugged, munching a cookie. For her, this was a pretty good apology, but she'd managed simultaneously to accuse me of failing at life.

"When I talked to Seth last night," she said, "he indicated that Aidan is really regretting asking you for a break."

"He did not ask," I said.

"Well. And I'm sure your feelings about this are still very raw. But Seth seemed to think the whole problem started because you made an error with the yearbook elections."

"Mr. O'Neill thinks so because that's what Aidan told him," I pointed out.

She nodded. "Aidan also told him you and Sawyer had been connected in some way in one of the polls. You and Sawyer have been spending more time together because of this cheerleading business, and now in student council. Aidan grew jealous and let his feelings get the better of him. He's going to ask you to take him back."

"I'm going to say no."

"And if you do," my mother said, "Seth and I won't interfere."

"Gee, thanks," I said.

She glowered at me again. This time I didn't say I was sorry.

Finally she went on. "But I want you to think about the three years you and Aidan dated. You told me time and time again you were going to marry him. Of course, that's a silly thing for a fourteen-year-old to say, but you were together so long that I began to think you'd found true love after all. You planned to go to Columbia together. Don't throw this away over one silly fight about a boy you're not going to date anyway."

We exchanged a long, unblinking look. She was making sure I'd gotten her message. I was thinking I wanted to try out Sawyer more than ever.

"When I was in high school," she said, "there was a boy I liked. He was *so fine*."

"Fine?" I asked skeptically.

"It was the eighties," she said. "Anyway, he was bad news. I knew he would take me down the wrong path, so I made a conscious decision to stay away from him."

My heart stopped. "And now you regret it," I said softly.

She side-eyed me. "No, he's in prison. If I'd done what he wanted, I would have ended up a single mother without a college degree, much less an MBA, working for minimum wage and struggling to make ends meet."

Oh, good Lord.

"What happened to letting me make my own mistakes?" I asked.

She shrugged. "You're right. I told you, it's hard for me to let go. I do want you to enjoy high school. But this year will fly by, and then your life will really start."

And with that she reached into the container for her own cookie.

I spent the rest of the night working on my pitch to Principal Chen for saving the dance. The student council had already put down deposits on the DJ and the caterer. If we canceled the dance altogether, we'd lose those student dues dollars with nothing to show for it. The best solution, both for fiscal responsibility and school morale, was simply to move the venue to the property of a local business owner and Pelican alumnus.

This speech made perfect sense. If Aidan somehow convinced Ms. Yates that I should be fired as student council vice president, Ms. Chen would never allow it, because I was obviously such a great school leader.

But as I rehearsed my speech in my head, I began to have misgivings about telling Ms. Chen we were moving the dance to a gay bar. If she didn't like this idea, she might not give me another chance.

And even if she did approve the move, the likelihood was high that someone's parents would complain. Our town was generally pretty accepting, but back in ninth grade, Angelica's mom had told Ms. Yates she shouldn't be teaching her impressionable child about evolution.

If we held homecoming at the gay burlesque club, there would be a stink.

The stink would lead to a petition.

Someone would post the petition online, where it would go viral.

Our school and our town would get a national reputation as closed-minded and backward.

It would be all my fault.

And my mother would look at me and say, *I told you so.*

Honestly, why didn't I leave well enough alone?

I lay on my bed, curled into a ball, staring out my window at the neighbor's yard, late into the night. When my mind was exhausted from weighing those options and mulling over the problem, it moved on to the conundrum of Sawyer. Maybe my mother was right. I was still furious with Aidan, but did I really want to throw our whole lives together away? We could take a break for a little longer and see if time healed our wounds.

But if I went out with Sawyer, or even acted like I wanted

to, I could easily ruin everything with Aidan. I didn't buy Tia's argument that dating Sawyer would make Aidan jealous and bring him closer. Aidan's ego wouldn't survive that insult.

Besides, what proof did I have that Sawyer wanted to go out with *me*? He'd been sweet to me last night. He said he'd gotten flustered when he saw me. He'd acted like he wanted me to visit him today. But he hadn't asked me on a date. There were a lot of things I didn't understand about Sawyer, but this I knew: He went after what he wanted.

I got so little sleep that, in the morning, I put on clothes and makeup and stumbled downstairs in a haze. But I'd decided two things. I would tell the student council that Aidan had been right. I'd looked for a venue where we could hold the dance, and the only alternative I'd found wouldn't be acceptable to everyone. We should cancel after all.

And I would tell Sawyer it would be better that we didn't get together.

If he even asked.

"I hope your paper on *Crime and Punishment* turned out well," my mother said as I was walking out the door to my car.

My response was to gasp, which gave away to her that I'd completely forgotten about the paper.

"I thought that's what you were doing up in your room

last night!" she shouted, anger flashing in her eyes. "You spent this entire weekend on everything *except* your paper?"

Dad had left early in the morning to drive to Miami for research on his new book. There was nobody left to say in a calming voice, "Sylvia," and stop my mother from freaking out.

"If you can't complete your basic assignments," she said, "we should definitely rethink this cheerleading mess."

I cried so hard on the drive to school that I thought several times about pulling off the road. Finally I parked, killed the engine, and searched the glove compartment for a tissue to clean up my mascara before I went inside.

I was blowing my nose in a fast-food napkin when I spotted Harper and Brody sitting on a bench near the school entrance, shaded by palms from the bright morning sun. He was talking close to her ear. Her hair was long and glossy, flowing over her shoulders, her dark eyes shining into the sunlight. A smile was frozen on her face because of something he'd said, but now she'd gotten distracted by a bird, a cloud, or the way the palm fronds waved in the breeze.

Farther away, walking across the parking lot toward school, Tia laughed loudly with Will. I could hear her even with my windows rolled up. She didn't look much different than she had in third grade: tall, disheveled, with her auburn hair pulled away from her face anyhow, laughing.

My favorite things about my friends, Tia loud and laughing and Harper daydreaming, were things my mother would have scolded me for doing. *Inside voice. Pay attention. Ivy League manners.*

I didn't even *have* a favorite thing about myself. I loved to dance. I loved to cheer. My mother made me feel like those activities were nonsense. All that was left of me was organizational skills and the ability to follow directions. My only two talents had had a fatal shoot-out in my brain overnight. Now I was an empty shell.

The bell rang to call everyone inside. My classmates who'd been moseying across the parking lot quickened their step. Tia and Will jumped the curb and high-fived Harper and Brody, who stood and stretched. They all disappeared beneath the parallel lines of palm trees leading into the school.

I had to go inside too, to face Mr. Frank with no paper and accept my first-ever zero. I knew this. But as I took one last breath of sticky air inside my car, I entertained a fantasy of turning the engine on again and driving in the opposite direction to play hooky at the beach. How much more trouble could I possibly get into this morning? Might as well enjoy myself, for once.

Two minutes later I was inside the crowded school hallway like a good girl, of course. I pulled my books for my first two periods out of my locker. Aidan leaned casually against the locker next to mine, just as he had countless times before, like we'd never broken up. When he saw my face, though, he straightened and asked, "What's wrong?"

"I forgot to write my paper for Mr. Frank," I said, hoarse from crying.

"Ha!" Aidan crowed. "That's one step closer to valedictorian for me."

I just looked at him with my mouth open. Aidan was competitive. He was callous. But until now I'd never known him to be cruel.

I slammed my locker as hard as I could and stomped down the hall.

"Hey!" I heard him calling after me. "I was *kidding!*"

I kept walking. The bell rang again, and the people remaining in the hallways slipped into classrooms. I was still moving. My history class was in the other direction, but I simply couldn't see myself sitting in a desk right now, facing the front, my stomach cramping with the knowledge that I'd just blown everything I'd worked for because of one crazy weekend.

Ahead of me, Sawyer stepped into the hallway and closed a door behind him. When he saw me, he froze with his hand on the doorknob, his face flushing bright pink.

I looked up at the nameplate on the door and saw why he felt caught. MS. MALONE, SCHOOL COUNSELOR.

But Sawyer was always quick to recover. The next second he didn't look self-conscious anymore. His hands were on my shoulders. "Wow, what's the matter?"

I flung myself into his arms.

9

AS SOON AS HIS ARMS ENCIRCLED ME, I WAS trying to pull away again. Nobody but us was in the hall right now. I could hear Ms. Chen's morning announcements echoing through an open door. But a teacher was likely to peek out at us any second, see us embracing, and send us straight to the principal's office. Plus, surveillance cameras frowned from the corners of the ceiling, keeping everyone safe from school shooters and public displays of affection.

Sawyer didn't let go of me. He held my head to his chest, saying, "Shhh. Tell me what's wrong, and we'll fix it."

I laughed and then coughed at the idea of Sawyer, with all his real problems, being able to solve any of my ridiculous ones. After a gargantuan sniffle, I said shakily, "I forgot to write my paper for Mr. Frank."

He held me at arm's length and looked into my eyes. "That's a major grade." Before I could cry again, he ordered me, "Stop. You mean you forgot to make your paper perfect, or you forgot to write it at all? How many words do you have?"

"None." I was about to lose it.

"Stop," he said again. "But you have your thesis statement and your notes and your outline, right? We did that in class."

I nodded.

"That's your blueprint. All you need to do is fill in the blanks. You have hours to get that done. We don't go to Mr. Frank's class until second-to-last period. You can write it on your computer and e-mail it to him while he's taking roll."

"But Sawyer," I wailed, "I have class until then. I'm doing class during class."

"You've got study hall," he pointed out, "and lunch."

"I was going to talk to Ms. Chen about the homecoming dance during lunch," I said.

He shook me gently. "Kaye. Listen to me. You've got to let go of that shit and prioritize. Save your grade today. Do homecoming tomorrow." He released my arms and rubbed where he'd squeezed me. "There's lots of downtime during class, too. Even when teachers are talking, you can be working on your paper."

"What if one of them calls on me and I get in trouble?"

"To save your GPA, it's worth it," he declared. "And if things really get hairy, take your computer to the bathroom."

"This isn't going to work," I whispered.

He gave me an exasperated look. "Do you know how much homework I've done at the very last second in the bathroom? You can do this, Kaye. You just have to believe it. Isn't your dad a famous writer?"

"He's not famous," I mumbled.

"But he works on deadline," Sawyer pointed out. "Just because you didn't obsess over this paper doesn't mean it won't be any good. Even if it does turn out to be shit, you'll get a fifty just for turning it in, which is way better for your average than a zero."

"Right." With a grade of fifty rather than a zero, I'd get a B for this grading period and lose hope of making valedictorian. But there was always salutatorian. That might be good enough for admission to Columbia, with my alumni parents backing me.

But nothing would save me in the eyes of my mother.

"Whatever you're thinking right now," Sawyer said, "snap out of it. Let me tell you what needs to go through your head for the next five hours, until you turn this paper in." He tapped one finger. "Dostoyevsky."

"Dostoyevsky," I repeated.

He tapped another finger. "Raskolnikov."

"Raskolnikov," I said.

"Alyona Ivanovna, Porfiry Petrovich, Sonia Marmeladov. Got that? Now, what's going through your head? Hint: The answer should be Dostoyevsky."

"I'm tardy for history," I sobbed, "and I don't have an excuse."

Sawyer gave me his crazy face with one eyebrow up, clearly at the end of his patience. "I'll write you in on the one Ms. Malone gave me."

"That's forgery!"

Shaking his head, he grabbed my hand and knocked on Ms. Malone's door. When we heard "Come in," he pulled me inside.

"Back so soon?" Ms. Malone asked from behind her desk. She saw me and said, "Oh, hi there."

"Ms. Malone," Sawyer said, "this is Kaye Gordon."

Ms. Malone came around her desk to shake my hand. "We were just talking about you." Too late she realized this was not the right thing to say. Her eyes darted to Sawyer, who was blushing intensely all over again.

His flushed cheeks were the only clue Sawyer was morti- fied, and he continued smoothly, "Kaye would like to make an appointment to talk with you about stress management techniques."

"Yes, I see you're having a problem there," Ms. Malone agreed, scanning my tearstained and probably mascara-streaked face. "How about today?"

"Not today," Sawyer said quickly, "or anytime before homecoming, because that will just stress her out more. How about the Monday after homecoming?"

Ms. Malone stepped behind her desk again and flipped through her calendar. She looked up at me. "Is this period okay?"

I nodded dumbly.

She wrote my appointment time down on a card.

"And can she also have an excuse that says she was here talking to you?" Sawyer asked. "She's late for history."

Ms. Malone gave Sawyer the briefest look that let him know she saw right through his ploy.

But she paged through her book of preprinted excuses and filled one out for me. Handing it across her desk, she said, "All right, dear. You come see me sooner if you need to." She turned to Sawyer. "And you, here, tomorrow."

"Yes, ma'am." Sawyer put his arm around my shoulders and steered me out the door.

"Thank you," I breathed as we walked down the hall.

"You're welcome. I earned my shoulder rub."

"You did." I laughed and felt better, even though I had a horrible five hours in front of me, and my face was still wet with tears. "Did Ms. Malone help you? What did she say?"

"Don't think about that right now. Until one o'clock when you e-mail this paper to Mr. Frank, your only thoughts are Dostoyevsky, Raskolnikov—"

"Okay." I stopped in the hallway. He stopped too, in surprise. His eyes were full of concern.

I wanted to kiss him—not a show of lust, but of appreciation. I would get us both in hot water, though. I only kissed my finger and placed it on his lips.

He looked shocked for a moment. But as I pulled my hand away, he said solemnly, "I know. I feel that way too."

And we walked to history together.

The following Friday, I skipped out of calculus even earlier than I had the previous week for the student council meeting. I waited outside Ms. Yates's classroom. Sure enough, I'd beaten Sawyer by a hair. I watched him saunter up the hallway, walking more like the jaunty pelican than his usual cool self while he thought nobody was watching. His backpack hung heavy over one shoulder. It probably contained six different library books explaining *Robert's Rules of Order*. He wore the madras plaid shirt with the blue stripe that I loved so much. When he looked up at me, his blue eyes were arresting in the blank white hall. He broke into a wide grin.

He'd been kind to me Monday while I was writing my paper, checking on me between classes. During lunch I'd e-mailed him my mostly finished draft. He'd read over it on his phone while I was still typing the end, and he suggested places I could clarify my statements or add more detail. Best of all, he told me my paper wasn't crap. That kept me going. I didn't have time to eat lunch, but I typed my closing statement just as the bell rang to go to Mr. Frank's class, where Sawyer slipped me a candy bar underneath our desktops.

The way he'd treated me, and the way *Aidan* had acted when he found out I'd forgotten to write my paper, made me question my decision not to date Sawyer if he asked. The problem was, he didn't ask. All week we hung out during lunch and the classes we had together. People certainly saw *something* between us. Tia and Harper, wide-eyed, asked me for updates three times a day. The cheerleaders and my other friends who hadn't heard about everything that had passed between Sawyer and me demanded to know whether we were hooking up. Several of them told me they'd voted for Sawyer and me as Perfect Couple That Never Was, and they were disappointed when I was named Most Likely to Succeed with Aidan.

Me too. I hadn't felt that way when the Superlatives titles were first announced, but hindsight was 20/20.

Maybe I should have taken the plunge and asked *Sawyer* out. But he was holding back with me. That was unlike him. He must have some good reason. And I was enjoying being close to him so much that I was afraid of messing things up if I pushed too fast for a change.

"Hey," I said as he stopped beside me at Ms. Yates's door. "I wanted to catch you before the meeting. Were you planning to sit at Ms. Yates's desk again?"

"I don't have to," he said. "I only did that last week to make Aidan mad."

"Great minds think alike."

He didn't laugh. He watched me carefully, as if talking about Aidan was making him as uncomfortable as it was making me.

"I don't want to argue with him anymore," I said in a rush. "I'm just not interested. And I think it would help us get along with him if we let him have the desk. We're trying to get stuff done in student council, and we should pick our battles."

The bell rang. Sawyer and I stepped back into safety

against the wall as Ms. Yates's freshmen streamed into the hall, followed by Ms. Yates, who hurried toward the teachers' lounge. She obviously couldn't deal with these meetings without a fresh cup of coffee. Considering the last meeting and Sawyer pulling out the rule book, I didn't blame her.

After the flood of freshmen had passed, I walked into the room and sat in a desk in the front row. Sawyer slid into the desk behind mine. Goose bumps rose on my skin as he whispered so close that I could feel his breath on my neck. "Will you marry me?"

"Yes," I said without hesitation, turning to smile at him. "I already told you."

He glanced up as the first reps walked in. Then he lowered his voice and asked, "Will you go to the prom with me?"

For the first time I really thought about our senior prom with Sawyer as my date. It could actually happen now. He would look dashing in a tux, a combination of handsome elegance and dangerous energy. I wanted to say yes.

Instead I said, "Prom is in April. A lot could happen before then. It's too soon to tell."

"Excuses, excuses," he said dismissively. "Nothing can happen before tonight, though. Will you sit in the van with me on the drive to the game?"

"I have to," I said, "because I owe you a shoulder rub."

He raised his eyebrows provocatively as if I'd said something very sexy. That's what I'd been counting on. Granted, he hadn't asked me out in the past week, or made anything that could be called a move on me. But we'd also seen each other only in public, usually fleetingly, like touching hands as we passed in the hall. Maybe we just needed some quality time together. We wouldn't be alone in the cheerleading van, but we'd definitely be stuck next to each other.

And I intended for something to happen.

When the classroom had filled with reps, Aidan swept in to take his proper place on the throne. As he sat down in Ms. Yates's chair, Sawyer sent him a message by noisily unzipping his backpack and thumping *Robert's Rules of Order* onto the corner of his desk where Aidan could see it.

Sawyer's threat worked. Aidan didn't deviate from the rules. He simply called on the committees to report about the student council's homecoming responsibilities. That is, he called on *me* to report on the various committees I headed.

I told the classroom that preparations for Monday's election of the homecoming court were going well. This meant I'd put some junior cheerleaders I trusted in charge. Preparations for the parade float build were also going well, because I'd delegated Will to handle them. He'd designed a gorgeous beach scene that he swore we could pull off with nothing but wood, chicken wire, and crepe paper, and he'd drafted Tia's contractor dad to take off work for once and supervise construction. Finally we got around to the dance.

"The dance preparations aren't progressing as I'd planned," I admitted. "I did find a potential place to hold it off campus." No need to bring up that the place was a gay bar. "But when I spoke with Principal Chen on Tuesday about moving the dance, she said we couldn't hold it off campus for liability reasons. If the dance is an official school function paid for with student dues, it needs to be held here on school grounds unless our lawyers okay a new location, and we don't have time to call them in."

"So it's dead?" Will called from the back of the room. "If we can't have it here, and we can't have it elsewhere, it's dead."

"It looks dead," I admitted. "I hoped one of you would have a brilliant idea. Throw me a Hail Mary pass here." I held up my hands, ready to catch the last-minute idea a rep would toss at me.

Nobody said anything. All eyes were on me, waiting for me to solve this problem myself.

"Well, y'all have my phone number," I concluded. "Text me over the weekend if you come up with something. If we don't have a solution by Monday, we won't have time to get the word out to students and parents, and the dance will definitely be dead."

The meeting progressed normally after that. Aidan didn't make a sarcastic comment about the dance or question why I'd pursued it in the first place. He didn't have to, because he'd already won.

But when he dismissed the meeting and the reps were filing out to the lunchroom, he walked over and put both hands on my desk, bending close, his face inches from mine. "Will you eat lunch with me today? We need to talk."

I eyed him. "About student council?"

"Of course," he said.

"About me resigning as vice president?" I asked. "I refuse to have that discussion again."

"I don't want you to resign as vice president," he said soothingly. "I was angry that night." This was as much of an apology as I ever got out of Aidan unless he also dropped his suave politician facade. This time he didn't.

"Will Ms. Yates be there?" I snapped. "I really enjoyed the last time I tried to eat lunch with you two."

"Just you and me," he said.

"All right. Let me do something first." I watched him return to Ms. Yates's desk to gather his papers. Then I faced Sawyer.

He was watching me, like he'd heard the whole conversation and expected an explanation.

"I'm eating lunch with Aidan," I said.

Sawyer nodded. He had no expression on his face, which was never a good sign.

But if he had nothing else to say, I wasn't going to hang around and try to draw him out. He *still* hadn't done anything to make me think he wanted us to get together. As far as I knew, the crush was all on my end.

I walked to the lunchroom with Aidan and a crowd of reps. Aidan went through the hot food line while I visited the salad bar—mainly because I was hoping for another word with Sawyer, not because I wanted salad. So much for not caring what Sawyer thought. I hadn't lasted five minutes. But I didn't see him anywhere.

Eventually I slid my salad onto a table across from Aidan, not in the teacher section but far away from our usual table too, in an unpopulated corner. As I sat down, he asked, "What'd you get on your *Crime and Punishment* paper?"

He uttered this like it was a casual question. It wasn't. He'd asked me all about my grades when we'd dated. But looking back on our time together, I realized my shoulders had tightened and my stomach had twisted with stress every time he'd grilled me. The constant competition with him over the years had been no fun. Being his girlfriend had made it worse.

I knew from experience, though, that not answering him would lead him to accuse me of getting a bad grade. That was something *my* ego couldn't withstand. I told him the happy truth: "A ninety-two." Not a grade up to my usual standards by any means, but way better than the zero I would have received if Sawyer hadn't stepped in to buoy me that day.

"Wow," he said between french fries, "you should get Sawyer to write your papers for you every time."

This was an insult meant to stab me in the heart. It didn't, because I knew I'd written my own paper. If he'd accused me of cheating two weeks ago, I would have been upset. His grip on me was slowly slipping.

And his mention of Sawyer turned me on. What if Sawyer *had* written my paper for me? Sure, that would be cheating. I would never do that. I didn't need to. But the idea suggested an intimacy between Sawyer and me that was more exciting than our tame reality.

So far.

"What did *you* get?" I asked Aidan.

"Are you scared?" he accused me. This meant he'd gotten lower than a ninety-two.

"All right, then," I said dismissively. "What's the student

council business you wanted to discuss?" I took a bite of salad.

"It looks like you're not going to get your homecoming dance after all," he said.

I nodded without looking up.

"But if we do have one," he said, "I don't want you to go with Sawyer."

As he said this, I finally spotted Sawyer across the lunchroom. He stood behind a table where a lot of the cheerleaders sat, one hand on the back of Grace's chair and the other on the back of Cathy's, laughing with them. It wouldn't be long before I heard yet another rumor about his sexual exploits, as if my friendship with him was an addition to his life, not a change.

But I wasn't about to admit that to Aidan. I said, "You broke up with me. What I do now is none of your business."

"I didn't break up with you," he said, pointing at me with a french fry. "I said I wanted to take a *break*. I thought dating other people for a while would strengthen our relationship, but I didn't mean you could date *Sawyer!*"

I put my fork down. "You said you wanted to talk about student council business. I wouldn't have agreed to eat lunch with you otherwise."

"This *is* student council business," Aidan said. "When

you and I were dating, people knew we were on the same page, president and vice president. Now people are coming up to me constantly, asking whether you're dating Sawyer. I tell them, 'Yeah, she's obviously had an aneurysm or a small stroke, and suddenly she's decided she wants to date a loser.'"

"Why do you say he's a loser?" I demanded. "He's in the upper-level classes with us." I had no idea what sort of grades Sawyer got, but he must have tested well enough at *some* point to be placed in the college track. "He's the school mascot, a student council rep, and the parliamentarian. He doesn't sound like a loser to me."

Aidan's eyes were cold as ice as he said, "I don't like him, okay? I don't like the way he talks to you."

I had no idea what Aidan meant. Frowning, I asked, "How does he talk to me?"

"He stands very close to you," Aidan said, moving closer across the table himself. "He leads with his pelvis. And I don't understand what you see in him. Of course, there *are* ladies who marry men in prison."

"He's not in prison," I pointed out.

"He will be."

We stared each other down across our almost untouched food. I'd had plenty of conversations with Aidan in which he lobbed witty insults at me to make me feel bad. But he didn't usually *want* something from me. This time he was intense and certain. Whether or not I was a part of his life, he wanted Sawyer out of mine.

"Tell me something," I said, acting casual by picking up my fork again and stirring my salad. "Did your dad help prosecute Sawyer's dad when he went to jail?"

I wasn't looking at Aidan, but his hesitation told me I'd surprised him. After a few seconds, he said, "Yeah."

"And when Sawyer moved to town, your dad told you who he was. That's how everybody knew on Sawyer's very first day at school that his dad had been to jail. You made *sure* they knew."

"So?"

I looked up at Aidan. "Sawyer might be a different person today if you hadn't done that. He didn't know a soul in town except his dad. He hardly knew his dad, I imagine. And you ensured he was teased by the entire student body the second he stepped on campus. No wonder he's so defensive. Some school leader *you* are." I shouldered my book bag and picked up my salad. Ignoring Aidan when he called to me, I walked away.

I wasn't sure where to go, though, which put a damper on my dramatic exit. I'd almost forgotten that the last time I'd seen Sawyer, he was cozying up to Grace and Cathy. But he wasn't sitting with them now. After a quick scan of the room, I spied him at our usual table, working through an enormous salad and speaking an occasional word to Quinn next to him.

When I approached, he glanced up at me. He looked down again without smiling, as if I wasn't welcome. He really *was* mad that I'd eaten lunch, however briefly, with Aidan. As I slid into the seat across from him with my salad in front of me, he concentrated on his own food. Then he asked flatly, "Did you finish with your student council business?"

"Yes."

"I've told you, I'm good at reading people. Don't tell me you were talking about student council."

Quinn looked at Sawyer, then at me, then wisely pretended to pay attention to a dirty joke Tia was messing up farther down the table.

I told Sawyer, "I don't know what you want me to say."

"Get back with him if you want to, Kaye." Sawyer sounded bitter. "I don't own you. That's your choice. But don't lie to me about it."

Now Noah beside me was eyeing us too, and Brody beyond him. I glared at Sawyer, letting him know I didn't find this public fight amusing.

He raised his eyebrows at me. He didn't care.

"Aidan and I were together for three years," I said. "We

dated for a year before you even moved here. The way he broke up with me was ugly and open-ended. It's hard to pretend that didn't happen."

The angry expression in his eyes faded. He took another bite of salad, considering. Finally he said, "I get it. But don't expect me to be polite about it."

I almost laughed and told him that was fair enough. But it *wasn't* fair. He was acting like a jealous boyfriend, except he wasn't my boyfriend, as far as I knew. I *wanted* us to be friends with bennies, but our bennies had gone missing.

I wasn't going to point this out with ten of our friends listening, though.

Instead, watching him reach the bottom of his salad plate, I asked, "Why did you become a vegan, anyway? Are the pelicans your brothers?"

He slammed his chair backward so suddenly that everyone at the table turned toward the screech. Rising, he said, "I'm tired of people telling me I'm a dumbass for going vegan. I know."

"I didn't say you were a dumbass!" I exclaimed.

"You didn't have to." He grabbed his backpack and his empty plate and stalked away.

As he went, I finally realized what he was telling me every time he got angry with me. People at school thought

Sawyer had a thick skin, but he was sensitive after all. And he was upset that I'd found out.

Near the other end of the table, Tia caught my eye and jerked her thumb over her shoulder, asking if I wanted her to go after Sawyer and smooth things over.

I shook my head and returned to my salad with a sigh. I was beginning to think whatever was wrong between Sawyer and me was something that couldn't be fixed.

10

BY THAT EVENING, I WAS EAGER TO TRY AGAIN.
I watched out the window of the cheerleading van for
Sawyer's beat-up truck to appear, lumbering over curbs in
the school parking lot. Just like last time he stopped right
next to my car. That was no accident. He looked up at the
window and saw me. I didn't turn away.

He climbed into the van wearing gym shorts and his
Pelicans T-shirt, with his huge costume bag slung over his
shoulder. He stood next to me in the aisle.

"Do you need to put your costume on before we make
up?" I asked drily.

He glanced toward the rear of the van as if he was considering this.

"Go put it down," I said. "I owe you a shoulder rub,

remember? Or is staying mad at me too important?"

"It's not *that* important," he admitted, already moving into the back to dump his bag.

He didn't make it all the way. He took two steps and chucked the bag over Ellen's head, making her squeal in fear. It landed on the back seat with a rustling of pompons.

He sank into the seat beside me. Before he could change his mind or feign anger again, I gripped both his shoulders and kneaded those tense muscles. He melted under my hands as if he'd never been touched before.

The ride home was even better. The cheerleaders were in a great mood after Brody led our team to yet another win. The highlights of the game had been Brody bulleting an impossibly long pass to our best tailback for the winning touchdown, and Sawyer directing the band. Usually when he wandered into the band's section of the stands, the band director, Ms. Nakamoto, made him leave, or DeMarcus, the drum major, wouldn't let him direct. This time everyone had been elated enough about our pending victory to forget all the times Sawyer had stolen flutes, disassembled them, and hidden them in the pelican's mouth. Ms. Nakamoto let Sawyer through. DeMarcus moved aside. The pelican directed a funny version of "Fight, Pelicans, Fight," speeding way up and then slowing way down and accelerating again. The cheerleaders, laughing, finally gave up trying to dance to it.

After the game, Sawyer disappeared into the locker room to take a shower. I carried his dead carcass of a costume back to the van, then retrieved his T-shirt and waited outside for him so he didn't have to look quite so buff and manly by walking across the parking lot bare chested. That's what I told him, anyway. Personally, I wouldn't have minded. When he was dressed, I extended my hand to him, and he took it. We held hands as we walked back to the van.

Ms. Howard already had the engine running. Sawyer and I were the last ones in. Before we'd even sat down, the van started moving, and the lights blinked out. This time he got into the seat first, taking the window. He propped his forehead against the glass, anticipating what I would do next, as I took his shoulders under my hands. The groan he let out caused Ellen and Grace to stand up from the seat behind us to see what was going on. Grace made a motion with her hand indicating I should jerk him off next. Grace. Sigh. If Sawyer had seen her do this, I would have died.

But she was right about one thing. I was giving Sawyer some pretty intense physical pleasure. And he was letting me know. I felt his groan in my crotch. I curled one thigh up and over his, letting my lower leg curve around his calf, as if this gave me better leverage.

"Oh God, Kaye," Sawyer said, guttural and appreciative.

"Ms. Howard!" Grace called. "I can't sleep because Kaye and Sawyer are having sex."

As a *wooooooo* echoed through the van, Sawyer straightened slowly so he wouldn't knock me onto the floor with a sudden movement. He pulled off his shirt and tossed it over the back of the seat at Grace.

"It's not a rock concert," Ellen said. "Geez." The shirt came sailing back to land on Sawyer's head.

"We want the shorts," Grace yawned.

Sawyer put his shirt back on—but not before I passed my hand down his bare back.

And he felt it. With the shirt over his head but not yet pulled down to cover his back, he looked over his shoulder at me. Our eyes met as the van passed under a light on the interstate. A shadow descended over his face when we drove away from that light and approached the next. Then his blue eyes lit up again.

I moved my hand down his arm and felt chill bumps.

He pulled his shirt the rest of the way on. "Your turn," he said, shifting in his seat.

"Here." I fished around in my bag and pulled out the

pillow I brought on long trips. He propped it behind his back against the wall of the van. With one of his legs extended along the seat, he pulled me by the hips until I settled back against him.

His hands gripped my shoulders and massaged. Now I understood why he'd groaned under my touch. Aidan had never bothered to give me a sexy rub like this (and in his defense, I'd never given him one, either). Sawyer turned me to water under his fingers. I nearly groaned but stopped myself so Grace wouldn't holler any more orgasm jokes across the van. My groan came out as a squeak.

"And you said *I* was tense." Sawyer's voice was a low rumble in my ear. "What's this knot right here?" He kneaded a spot in my neck.

"Ah," I gasped.

"Put your head down," he said gently, his hands working their way up my neck, then down into the neckline of my cheerleading top. "I wish I could take this off."

"That could be arranged," I murmured as if I were Grace, or Tia.

My face flushed hot. He'd only made a joke. Maybe he hadn't even meant anything risqué, and I'd ruined the mood by going too far. I wondered if he could feel my neck and shoulders tensing up again.

He placed one kiss on the back of my neck, at the lowest dip of my neckline.

I shivered.

And then he passed one arm around my chest, drawing me even farther against him until I relaxed into him, and he eased back against the pillow.

The heat of his body soaked into me. He took one deep breath. My body rose and fell with his. He nestled his arm under my breasts, his hand resting protectively across my hip.

In the silence that came after, I didn't know what to say.

Finally I gave voice to what had been bothering me from lunchtime until he sat down with me in the van. I said quietly, "Aidan did tell me he wanted to talk about student council at lunch. You were there. You heard him."

"What did he really want to talk about?" Sawyer asked, his words vibrating through me.

"He wants to make sure I don't go out with you."

"Hm," Sawyer half laughed.

I waited for him to ask me out, or to tell me the idea of us going out was ridiculous, but he did neither. He only flattened his palm on my hip, then gripped me more firmly, which sent a jolt of electricity down my leg.

I said, "And he wanted to know what I got on my paper for Mr. Frank."

"Was he impressed?"

"He said you wrote it for me."

"He is an asshole," Sawyer said, "and he knows how to push your buttons. More importantly, was your mom impressed?" At some point during that horrible morning, I'd moaned to him about accidentally telling my mother what I'd done. Even if I pulled off a feat by scoring well on the paper, she'd still know I'd forgotten to write it until the last second—that is, failed.

And that's exactly how she'd reacted when I told her what my grade was. "No," I said, "she wasn't impressed. She's making me stay home tomorrow to write the next one."

"It's not due for two weeks."

"I know."

"We haven't even worked on the notes or the outline in class yet."

"Doesn't matter."

"How can you be in trouble when you're perfect?"

I nodded, careful not to bump his chin with the back of my head. "It's a question for the ages."

"*Most* importantly," he said, his breath tickling my earlobe and sending a fresh chill across my skin, "are you impressed with yourself?"

"No," I admitted, "and I know that's stupid. Ms. Malone

will tell me this when I meet with her about handling stress. I've already heard it in self-esteem lectures, especially for girls only. I just can't shake it, though. When I don't accomplish something, I know it's my fault. When I do make good, I feel like I don't deserve it."

"I know that," he said, "but why do you feel that way?"

I shrugged automatically, then hoped I hadn't elbowed him. He put one hand up to rub my shoulders again, very gently.

I said, "People give me stuff because of what I've already done, or because of who my mother is."

"That's definitely not true," he said. "People don't want dipshits leading the student council. Well, scratch that. We elected Aidan president. But people definitely don't want an ugly, unpopular head cheerleader. When the school voted for you, nobody was thinking, 'Kaye's mom runs a bank.' They were thinking, 'Kaye has a firm ass.'"

This time I did elbow him softly in the ribs.

"Oof. Maybe that's just what *I* was thinking. But *nobody* was thinking about your mom. And you're in all the upper-level classes. That's no accident. You were in the Loser class way back when, right?" *The Loser class* was Sawyer's term for the gifted class. "If they put people in the Loser class based only on their hard-hitting parents, Tia wouldn't have been in it, because God knows whether her mom is dead or alive. Harper wouldn't have been in it. I love Ms. Davis, but she's not exactly playing with a full deck."

"She's an artist."

"That's one way to put it."

That's exactly what *I* thought of Harper's mom. I loved that Sawyer said he loved her. Everything I found out about him, every additional inch he pulled back the curtain on his life, made me like him more.

And every stroke of his skin across mine made me want him more. Yet if we followed our recent pattern, the closer we felt to each other, the sooner we'd have a dumb fight and push each other away again.

So I brought up the other thing that had been bothering me since lunch. "I didn't mean to offend you today when I asked if the pelicans were your brothers. I was just trying to snap you out of being mad about Aidan, and I picked the wrong thing to make a joke out of. I didn't know you were so serious about being a vegan."

"Why not?" he asked, dropping his sexy tone for the first time and sounding more like his normal self. "I have to eat, like, four gallons of salad to get any calories. Doesn't that seem serious to you?"

"You're never serious about anything."

"I'm serious a lot," he said.

"It looks exactly like kidding."

His sultry tone was back as he whispered, "Maybe you just don't know me that well."

"Maybe not." I pulled away from him and turned around in my seat.

"Don't go," he murmured.

I wasn't going anywhere. He was right. After two years, I felt like I hardly knew him at all. If he was as good at reading people as he claimed, he had me at a disadvantage. I wanted to look him in the eye when I posed my next question. I sat sideways, one knee bent and my foot up on the seat, open to him. "When did you go vegan?"

His eyebrows rose in surprise. "Last spring."

"Why?"

"I was about to try out for mascot. I was up against five other people, really funny characters—"

"Like who?"

"Chelsea."

"Oh, right! I'd forgotten she'd gone out for mascot." My friend Chelsea was a majorette in the marching band. Majorettes and cheerleaders tried out in front of the whole school, and students voted. These definitely were more popularity contests than any measure of talent—though I'd probably clinched the wow factor among cheerleaders with my ability to do ten back handsprings in a row. This boggled boys' minds.

Mascot selection was different. These candidates tried out in front of the principal, the football coach, and the cheerleading coach only. I guessed the faculty wanted to make damn sure the mascot would do a good job of representing the school. They weren't taking any chances on getting a lame pelican by letting students vote.

That meant the mascot selection had flown under my radar. I vaguely remembered the announcement that rising seniors could try out, and later, the shocking announcement that Sawyer had won. But this event had been as big a part of Sawyer's life as the cheerleader tryout had been for me.

Maybe bigger.

"They let us put the costume on for two minutes to see what it was like," Sawyer said, "and that was all. The next day we had to come back, get in the pelican suit, and convince them to give us the job. But my two minutes in the suit had taught me that a lot of the gags I'd been planning weren't going to work. You've got so much padding on that your movements have to be hugely exaggerated for the crowd to see what you're doing. I left wondering if I should even come back the next day."

"Really!" I exclaimed at the idea of Sawyer, discouraged. This was a new concept for me. Every time he identified a real emotion he'd had, I was shocked all over again.

"After school, before I went to work, I drove down to the marina and sat on the dock for a while, watching the pelicans, looking for inspiration." He moved one hand up, swooping like a seven-foot wingspan. "And—"

He stopped in midsentence, hand in midflight, lost in thought. In the dim van, his eyes were darkest blue, watching imaginary birds above us. I'd never seen him so unguarded before. I loved to look at him when he'd forgotten he was being watched.

He blinked and put his hand down. "Pelicans are dorks on land," he said, "little trolls waddling around. In the air they unfold their wings and grow huge, soaring and then diving for their dinner. It occurred to me that they're like a lot of students at this school. We're not so good at sitting in desks, staying still, and paying attention to a boring lecture."

He cut his eyes to me, and I knew the same thing was going through both our minds: *I* was good at that. But, granted, *he* wasn't.

"That doesn't mean we'll never be good at anything, though," he said. "There's almost no job out there where you sit at a desk and pay attention while someone else talks. I mean, I've already got a job I'm way better at than school."

True—Sawyer was a terrific waiter, as long as he wasn't mad at the customers.

"That's how I played the pelican," he said. "The other people trying out were just bopping around in this big padded suit, walking funny. I made the pelican into a character, a student at our school who gets no respect but who's a lot smarter than the teachers give him credit for. After I got the suit on, the first thing I did was walk behind the judges and try to look over their shoulders at everyone's scores."

I laughed. "That could have backfired." Principal Chen had her panties in a wad most of the time, and the football coach wasn't exactly open-minded, either.

"I knew that," Sawyer said, "but I figured I had to do *something*. I mean, all else being equal, would *you* pick me for *anything* over Chelsea?"

"No." But as soon as I said this, I felt the blood rush to my face, as it did so often when I was around Sawyer. I'd thought of several things I would pick Sawyer for over absolutely anybody, and all of them required sitting very close to him in the dark, just like this.

To cover up my embarrassment, I asked quickly, "How did this make you into a vegan?"

"Oh." He nodded. "It was when I was watching the pelicans. I felt like I was borrowing something from them. Like I was *one* with the pelicans, or something? I know that sounds stupid."

It didn't sound stupid, exactly, but it sounded like something Sawyer was making up to see if I would believe it, teasing me. I said carefully, so he couldn't tell whether I was buying it, "But people don't eat pelicans, do they?"

"Not unless they're desperate. I guess I was also thinking of a deer hunt I went on before I left Georgia. I've regretted it every day." He turned to look out the window at the interstate, lights and palm trees flashing past at even intervals. I could tell, though, that in his mind, he was lost in a dark Georgia forest.

I found his hand and covered it with mine. This was hard for me, making the first move. I'd never gone out of my way to touch Aidan like this. He hadn't ever tried to comfort *me*, either, which was probably why my three years with him seemed so sterile when I looked back at them now.

Sawyer turned away from the window. He took my hand in his and rubbed his thumb over my palm, watching me.

"What do you eat, as a vegan?" I asked. "Besides gallons of salad."

"Cereal, mostly."

"Dry? Vegans can't have milk or anything that comes from an animal, right?"

"Right."

I shook my head, disapproving. "Where do you get your calcium and vitamins and protein?"

"I guess I don't."

It occurred to me that, except for salad at lunch, I'd never actually seen Sawyer eat anything. "What did you eat before the 5K on Labor Day, when you nearly passed out?"

"Nothing."

I slid my hand out of his and poked him angrily in the leg. "You can't run three miles on nothing, Sawyer."

"Ow. I found that out, thanks."

"What did you eat the day you passed out at school?"

He shrugged. "I had a Bloody Mary for breakfast."

"With *vodka* in it?"

"And tomato juice, which is full of antioxidants." He cut his eyes sideways at me. "I know, I know. That's the day I realized I might have a problem."

Normally I would have interjected a sarcastic comment here: *Oh,* that's *when you realized you had a problem?* Sawyer's problems had been obvious to me and everybody else the entire time he'd lived here. Some other guys in our class drank, but most of them didn't make alcohol their favorite hobby.

I amazed myself by not saying a word. It took a lot of self-control, but I simply moved my hand low on his back and slid my arm around his waist.

He set his head down on my shoulder.

We sat that way for a while. This was a serious step past holding hands. It would have attracted attention in the van if any of the cheerleaders had been awake to see. But they'd bedded down, propping pillows against each other and the walls of the van. The silence seemed heavy, like a question mark.

My skin burned underneath Sawyer's cheek, and my face felt flushed everywhere his soft hair brushed against it. I wondered if this truce signaled that we'd reached a different level of our relationship. I wondered if I wanted it to. I took a long breath through my nose, easily enough that he might not notice, and exhaled, trying to relax. I wanted to enjoy the sensation of him cuddling against me. I might not get it again.

I'd thought he'd fallen asleep, but he finally spoke. "You think being a vegan is stupid."

"I don't," I said. "I think you're not doing it right. Starvation, dry cereal, and alcohol do not equal a diet of any kind. My God, at least have some hummus."

He chuckled—a sound I loved.

"What made you decide to sober up?" I asked. "Being in the hospital?"

"Being in the hospital made me realize that nobody has my back." He sat up and leaned against the pillow again. We weren't touching each other anymore, for the first time since he'd come out of the locker room. He *looked* alone, the only boy in a van full of girls, his blond hair lit by the streetlights behind him like an ironic halo, his features dark and inscrutable.

"My dad was up in Panama City," he said. "Anybody else's dad or mom would have rushed home if their kid was hospitalized with heat exhaustion. Not mine. The nurse—DeMarcus's mom, actually—made me give her my dad's cell phone number. I told her it wouldn't do any good. She called him anyway, then came back in the room outraged that he wasn't coming home. Outraged at *me*."

"She wasn't outraged at you," I said.

"That's how it felt. Like, *What kind of family are you from?*" He took a long breath, still needing to calm himself down when he talked about this, even though it had happened a month ago. "My brother was in town, but he wouldn't take time off work to check me out of the hospital when they said I could go home. He needed the hours."

I nodded. *Needing the hours* was a foreign concept to me. My parents wanted Barrett and me to concentrate on school instead of getting jobs. Both of them had worked professionally since college. They hadn't been paid hourly in decades. My understanding of hourly work came solely from Tia talking about her dad. He'd worked at a factory until recently, *needing the hours* and missing her marching band performances. But he would never have stayed at work if she'd been hospitalized. Neither would her sisters, even though she didn't always get along with them.

The closer I got to Sawyer, the more isolated he seemed.

"Yeah," he said, "I realized while I was in the hospital that I had a short-term goal, to be a really good school mascot in ninety-degree heat, and I couldn't meet that goal without making some changes. But I also came to this new understanding of what could happen to me later. The biggest stoner in school is Jason Price, right?"

"I hope." Actually, I hadn't seen a lot of Jason lately. He'd gradually dropped out of the advanced-level classes. The last I'd heard, he was trolling business math and remedial English.

"Jason's parents are both doctors. If he ever gets arrested, they'll hire lawyers to have him released. Hell, they'll probably sue the police department for taking their baby in. If I get arrested, my family will leave me there to rot. Nothing will make you clean up your act like your parents abandoning you completely."

I didn't realize I'd tilted my head and lowered my shoulders in disbelief until Sawyer imitated me.

"Come on," I said. "Do you really think that?"

"You would hope my dad learned something during fifteen years of hard time," Sawyer said. "But he treats me like his family treated him. I try to understand where he's coming from. He didn't exactly have every advantage when he was growing up. But not everybody raised in adverse circumstances decides to make a better life for themselves and their kids, like your mom did. A lot of them are hell-bound to repeat the process for the next generation. Somebody has to put their foot down and say, 'I'm not playing that game.' That somebody is me.

"I've known that for a long time. I felt like an outsider up in Georgia, when my mom was dragging my brother and me around to mooch off one relative and then another. If you're on the outside looking in, it's easy to judge and to feel superior. It wasn't until I was lying in the hospital that I realized what I'd done. Instead of getting away from my relatives, I was becoming them. And if I got arrested at age twenty like my dad, my family would give me exactly as much help as his family gave him. I remember the exact moment it hit me."

I went very still, hoping that moment hadn't been some

cruelty I'd paid him, one of those casual insults I'd lobbed at him before I knew the truth.

"You and everybody from school hadn't gotten to the hospital yet," Sawyer said. "It was just Will and me in the room. You know, he rode in the ambulance with me."

I nodded. Sawyer had passed out on the football field. Will had hefted him over one shoulder and carried him all the way up the stadium stairs, into the parking lot to meet the ambulance. I'd just stood there among the other cheerleaders with my hands pressed to my mouth, impressed and terrified. I hadn't known Will had this he-man superhero side. And up to that point, I'd never seen Sawyer vulnerable. Ever.

"I don't remember passing out," Sawyer said, "or throwing up in the parking lot, or being in the ambulance, even though Will says I was conscious for the whole ride. The first thing I remember is, Will's in the chair next to my hospital bed, making small talk. Whether the Buccaneers will suck less this year, what the Rays' chances are for a pennant, whether we can sneak past security to watch the Lightning practice. And I'm thinking what a shit I've been to this guy, and how little sense it makes for me to treat him that way. I mean, I want to *be* this guy. He has everything I want."

"Tia?" I breathed.

"No! A future." Sawyer frowned at me, only now understanding my question about Tia. His face softened.

"And then *you* walked into the hospital room," he said. "You looked beautiful in red."

"Ha," I said. "I came straight from cheerleading practice. I was wearing a Pelicans T-shirt."

"Yes, you were." He laid his arm along the back of the seat and put his hand in my hair.

I smiled at the sweet feel of his fingertips rubbing my nape. "You might have sworn off mind-altering substances that day, but it's not like you've changed personalities. You're still really mean to Kennedy," I pointed out.

His nostrils flared. "I strongly dislike Kennedy."

"And Aidan."

His hand stopped in midair, pulling one of my curls. "I hate Aidan." He let my curl go. It sprang back into place.

"You haven't changed as much as you think," I said. "You're incredibly smart and responsible about some things, like quitting drinking. On other things, like your diet, and getting along with certain people, you act like you're from another planet."

"Oh," he said, lifting his chin defiantly, "and *you're* not like that?"

"I'll bite," I said. "What am I smart about?"

"Almost everything," Sawyer declared. "Though, as you pointed out, you don't believe it. Is there anything you honestly think you're good at?"

"Being a cheerleader." I smoothed my hands over my short skirt, then lowered my voice to a whisper. "Not the part where I babysit Grace and Cathy and Ellen." In a normal tone I said, "The part where I actually cheer and dance. I love dancing. And of *course* this would be what I really enjoy, because my mother makes a comment every time I leave the house for practice. 'That's really going to help get you a job as a professional cheerleader.'"

"It could be a backup career if your corporate takeover falls through," Sawyer said.

"You laugh," I said. "But lately, every time I'm on the field during a game, I'm thinking, 'I don't want high school to end.' It's partly because I don't want to leave my friends. But I also don't look forward to spending the rest of my life sitting in a tiny room, ciphering. That's what my career is going to be like. That's what my college experience will be, too."

"Surely Columbia has cheerleaders," Sawyer said.

"I never really thought about it," I admitted. "But their football team sucks. Cheering them on wouldn't be much fun. The whole school seems focused on academics. They put classes ahead of sports in a way the entire state of Florida doesn't really comprehend."

"What about actually trying out as a professional cheerleader?" he asked. "You could do that while you're in school. I don't think it pays much at all. Those girls are trying to get discovered as models. But if you were just doing it for fun . . ."

"My mother would disown me." I enjoyed saying these words more than I expected. After picturing myself for half a second in a low-cut bra top and shorts the size of panties, I shook my head sadly. "I'll bet I can't try out until I'm twenty-one."

"I'll bet you're wrong," Sawyer said. "Men still make most of the rules in this country. Men aren't going to prevent an eighteen-year-old from being a professional cheerleader. It's her God-given right."

I stared at Sawyer, who watched me with his brows raised. The interstate lights caressed his face and released him, then slowly moved across his face again. I was so accustomed to Aidan talking me out of crazy schemes that I hardly ever came up with them anymore. This one was so nuts that I was having a flashback to eighth grade, before I started dating Aidan, when my friends laughed and called me a live wire. At some point along the way, the life had gone out of me.

And here was Sawyer, calmly encouraging me to do exactly what I wanted.

I fished in my bag for my phone, then looked up the Giants. "The Giants don't have cheerleaders." I typed the Jets into the search engine. "The Jets have a cheerleading squad called the Flight Crew. That's adorbs." I thumbed through to an information screen and enlarged the tiny print. "I can't do it. Tryouts are in March. My mother would never let me go up to New York for that. And I won't be eighteen by the deadline. But I could try out the next year, when I'm already at Columbia." I took a closer look at photos of the current squad. "They would make me relax my hair."

"You don't know that," Sawyer said, "but it makes an excellent excuse not to try."

I eyed him. "You're daring me."

"I'm definitely not. You'd be wearing next to nothing, and men would leer at you. I wouldn't encourage you to do it, except that you obviously want to. I think you understand the leering aspect and accept it, even want it. And that's okay."

"You wouldn't be jealous about the skimpy uniforms and the leering men?" My tone was teasing, but suddenly I wanted so badly for him to acknowledge that the thought made him crazy.

"Your body belongs to you," he said solemnly, "not any guy, and not your mom. You really don't seem to understand that."

Across the aisle from me, Cathy shifted in her sleep and

nearly fell off her seat. Instinctively I dodged away from her, cupping my hands over my phone screen.

"It's not a joint," Sawyer said.

"I feel awful even looking this up, like my mother is watching me and doing calculations about how much money I'm wasting if time is money."

"Anything making you feel that guilty is definitely worth doing."

I looked over at him, at his sharp nose and soft mouth coming in and out of focus as the van moved through the interstate lights. My lust for him had grown as the ride went on. I wondered if he meant we should indulge our own guilty pleasure. I'd reached the point that I wouldn't be able to sleep tonight, or ever, if I didn't find out.

I bent to slip my phone back into my bag. Then I moved toward him.

His eyes widened, but he didn't back away.

I cradled his chin in my hand, his blond stubble scratching across my fingertips.

His lips parted. He looked a little outraged, honestly, like this was unseemly behavior for a future valedictorian.

If I'd thought about the expression on his face, I would have backed away. But I was sick to death of thinking. I kissed him.

He opened his mouth for mine. I swept my tongue inside. He didn't pull away, but he didn't reciprocate, either. I knew I could kiss. Aidan and I had had plenty of practice. But I felt as if I was initiating Sawyer in a decidedly unsexy way, like when DeMarcus had taught me to French kiss in front of an audience of our peers at his Halloween party in seventh grade, directly after Tia had taught DeMarcus.

I broke the kiss and pulled back until I could see Sawyer. His face was mostly in shadow. I wished yet again that I could gauge the look in his eyes. "I feel like I'm taking advantage of you, which is no fun at all. You don't want to kiss me?"

"I do." He swallowed, and he actually looked like he was in pain as he said, "I don't want to get hurt."

"This won't hurt." I slipped my hand into his hair and kissed him.

Again I felt that I was leading the dance. I was about to give up on him. That lasted about five seconds.

Then he was kissing me back. He pulled me closer, deepened the kiss, and explored my mouth. He bit my lip, almost hard enough to hurt. As I opened my mouth wider to protest, he gave me a taste of what other girls were talking about when they said Sawyer turned them on. In one minute he had controlled me completely.

He took his hand out of my hair and placed it on my

breast. I broke the kiss to gasp at the intensity of tingles racing through me.

Just as suddenly as he'd started, he let go of me and backed away, his shoulders rising and falling rapidly as he panted. He said hoarsely, "We just can't. I want to, but I know this isn't going to work out."

I gaped at him. I could not *believe*, after everything we'd been through to get to this point, that he was dumping me when we'd hardly gotten started.

I'd heard so many reports of him having trysts like this with different girls. Strangely, those accounts included the beginning, and the good stuff, but never the ending of those relationships. Maybe that's because they all ended like this.

I jerked my pillow out from behind him, then grabbed my bag from the floor.

"Kaye." His hand circled my wrist.

I glowered at him. I wasn't sure he could see my face in the dark, but he knew what the sharp jerk of my head meant. He let me go and put his hand up, surrendering.

I stood and shuffled to the back of the van. Normally I was the one who told the other girls to treat their pompons right, leaving them in clean places rather than in pools of half-dried Coke on the concrete steps of the stadium. This time I was the one who unceremoniously knocked Sawyer's costume bag and a pile of pompons to the floor in a hiss of plastic streamers. I lay down with my pillow underneath my head and closed my eyes, listening for Sawyer over the drone of the van motor, and hating him.

What I heard was a grunt near the floor. After a few seconds I realized it wasn't a rogue bullfrog that had found its way onto the van but my phone vibrating in my bag and bouncing against the van's carpeted bottom. I snatched the phone out. I knew Sawyer was texting me.

Sawyer: I never had a chance to tell u what ur stupid abt.

I waited. I wasn't going to give him the satisfaction of prompting him: What's that, Sawyer? But he'd heard me take my phone out. He knew I was hanging on what he would say next.

Sawyer: Me.

I texted back so angrily that my thumbs pressed rogue characters and my message was full of)$&@. I had to take a deep breath. I wasn't going to send him an answer that was less than perfect. Finally I got it cleaned up and texted this:

Me: I'm not stupid about u. YOU lead me on and then shut me down. U have done that for the last time. 3 strikes and ur out.

I turned my phone off, threw it in my bag, and rolled over with my back to the van.

As soon as I'd done this, I regretted it. "3 strikes and ur out"? That was the kind of draconian statement my mother would make, setting limits and sticking to them no matter what, even if they had no meaning later and caused everyone misery.

But I wasn't wrong, was I? Showing Sawyer how much I liked him was hard for me. There were only so many times I could go out on a limb like that, only to have him cut off the limb at the trunk and watch me fall. I'd been worried at lunch that his problems were too serious for us to get over. Well, I was done. Now he could start worrying about *my* problems.

I pictured my life as I would start living it tomorrow: single. I wouldn't go after Sawyer. I wouldn't worry what Aidan was up to. I wouldn't try desperately to find a date for my nonexistent homecoming dance. I had great friends and lots to do my senior year—too much, according to my mother—and I could enjoy it all by myself.

I sat up and peered around the seat in front of me only once to see what Sawyer was doing. His worried face was lit clearly by the glow of his phone. He was still typing.

An hour later, the instant I arrived home and escaped to my room, I turned my phone back on and opened his texts.

Sawyer: 3 strikes makes it sound like ur playing a game w ME.

Sawyer: Kaye

Sawyer: We need to talk abt this. You can't just pretend I'm not here. I'm RIGHT HERE & if u don't answer I will do something inconceivably cruel to ur pompons.

Sawyer: Kaye

Sawyer: Kaye.

11

THE NEXT NIGHT HARPER CALLED ME AFTER dinner. "What'cha doing?" she asked.

"My next paper for Mr. Frank."

"Oh, shit. On Saturday night? Have I missed something? I thought it wasn't due for another two weeks."

"It's not," I said. "My mother is making me write it early, because she doesn't trust me anymore. Like she ever did." I wished Harper hadn't asked. I hated the bitter sound of my voice. "What's up?"

"I was wondering if you would help me buy a car."

I waited for Harper to explain what the hell she was talking about. When she remained silent, I said, "What?"

"Remember my cheapskate granddad's birthday present for me?" she asked. "The *use* of his car? Well, he's taking it back. Now that he's dating, he's using his car more. *I need it more too, because I'm getting photography jobs on week-ends. I told him he couldn't take back my birthday present. He gave me a thousand dollars basically to leave him alone."

"Nice!"

"Yeah. And I have a thousand of my own saved up, so I'm going to buy a car tonight. I have one picked out, and I looked up the blue book value. All I need is you."

"Why me?"

"Because your mom made you haggle for your own car."

"But you should haggle for *your* own car," I pointed out. "That's why my mother made me do it, so I'd have that adult experience under my belt and I wouldn't get taken to the cleaners later." At least, that's what she'd *said*. Actu-ally, she'd made me do it because she'd brought me up in a comfortable suburban environment, and periodically she decided she needed to toughen me up by throwing me to the sharks.

"Why in the world would I do that when I have you?" Harper asked reasonably. "You're so much better at hanging tough than I am. You'll get me another two-fifty off."

"Harper." I sighed. "You're basically telling me I'm your bitch friend."

"Kaye, I would *never* tell you that."

I rolled my eyes so hard that Harper could probably hear it through the phone.

"Spin it however you want," she said, "but come pick me up."

Truthfully, I was glad to have an excuse to get out of the house. Dad was back from Miami, but he wrote a lot on weekends, so he wasn't available to save me from homework by inviting me to watch football with him or taking me out for ice cream. My Saturday had been full of nothing but my disapproving mother and research on Stephen Crane's *The Red Badge of Courage*. Mr. Frank had a thing for white male protagonists who whined and waffled.

Which made me angry all over again at Sawyer. Until the past week I would have said he was the *least* likely guy in the world to seem to want a girl, then back out.

He'd never had a problem like that with girls before. He had a problem only with me.

Fifteen minutes later I cruised into the parking lot behind the B and B. Stepping into my car, Harper flashed me her wad of hundreds, which I told her was very gangsta. We chatted about the football game last night and Brody's stellar performance. Finally I asked, "Why aren't you with Brody tonight?"

"He went out with some friends," she said, seemingly fascinated with the scene out her window, the parking lot of the movie theater.

I glanced where she was looking. "There's Chelsea's car. She must be at the movie with DeMarcus."

"With Tia," Harper corrected me.

"Really?" I asked. "I wonder why Tia isn't with Will. It must be another girls' night out."

"Must be," Harper said vaguely, as if she was thinking about something else.

"We'll probably be done with your car about the time Tia and Chelsea get out of the movie. We should come back by and show them."

"Okay," Harper said absentmindedly.

Well, I had a question that would wake her up. "Do you think Tia and Will are doing it yet?"

Harper huffed out an embarrassed laugh. "Why don't you ask her?"

"Anytime I ask her about sex, she thinks I'm calling her a slut."

"That's because you *are* calling her a slut," Harper pointed out.

"I am *not*. I may have intimated in the past that she would get in trouble involving herself in such casual escapades with—" I stopped, realizing what I was about to say.

"Sawyer," Harper finished for me.

I felt all the blood rushing to my face.

To gloss over the uncomfortable moment, Harper hurried on. "I haven't asked Tia, but my sense is that she and Will haven't done it. They've done everything but. There's a lot of other stuff you can do if you're really into each other."

"It sounds like you speak from sexperience."

She laughed self-consciously. Bright pink spots appeared on her cheeks, noticeable on her porcelain skin. "I guess. I never expected dating someone I loved to be so . . ." She held up her hands. "Free. Dating Kennedy, I felt strapped down. Brody makes me feel good, and like there are more possibilities, bigger ones."

I envied her. But I supposed that's what she got when she and Brody were dating after a long, vague friendship, unlike the intense baggage that plagued Sawyer and me.

We reached the used car lot and peered into Harper's clunker of choice. The salesman didn't bother to come out of his little building to help two teenage girls. We obviously didn't have the money to buy anything. I understood now why my mother always dressed professionally in public. I should have gussied up tonight and made Harper do the same, but always doing everything the right way was too much hassle. I wanted to be seventeen sometimes, even if that meant doing things the hard way.

I hiked into the office with Harper behind me and told the

salesman we wanted to go for a test drive, carefully listing the make and model rather than saying "that red car." I sat in the back while Harper drove and the salesman rode shotgun. It sounded like a car to me. I couldn't vouch for the engine, but at least the sale included a warranty. Around closing time Harper and I drove back toward downtown in separate cars.

We both pulled in to the movie theater parking lot just as Tia and Chelsea were walking out. They oohed over Harper's new ride *and* over how smart she'd been to ask me along. Despite myself, I beamed with pride. My mother might not think I had much sense, but *somebody* did.

"We're glad you came by." Chelsea grabbed my arm. "Aidan is in the movie," she said in a stage whisper, "with . . . guess who."

"Angelica!" I said.

"I have a theory about what old Angelica's up to," Tia said conspiratorially. "She dated DeMarcus last summer. Then Xavier. Now Aidan. She's systematically cycling through all the likely candidates for valedictorian. She even hedged her bet by going out with Will once, just in case he comes from behind and pulls off a long shot. So you know who's next!" She looked pointedly at me.

I said in my best redneck accent, "Shee-yut, I ain't wasting no time with that girl. I hear she don't put out."

"Is sex all you care about?" Tia shrieked, putting the back of her hand to her forehead and pretending to swoon, at the same time Chelsea said, "You are a shallow, sexist person." Harper snorted.

"Speaking of putting out," I said, "why are all of your menfolks missing at one time?"

"They're with *your* man," Chelsea said. "Didn't you know that?"

"What?" I asked, glancing from Chelsea to Tia, who was giving me shifty-eyes, to Harper, who looked downright alarmed. I prompted them, "DeMarcus and Will and Brody are all with Sawyer?"

"Well, you're obviously not supposed to find that out," Chelsea said self-righteously. She slapped the back of Tia's head. "Thanks for warning me before I blabbed."

"You already blabbed it to Aidan and Angelica," Tia said. "Could I have stopped you?"

I raised my brows at Tia, waiting for an explanation.

Exasperated, she said, "Sawyer is so in love with you."

Harper nodded vigorously at me. "He is."

Again I looked from one of them to the other. I'd been to this movie theater and stood in this parking lot a hundred times in my life, but suddenly the everyday scene seemed foreign because my heart was pounding and my life was shifting around me. I put one hand up to my face and repeated, "He's in love with me?"

"That's why he moved out of his dad's house in the first place," Tia said. "His dad said something about you that Sawyer didn't like."

I didn't ask what that something had been. I knew. For a white person insulting a black person, that something was always the same. The only part of this revelation making no sense to me was the timing. "Sawyer moved out before Aidan even broke up with me."

Tia and Harper nodded solemnly. And that meant Sawyer had been into me, intensely enough that his mean dad knew about it, before we'd even doubled down on toying with each other.

"Why doesn't he *act* like he's in love with me?" I cried. "I threw myself at him last night, and he dissed me. *Again!*"

I must have sounded hysterical. Harper put a hand on my shoulder. Tia said as gently as she could, "He's terrified, Kaye. He doesn't want to start something with you. He's certain it won't work out."

"Well, it's too late. He's already started it!" I exclaimed. "And why are y'all keeping me in the dark about this?"

"I promised him," Tia said solemnly.

"I promised him too," Harper chimed in.

"I had no knowledge of any of this shit," Chelsea said.

"Where are the boys?" I demanded, turning to Harper. "Are they at your granddad's beach?"

Harper looked at Tia hopelessly. They were at her granddad's beach, all right.

I headed around Harper's car to reach mine.

"Don't go to the beach," Tia pleaded.

"Why not?" I asked, opening my door. "Are they drinking?"

"Will's not." She was stalling. Will didn't drink.

"Is *Sawyer* drinking?" I clarified. "Because that would be a great way for me to get over him. Problem solved." I started my engine.

I already knew I wouldn't be catching him by surprise, though. Before I'd driven out of the parking lot, Tia was on her phone.

As I drove the few short blocks down the main road through town, my mind raced with everything that was happening behind my back. I could hardly comprehend it all. Sawyer was in love with me. He wanted to be with me. But he was afraid I would break his heart. All my best friends knew. He'd gone drinking down at the beach to find solace with his guy friends. And he was content to leave me at home, out of the loop, innocently obsessing over *The Red Badge of Courage*. Was he even worth the trouble?

I pulled onto the sandy road that led to Harper's grand-dad's property, punched in the combination to open the gate, slowly drove through, and pulled the gate shut behind me. My car crept through the palm grove. No trucks were parked ahead of me. Possibly the boys had left when Tia sounded the alarm. More likely, especially if they were drinking, they'd walked here from their houses downtown.

I swung my car around to park exactly where Aidan and I had parked all three times we'd had sex. My headlights caught Sawyer waiting for me.

He stood on the threshold. The dark palm forest was in front of him, and behind him, the open beach, bright with moonlight. He wore his usual flip-flops and shorts, plus his blue polo shirt that matched his eyes exactly. This shirt didn't make an appearance as often as his madras one, presumably because it was so old that the collar was turning white at the edges.

His arms were folded across his chest. His blond hair played across his forehead in the ocean breeze. His eyes were on me, and he looked miserable.

Good.

I turned off the engine and the lights, got out, and slammed the door. His expression didn't change as I stomped toward him as best I could in slick flat sandals on mounds of sand. I stopped right in front of him and poked him on the forearm he was using to protect himself. "Why does everybody in the senior class know about this except me, huh? Am I just a big joke to you?"

He looked over his shoulder. The other guys—I recognized the three I'd known about, Will, Brody, and DeMarcus, plus Noah and Quinn—sat in a circle about halfway down the beach. The sound of the ocean must have muffled my voice, but they still heard me and turned. Will's dog thumped her tail in welcome.

Sawyer faced me again. "No!" Eyes wide, he sounded almost desperate. "It's just that I'm going to ruin your life, Kaye."

"Don't you think that should be my choice?" I shouted. "Do I get a say at all? In *anything*?"

He bit his lip, frustrated. "Come on," he said, grabbing my hand. He pulled me into motion down the beach.

We passed within a few yards of the other boys and the dog, but I was too mortified by this entire fiasco to say hi. I did notice a beer bottle next to Brody, and across the circle, the tiny orange glow of a cigarette or a joint. I called to Sawyer, "Are you stoned? Getting stoned because of me is not the way to win me over."

He stopped so suddenly that I smacked into him. He

grabbed me by both arms to keep me from sliding down. "I told you, I quit all that," he said over the roar of the tide. "You don't believe anything I say."

"I *have* believed you," I snapped. "That's the whole problem. You've acted like you wanted us to get together. I bought it. I tried to follow through, and you decided on your own that you don't want me anymore."

"I *do* want—" He looked over my shoulder at the guys behind us. "Come over the hill." He took my hand again and led me up and over a rise in the beach, where we were hidden. Now we could see the pier and the pavilion of the public park. It was closed for the night. We were alone.

He pulled me toward the ocean until the water lapped at my toes and made the bottoms of my sandals slimy.

"You're getting my sandals wet," I said.

Toeing off his flip-flops and kicking them up the beach, he said, "For once in your life, kick your shoes off." He made it sound like a challenge.

I rolled my eyes to show him that he didn't fool me. What I meant was, it was okay with me if he manipulated me, as long as he knew I knew he was doing it. I wiggled one shoe off the end of my toes, then the other, and stepped into the water with him. The warm tide raced around my ankles.

He walked forward into the ocean, tugging me after him. I thought we were just going for a wade. But he kept going until the warm water reached the middle of my calves and crept toward my knees.

"Sawyer," I called, digging my heels into the sand and pulling against his grip. "My skirt's getting wet."

He turned to me with an evil grin. "Take your skirt off for once."

Oh, as if he thought I was innocent, and Aidan and I had never done it? "I've taken my skirt off before," I said archly, before I gained complete understanding of how stupid that sounded.

"That's what I heard about you," he said.

I gaped at him. What had he heard? I was furious with Aidan now, and sorry I'd gone as far as I had with him. But I'd never suspected he'd given a third party the play-by-play—especially a third party who wouldn't keep that information in confidence, with the description eventually getting back to Sawyer.

"I'm joking," Sawyer said. "Take your skirt off anyway."

I might have if he'd given me any assurance that he wasn't setting me up again. I put my hands on my hips. "I thought you were afraid to get too close to me, and we were mad at each other. You wanted to talk it out."

"I *do* want to talk it out, but knowing us, we'd be mad at each other again in an hour. Maybe it would help if you took your skirt off."

"If you take your shorts off."

I made a mental note never to use Sawyer taking his clothes off as a countermeasure. Instantly he was wading closer to shore, where he could take off his shorts without getting them soaked. He unbuckled his belt and shoved his shorts down his hips, exposing his plaid boxers. Most girls would stare at him, straining to gauge the shape and size of him in the darkness. I got stuck on the fact that he was wearing a belt. He often wore a belt, in fact. It showed whenever his shirt rode up or he tucked it in. Knowing his personality, I would have thought he'd dress like a slob, but his casual clothes were neatly pressed. I felt like I was having another epiphany about the puzzle that was Sawyer, but really I was standing in the ocean, avoiding thinking about what was about to happen.

He snapped me out of it when he held out his hand for my skirt. "Hop to it, Gordon. We ain't getting any younger."

I waded after him, shimmied my skirt down my hips, and stepped out of it. Shining drops of ocean dashed dark stains across the fabric.

He bundled it with his shorts and tossed both to the

shore, which was sandy and wet. So much for keeping my skirt dry.

He turned back to me. He looked me up and down, and his lips parted. "The bottom of your shirt's going to get wet. Why don't you take that off too, while we're at it."

My knee-jerk reaction was to be offended that he was using such a thin excuse to get my clothes off. But I loved that he wanted this. And I did feel a little silly standing in the ocean in my shirt and panties. A bra and panties were more like a bikini, at least.

Before I reached for my first button, I said, "You first."

Gamely he pulled his shirt off over his head, exposing his flat stomach, then his strong pecs, and finally his arms made of muscle. He balled up his shirt and nodded, prompting me.

I fumbled with the first button of my blouse, fingers shaking. Sawyer had seen me with less on than this. When I got undressed, I'd still be exposing exactly as much in my bra and panties as I did in a bikini. There was no reason for me to feel so nervous as I moved my fingers down to the next button, except for the way Sawyer watched me, jaw hard, eyes serious. The breeze off the ocean toyed with the top sections of his hair, bright blond in the moonlight, and moved one lock back and forth across his forehead. He didn't brush it away.

He stared at my fingers until they reached the last button. As I pulled the shirt backward off my shoulders, his eyes rose to my face. Still looking at me, he held out his hand for my shirt. He wrapped his own shirt around it and tossed the bundle toward the shore, not looking to see where it went. Neither did I.

"Now we're seaworthy," he said, reaching out again, this time for my hand. Facing me, he backed deeper into the water, pulling me with him. I began to wonder if this was one of his practical jokes.

He stopped backing up but kept pulling me toward him until our bodies pressed against each other in the water. His lips found my neck, making me gasp and sending chills rushing across my skin. I felt my nipples tighten, straining against the lace of my bra.

"This is why we needed to come out here," he said in my ear, "where the guys couldn't hear or see us. I wanted to tell you how bad I am for you. I'm going to corrupt you. I wanted you to understand that and feel it for yourself." His hand slipped inside the front of my panties. His fingers found me and started circling.

"Ah." This was something Aidan had never done to me. In thirty seconds with Sawyer, I already understood why girls went crazy over him. Weak with pleasure, I collapsed into his shoulder, only caring about the position of my hips so he could still reach me.

With his other hand he lifted my chin from his chest and kissed me. The tentative boy from the van was gone. His mouth was hard on mine, his tongue exploring me. He slid his hand into my hair and tilted my head exactly where he wanted me.

Every minute this went on I got closer to climax—my first in front of anyone. I wasn't embarrassed. I had stopped thinking. My hands found his boxers on their own, and it was the shocking hardness of him, and the strange possessiveness I felt when I put my fingers around him, that finally sent me over the edge.

He kissed me harder, holding me up against him, knowing exactly what he was doing to me.

When it was over, I leaned against him, catching my breath, and finally pulled away to stand upright. Barechested, with the black ocean and the blue night behind him, his golden hair whipping in the wind, he looked like a god. A sarcastic one, smiling smugly at his accomplishment.

I took a deep, shaky breath. "Was that your way of getting rid of me once and for all? Because you have totally fucked that up."

"Good." He kissed my cheek. "It was just my one last,

futile attempt to save us both." He kissed my neck. "I'm glad it didn't work." He kissed above my breast, his mouth lingering as if this was going to be his next thorough exploration.

A bright light shone in our eyes from the beach. "Police," said a man's voice through a megaphone. "Come out of the water."

12

"STAY BEHIND ME UNTIL WE KNOW WHETHER they're really cops," Sawyer ordered me, leading me by the hand toward the beach.

He didn't have to convince me. I'd told myself before that wearing a bra and panties in the ocean was no worse than wearing a bikini. But now that men in addition to Sawyer were going to see me, I wondered how opaque the wet lace of my undies really was.

When we reached shore, the light was still too bright to discern much about the figures who'd found us, but they were big. Sawyer said, "Get your light out of my eyes, and show me your badges." His words were forceful, but his tone was reasonable enough that the light shifted to the police badges on their shirts. The names appliqued above their badges were, I swear to God, Sterns and Sorrow.

"Ma'am," Sorrow said to me, "will you step over here?"

"Don't make her do that." Sawyer sounded annoyed now, which I didn't think was a good idea when talking to policemen. "We're obviously not hiding anything."

Sterns said, "We got a call because you're on park land."

"We're not," Sawyer said. "We're on Hiram Moreau's land, and we have permission to be here."

"You're on park land," Sterns insisted. "The line's right there." He shone the flashlight toward the palm trees. I had no idea exactly what he was pointing at or how he knew this. Maybe we'd walked far enough that we'd crossed the property line, but we shouldn't be arrested for trespassing when it had been an innocent mistake.

Well, maybe not an innocent one, considering what we'd been up to—but a genuine one.

"We were on Mr. Moreau's land," I insisted. "He's my best friend's grandfather. We were with—" I was about to name the other boys, hoping the police would recognize the name of one of them. Surely they'd heard of Brody. Articles about his football performances had filled the local paper lately.

"With her car," Sawyer interrupted me loudly. "You can check, and Kaye's car will be right up there."

I was still standing behind him, so I couldn't see his face. But he squeezed my hand. He was telling me he didn't want me to mention the guys. Some of them had been drinking underage, and I'd almost gotten them in trouble.

"Let her put her clothes on," Sawyer said.

The policemen allowed this. The catch was, they continued to grill Sawyer while I tripped along the beach in my undies in search of our clothing. I was able to shake the sand off my skirt and wiggle into it without much trouble, storing Sawyer's shorts under my elbow. But our shirts had hit the water. The tide had rolled them in and out and gotten them thoroughly soaked. I washed the sand out of them as best I could, squeezed out the salt water, and buttoned my shirt with my back to the policemen, wondering how in God's name I was going to explain this to my mother. I slipped on my sandals and snagged Sawyer's flip-flops. This was not how romantic trysts were supposed to end.

As I walked back to them, Sorrow was asking Sawyer, "Is she your girlfriend?"

"Of *course* she's my girlfriend. Look at her." Sawyer glanced over his shoulder at me and winked. I wasn't sure whether he was trying to reassure me because things were going to be okay, or comfort me because things were very, very bad.

"Do your parents know you're here?" Sterns asked. We both shook our heads. "Then give me your phone numbers. I'm going to let them know."

While he wrote on a pad, I recited Dad's number, not my mother's, because I wasn't insane. Sawyer said, "I can give you my dad's number, but he won't answer because he's drunk, and if you did reach him, he sure as hell wouldn't care I was making out with my girlfriend at the beach *legally*. But you're welcome to call Hiram Moreau, whose property *you're* trespassing on right now."

That was a lot of bravado for him to throw around while wearing wet underwear.

"Let's step up here to the patrol car while we figure this out." Sterns led the way over to the park while Sorrow fell in line behind us as if we were already jailbirds being marched from one cell to another.

Sterns put Sawyer in the back of the waiting patrol car. Sorrow led me to the opposite side and asked as I sat down, "What's the make and model of your car? Do you know the license plate number?" I gave him all that information. He closed the door with a frighteningly permanent-sounding *thunk*, shutting out the roar of the ocean.

"I hope the guys saw the flashlight and left," Sawyer told me quickly. "Quinn had a joint. I'm about to give them a little more time before the cop walks over there to look at your car, okay? Don't freak out."

"Okay," I breathed. I'd thought I couldn't be more horrified at what was happening. I was wrong.

"Hey!" Sawyer shouted at the cops. My ears rang.

Sorrow had taken two steps toward Harper's granddad's land. Sterns was on the phone. Both of them turned to look.

Sawyer held up his soaked shirt, which they'd thrown into the car with him. He wrung it out. Seawater streamed onto the floor of the car.

The policemen spoke to each other. Sterns put his other hand up to his ear to have a conversation with Dad. Sorrow stormed to Sawyer's side of the car. "Come here, bro," he said, yanking Sawyer out.

The door slammed. Sawyer's body slammed against it. His bare chest pressed against the window. Sorrow moved up and down behind him, searching him, I supposed. Then Sorrow opened the door again and threw Sawyer in, handcuffed.

Sawyer was wearing that blank expression he got when he was beyond fury. He stared out the window as Sorrow trekked off in search of my car.

Shivering in my wet shirt, I said, "I hope Quinn appreciates what you did."

"It was my fault he was there in the first place," Sawyer muttered. "I asked him to come."

It wasn't Sawyer's fault Quinn was smoking pot, but I didn't argue that point. I said, "I'm afraid it's my fault we got caught in the first place."

Sawyer's face softened as he turned to me. "Not everything that goes wrong can be your fault, Kaye."

"Why would anybody call the cops on us?" I asked. "You had permission from Harper's granddad to be here. The park is closed, so nobody could have seen us from there. But Tia and Chelsea ran into Aidan at the movie. Chelsea mentioned you were here. Aidan had no idea *I* would be here. He just wanted to get *you* in trouble."

Sterns opened my door. I asked, "Officer, did you hear who called you down here? Sawyer has permission to be here, and the park is closed. I think my ex-boyfriend just wanted to get revenge on Sawyer. If you take us to jail, you'll be contributing to prison overcrowding, all for nothing."

Sterns shrugged. "All I know is, you are in serious trouble, young lady. I was talking to your dad at first, but then your mom got on the phone." He shut the door.

"Okay," Sawyer said soothingly, but I was already gasping for breath, trying not to cry and failing miserably. "Kaye," he called over my sobs. He was the one with his hands behind his back in cuffs, trying to make me feel better, and I was the one who was losing it because I'd gotten him into this.

"On a happier note," he said, "I think I've solved the problem of where to hold the homecoming dance."

Now I was crying and laughing at the same time, and hiccupping as a result. Wiping the tears from my cheeks, I said, "That is of absolutely no use to me in jail."

"You could hold the dance here," Sawyer said anyway. "People could leave their cars along the road and walk down here, and we could have it on the beach. Or maybe the city would let us leave our cars over there in the lot at the public park if we told them ahead of time. We could even hold it on the city's part of the beach. Just have everybody kick their shoes off, string some lights through the trees—"

"We can't have it off campus," I said. "Remember? Ms. Chen already shut that idea down. Too much liability."

"Then what if we made the football field look like the beach?" he suggested. "String some lights across the field, bring in some palms in pots, turn off the floodlights overhead—"

"I thought of that, too," I said. "I mean, I didn't think of making it look like the beach, but I already suggested having the dance in the stadium. The school doesn't want us standing on the grass and killing it. Grass is expensive and more important than our happiness." I sniffled.

"Then we hold it in the parking lot right outside the stadium," he said. "People don't even have to get back in their cars and drive after the game. It's on school property. There's plenty of room. We just cordon off a section—say, where the away team's buses will park, because they'll be gone by dance time—and string lights through the palm trees that are already there. It's not supposed to rain. No hurricanes in sight. If the school says no to that, they just don't want us to have a dance, and they should 'fess up."

I gasped. "Sawyer, that is a great idea."

"Some acknowledgment, please, that I came up with it while handcuffed in the back of a cop car, wrongly accused, in my boxers."

I patted his bare thigh, which was more solid than I'd imagined. "I'll give you all the acknowledgment you can handle if we ever get out of here."

He grinned mischievously at me.

"Our night together was so romantic, up to a point," I said. "We could recreate it for the dance."

"Would we ask the police to come and handcuff people?"

"Only if they're into that sort of kink. We could use it as a fund-raiser for the prom."

"Always thinking, aren't you, Gordon?" He glanced out the windshield. "Here they come. Now we're not trying to create a diversion. We only want to get out of trouble, so be humble and say nothing but 'Yes, sir,' and 'You're absolutely right.'"

Two minutes later we were hurrying back across the city beach and onto Harper's granddad's beach, hand in hand. Sterns had told my mother that I would drive straight home. I don't know what my mother had said to Sterns, but he'd seemed afraid for me.

"Listen," Sawyer said as we walked. "Whatever your parents tell you, you didn't do anything wrong. Don't let them make you feel like you did. They can punish you all they want, but don't let them convince you that you're a bad person, because you're not."

I nodded, hardly hearing him. I had a much more serious concern. "They're never going to let me see you again," I breathed.

"We'll see each other at school," he said gently. "And after we graduate in May, what they say won't matter."

I wasn't sure this was true. I'd planned to live with my parents until I left for Columbia in August. Even after that, conceivably they could continue to jerk me around by withholding my college tuition if I didn't do what they said.

Sawyer's words made me feel better anyway—because he considered how to get around unfair rules, which was totally foreign to my way of thinking. And because he assumed we'd still be together in May, no matter what.

At least, he talked the talk.

When he reached the passenger side of my car, he dropped his flip-flops and slapped his wet clothes across the roof. "Give me a sec to put my clothes on," he said. "I've moved from Harper's house into the B and B."

"Oh, have you?"

"Yeah, and I don't want to frighten the elderly."

While he got dressed, I fished in my purse and checked my phone. "I have a message from DeMarcus, and one from Brody," I said as he got into the car. "They must be worried about us. One from Noah, one from Tia—"

"Don't think about that right now," Sawyer said.

"—two from Quinn, four from Harper, six from Will." None from Aidan. Either he hadn't heard he might have gotten me detained by the cops along with Sawyer, or he didn't care.

"I'll call them," Sawyer said. "You've got to get home. I'll say the cops accused us of trespassing and let us go. I'll leave out all the near-naked parts. Nobody at school will ever hear about that unless the cops blab."

"Or my parents," I muttered.

I started the engine and cruised under the palm trees. It was a very short drive to the B and B, so I didn't waste any time before telling him what was on mind. "If we're going to date, Sawyer—"

"If? Wait, what?"

"—I want to make sure that we're exclusive," I said. "That's the only way I want to do this."

He was very slowly massaging his wrists where the cop had cuffed him, but he was looking at me. He glared at me so angrily across the car that my heart felt like it was failing.

"*What?*" he finally exclaimed again. "How long did you date Aidan?"

"Three years," I said.

"And in that three years, did you *ever* have a conversation with him in which you made sure you were both on the same page about dating exclusively?"

"No," I said meekly.

"Then why are you asking me?" he demanded.

"Sawyer!" I said, exasperated. "You have a reputation for getting around."

"When I wasn't dating *you*! Don't you think I would automatically stop going out with other girls if you and I were together? I said something like this to you before Aidan even broke up with you, because you said something like this to *me*. I mean, if you think so little of me, what do you want to date me for?"

I remembered, with a slow burn across my cheeks, the note I'd lost in Harper's house, in which Tia and I had discussed exactly this. I wondered again whether he'd found it.

I drove up to the gate and punched in the combination. But when it was open, I didn't pull out onto the road right away. I turned to Sawyer.

He had the same idea. "I'm sorry," he said. "We're both stressed out right now. I know that's not what you meant, and I didn't mean to—"

I leaned over and kissed him.

His arms wrapped around me and pulled me closer. He deepened the kiss, making it very, very sexy for a moment. Then he backed off and placed a series of light, sweet kisses on my lips. "You have to go," he whispered before kissing me again.

"I know."

His lips lingered on mine. "But I want to stay here forever with you"—kiss—"and get gawked at by passing motorists." A car zoomed by on the road.

"That is so romantic." I kissed him back, savoring what might be our last seconds together for a while. I truly wanted to stay there forever with him, too. Or, better yet, a hundred yards behind us, alone on the beach. The thought that finally made me leave was that if I stayed, I would make my punishment worse and, if I got grounded, my time away from Sawyer longer.

When I pulled in to my spot in the driveway, Dad was standing outside the garage in pajama pants and his ancient Columbia T-shirt. He said as I dragged my feet toward him, "I convinced your mother that she's too angry to speak with you tonight."

"Thanks." I sighed with relief.

"Are you okay?"

I nodded.

"You're wet."

I swallowed. "I didn't do anything wrong. I'm pretty sure Aidan called the police to get Sawyer in trouble for nothing."

"Whether you did something wrong is in the eye of the beholder," Dad said ominously. "In the morning, the beholder is going to be your mother."

Then he hugged me close and squeezed me. Immediately he let me go. "Ew, you're *really* wet." He took me by the shoulders and pressed his lips to my forehead for a long moment. "I'm glad you're safe."

But a conversation with my mother loomed in the morning. I didn't feel safe at all.

13

"GET. UP!"

Fight-or-flight adrenaline zipped through me. I sat straight up in bed. Morning light flooded my room. My mother, fully dressed, frowned at me with her fists on her hips. She was the definition of a rude awakening.

"Put some clothes on," she said, "and be in my car in two minutes." She stalked out.

In a minute and a half, I was at her Mercedes, but she was already waiting with the engine running like I was late and had a lot of nerve.

She didn't say anything for a long time as we drove through town. When we stopped at the intersection beside Aidan's house, I craned my neck and saw his car in the driveway. I'd never considered myself a violent person, but I would have loved to try a Molotov cocktail just then. A gasoline-soaked rag stuffed into a bottle, aimed to roll underneath and explode the car he'd screwed me in three times. I fire-bombed it with my eyes after we'd passed it, until I couldn't see it anymore.

"The police," my mother finally muttered as we cruised the interstate. "I get a call at eleven o'clock at night from the *police*, saying my seventeen-year-old daughter is half-naked on public property with the very boy I have told her to stay away from. This is not a poor grade we're talking about, Kaye, or a position at school. You are associating with a delinquent who has a bad reputation, and who is a bad influence on you."

"I agree he has a bad reputation." No arguing with that. "I don't agree that he's a bad influence. He's cleaned up his act lately. Anyway, you sound like you think I'm five, with no mind of my own."

"Because that's exactly how you're behaving, as if you can't see you're throwing your future away. Listen to me. I didn't go to school with anyone like Aidan."

"Oh, *Aidan*," I exclaimed. "You still want me to get back with Aidan? Let me tell you what he—"

She interrupted me. "I went to school with *lots* of boys like Sawyer."

"You don't know what Sawyer's *like*," I said. "You hardly know him."

"I've heard plenty about him. In fact, I've heard half of it from *you*."

She had me there. I put my chin in my hand and stared out the window, cursing myself for repeating the cheerleaders' rumors about Sawyer over the years to my mother.

I was so angry, and my mind was spinning so fast, that I didn't even realize where we were headed. But when she turned onto the exit in the seediest section of Tampa, I knew. "Mom."

She didn't answer, just kept moving her land yacht smoothly down the ramp. I could see one muscle in her jaw working as she clenched her teeth. She sailed into the slum, deserted of cars except for one 1980s model far down the long, straight street, its axles up on cement blocks. But the neighborhood was busy with young men hanging out in the shadows of the run-down apartment buildings, and riding kids' dirt bikes in circles. Any sane person *not* looking to buy a dime bag would have recognized what she'd stumbled into and hightailed it out of there.

My mother was not sane. And it was getting worse. In the past she'd only slowed long enough to point out her old apartment building to Barrett and me. This time she actually pulled alongside the curb, put the car in park, and pushed the button to turn off the engine. She looked over at me and raised her eyebrows.

Instantly the car was surrounded. A guy on a bike hopped down the curb, into the street, and pedaled back and forth in front of the car. A boy in a baseball cap with a marijuana leaf on the front knocked on my mother's window. She didn't react.

Watching this in horror, I jumped, startled at a knock on my own window. I didn't turn, afraid of what I'd see, terrified that I was separated from these people by one pane of not-bulletproof glass.

My mother watched me smugly.

"Fine," I said. "You grew up in that corner apartment." I pointed to the second story across the lawn of brown grass and packed dirt, strewn with cigarette butts and trash. "Your brother died at sixteen on this very street, selling drugs. Your dad was robbed and killed coming home from work. At age forty-five your mom died of cancer, which could have been caught early and treated if she'd been able to afford health insurance."

My mother gave me a curt nod.

"You got good grades, participated in every academic competition available, and snagged a full scholarship to Columbia, so you and your new family could live to their full potential, and you would never have to face this crushing poverty again."

She raised her chin to nod again, but stopped when I said this:

"You got out of here. You ensured your children would never have to live here. And yet you have driven your daughter back here, and we're both about to get shot in the head, because you don't like my boyfriend!" I was shouting now.

Even if my mother didn't care, the drug dealers around the car did. The guy at my mother's window and the guy on the bike said something to each other and took off, jumping the curb and speeding around the far side of the apartment building. I felt rather than saw the shadow of the man at my window moving away.

Another knock sounded on my mother's side. I started again, and this time she jerked her head in that direction too. A policeman's tan uniform filled the window. I looked behind us and saw the cop car, blue lights flashing.

"Oh, and *I'm* the one who always gets arrested," I said.

"You shut your smart mouth." My mother pushed the button to start the car, pressed another button to roll down her window, and then turned the car off. "Yes, officer?"

"Ma'am, do you live around here?" I couldn't see his face above the roof of the car, but he sounded young.

"I live at the beach," my mother said icily.

"What are you doing in this part of town?" came his voice. "Did you know this neighborhood is full of drug activity?"

"I grew up in that apartment right there." She pointed to the corner. "I like to show it to my children now and again. That is not a crime, not yet, not even in Florida."

"Yes, ma'am," he said. "If you ask me, if I grew up here and got out of here, I wouldn't come back. I definitely wouldn't bring my daughter to this neighborhood."

"Young man," she seethed, "I did not ask you."

This could not be happening. I was going to sit in the back of a cop car for the second time in twelve hours, because I had a habit of hanging out with people who couldn't keep their attitudes in check and their big mouths shut.

But cops were more leery of my mother than they were of Sawyer, apparently. "Yes, ma'am," this one repeated. "Y'all have a safe afternoon." I watched his uniform pass the back seat window. He got into his patrol car, shut the door, and put his head down as if he was writing something. I suspected he was really waiting for us to leave. I wouldn't put it past my mother to outstay him just to spite him.

She pushed the button to start the car again with one elegantly manicured finger. Her hand was shaking, but she didn't say a word. She pressed the button to roll up the window, flicked on the blinker, looked behind her so as not to pull into oncoming traffic while a cop possibly had her on camera, and headed down the street.

"I learned a lot from that," I said.

"You are grounded," she said. "Your father is not going to talk me out of it this time. You may go to school and come home."

"You just made sure I won't get into Columbia, then. Nobody's going to write me a stellar recommendation letter if I shirk my responsibilities for student council. We're building the homecoming float every day after school next week—"

"You may build the homecoming float," she said stiffly.

"—and I've figured out a place to hold the homecoming dance. Actually, Sawyer figured it out. Do I get to go to my own homecoming dance?"

"Yes," she said carefully, "but not with that boy. Your father and I will volunteer as chaperones to make sure."

"Fantastic," I muttered. I'd gone to all the trouble of saving this dance for my friends. I was rewarded with a date with my parents.

When we got home, Dad was watching a pro football pregame show with his feet up on the coffee table. "Did you bring me a rock?"

"Shut up." My mother disappeared into her office.

"Hey, my Kaye," he said. "Get changed and meet me on my boat in five minutes."

"Really?" I whined. "I just went through this whole thing with one parent."

"Please," he said.

Obediently I changed into a bikini and a hat, smeared on sunscreen, and galloped across the yard and down the pier to the sailboat. I was still angry and not looking forward to whatever Dad had to say. But at least his run-up to a scolding was more enjoyable than my mother's. He'd made me a picnic basket full of breakfast, for one thing. The boat puttered through the lagoon on its impotent motor, but as soon as we hit the open Gulf, Dad unfurled the big sail. We sped through the sea breeze, past the harbor and Harper's granddad's beach and the public park that had caused all the trouble. I sat in the bow, enjoying the wind in my face. The late morning sun was warm and kind.

Finally I asked, "Well? When's the lecture? Let's get it over with."

"No lecture," Dad said. "I thought it would do you good to get out on the ocean."

Moving with uncharacteristic speed, he wound and unwound ropes until the sails dropped and the boat slowed to a crawl. He offered me his favorite fishing pole. I shook my head. He baited the hook for himself and skimmed it out over the sparkling water.

I shifted to sit close to him on a lawn chair in the stern. "Can I ask you something?"

He glanced at me like he was very afraid.

"You and Mom both majored in finance at Columbia."

"Yes."

"You both worked in Manhattan for a couple of years. Then she got an offer for a great position with the bank here. She grew up here, but you're from Boston. You didn't want to move to Florida. She bribed you by buying you this boat, and the house on a lagoon with access to the Gulf."

"Yes."

"Why did you give up?"

He gave me a look like that was crazy talk. "I didn't give up, exactly. Everyone seems to forget this, but I do have a job."

"I know. I didn't mean—"

"And in that job, I wrote a headlining article for *GQ* on how the hardest thing about being a writer and the secondary breadwinner and the primary caretaker is that your own kids think you're a loser."

I raised my voice, and it echoed back to me over the

waves. "I don't think you're a loser. But you and Mom both had these power jobs in New York. She got her own bank. You became a writer. Something happened to you."

He reeled his line all the way in and flicked it out again before he said, "Being a stockbroker is very stressful. I couldn't handle it."

"What do you mean, you couldn't handle it?"

"I just couldn't."

I tried to picture what he meant, and what this had looked like. "Did you go to a counselor?"

He laughed bitterly. "Of course not. Men don't do that."

That sounded familiar. I said, "That's dumb."

He shrugged, zigzagging the line across the water.

"So what did you do, when you couldn't handle it?"

"I quit. In the worst, most public way possible, sabotaging myself so I wouldn't be able to work in the finance industry in Manhattan again for a while."

I'd never heard this story before. I was dying to know more about his meltdown. But he seemed so traumatized describing it, even now, that I decided to press him for details another day. I only asked, "Did Mom lose her mind?"

"No." He sounded surprised. I couldn't tell whether he was surprised at my question, or surprised that my mother hadn't blown her top two decades ago. "She helped me brainstorm for another job I could get with this degree, a job that wouldn't drive me crazy. We figured out that I loved writing. I could write books and articles about finance, interpreting the stock market for lay people. And she said I might like living in Florida and slowing down. She promised that if I would let her have this bank, she would let me have this boat."

That didn't sound like my mother at all.

"You've been traveling a lot more lately," I said. "Are you trying to get away from Mom? Truthfully."

He gave me an expression of utter shock. "No!"

"Would you tell me if you were?" I kept on.

"I don't know, but that's not why. Your mom and I aren't having marital problems just because *you've* suddenly decided that I feel emasculated."

"You've been gone a lot, that's all," I muttered.

"I have a *job*."

"It's the same job you've always had, but you didn't travel like this before."

"I'm doing research for the new book and, at the moment, three different articles. I can accept more projects now that Barrett is gone and you're old enough to take care of yourself."

"Oh, it's all about Barrett," I sneered. "That makes sense."

"Don't go bitter on me. Barrett is a lot more fragile than you are. I worried about him. Still do. I've never worried about you. I thought you didn't need me around." He reeled his line all the way in, set the butt of his pole down on the deck, and turned to me. "Obviously I was wrong." Rummaging in his tackle box for a different lure, he commented, "Thanks to the book deal, I'm going to make more money than your mom this year."

"You *are*? That is a huge amount of money."

He nodded. "It doesn't make up for the last nineteen years, when she made more than me."

"You're not in a competition," I pointed out.

He straightened. "You're right. It feels that way, though. And I don't really care. I only care because society cares, and I'm supposed to." Satisfied with the new lure he'd found, he deftly slung the line out over the water again.

It was soothing to watch him skip the hook over the surface, reel it back in, throw it back out, thinking of nothing, rarely catching anything. Just enjoying the sun and the water and the day. A flock of pelicans, the more common brown ones rather than white, skimmed past us, close over the water. Their wingspans were impossibly wide. I watched until I lost them in the far-off color and movement of the harbor.

I mused, "I think I'm a lot more like you than I am like Mom."

"I think it's taken you a long time to figure that out."

He was silent for a while. The ocean was full of sound, though. Waves lapped against the boat. Seagulls cried. The fishing line buzzed over the water.

"But listen, my Kaye," he finally said. "You and your mom are at each other's throats right now, and I'm just trying to hang on. You're going through some growing pains. You are not easy to get along with at the present time. Your mom has never been easy to get along with, and never will be. She's got issues." He looked pointedly at me. "And I love her with all my heart. Don't forget that."

A few hours later, I hiked back to my room. I had an appointment with Stephen Crane, I supposed, but first I checked my phone for signs of Sawyer.

Sawyer: How much trouble? :(

Me: Much. I got taken to downtown Tampa to gawk at the drug deals.

Sawyer: That shit is dangerous. Way more dangerous than me. Don't let her do that again.

Me: Ha, "let."

Sawyer: Biz is slow & the CL gave me the p.m. off. Can you go out?

Me: They don't want me to go out w u anymore.

Immediately I started typing an explanation, but not fast enough. I hated that I'd sent that text by itself, accidentally making him wait for more. I wished I could take it back. Finally I sent this:

Me: I will work on them. We just need to wait a while if u will wait for me.

Sawyer: Duh

Almost instant gratification after I sent my vulnerable text. Sawyer was a lot better at this than I was.

Sawyer: What if we went out in the daylight when I am less likely to get u arrested?

Me: I don't know.

Sawyer: What if we did something innocent?

Me: You?

Sawyer: Girl, it takes two. I didn't do any of that stuff by myself.

I tried to type "Touché" but autocorrect kept changing it to "Touched," which sounded even dirtier than I'd intended in this context. I finally backspaced over it.

Me: What did u have in mind?

Sawyer: Tennis

Me: U know how to play tennis?

Sawyer: What do u mean, why can't I play tennis

Me: I just can't picture u playing tennis.

Sawyer: The YMCA in Georgia thought tennis would save the poor children. I have played a lot of tennis.

Me: How do u know I play tennis?

Sawyer: Princess Country Club knows how to play tennis.

He was right about that. When we were twelve, Ellen and I had won the Pinellas County junior girls' doubles championship.

Me: Let me ask.

First I peered into my parents' bedroom. Dad was a lot more likely to give me permission for anything, ever, than my mother. However, his playtime was over. The door onto his porch had a sign taped to it that said NO, which meant he was working. He never put out the sign during the week, only on the weekend when my mother was home. He'd definitely been my primary caregiver on weekdays when I was growing up, but on the weekends "NO" meant "I am finally getting my time to write; go find Mother."

I skipped down the staircase and through the kitchen, my steps slowing as I approached my mother's office. I knocked politely on the open door.

She was already wearing a frown as she turned from her desk.

I swallowed. "Sawyer—"

"No."

"—wanted to know—"

"No."

"—if we could go out during the wholesome daylight hours—"

"Katherine Beale Gordon, I said no."

"—to play tennis, because how can anybody possibly get arrested playing tennis?"

"That boy would find a way."

Angry all over again, I tromped upstairs and texted Sawyer the sad news. He sent me a hilarious answer. My mother would have been horrified to know that we texted back and forth for the rest of the day, into the night. I wasted hours with him and lost some sleep despite her, and fell for him that much harder.

On Monday the school elected Sawyer and me homecoming king and queen. Since cheerleading practice was on the football field with the band, DeMarcus held his phone and read the announcements Ms. Chen had e-mailed to him. As soon as he made this pronouncement, all the cheerleaders mobbed me, squealing and hugging, along with all the majorettes (except Angelica), and Tia, who'd abandoned her snare drum halfway across the field—despite Ms. Nakamoto calling through her megaphone, "Ms. Cruz?

Let's keep it together until the end of practice, shall we?"

Sawyer had heard the announcement too, in football practice. A couple of guys who came to help with the homecoming float build after school told me the entire football team had ribbed Sawyer about what he and I were going to do to each other on homecoming night, which was kind of touching and kind of gross.

He called me from work. "What does this vote even mean?" he asked me. "We just sit on the float together?"

"And get crowned during halftime, yeah."

"Do we get a special prize at the dance?"

"Like my parents have a change of heart and let me go out with you? I seriously doubt it." I hated the way this sounded. I'd treasured every moment I'd stolen talking with him at school that day, but all I'd done while I was with him was complain bitterly about *not* being with him. If I kept this up, he wouldn't even *want* to date me for long, and my mother would have won.

"I'm wearing the costume, you know," he said. "Not at the dance, but of course at the game, and also on the float. The pelican has to make an appearance of some kind in the homecoming parade. Little kids might actually cry if he doesn't."

I planned to cheer during the game too. I wouldn't miss that to stand and grin at the crowd in a tiara for five minutes.

During the parade, though, the cheerleaders just waved from the back of Grace's dad's farm truck. I might as well play queen in formal wear.

And I didn't need my mother to help me with that. I had last year's prom gown. So I didn't even tell my parents about my achievement, which they wouldn't see as an achievement anyway. I just kept going to the homecoming float builds after school as if we weren't building it for me.

On Thursday night, Sawyer showed up at eight o'clock at the school's shop class, where we'd constructed the float. He said he'd gotten off work an hour early so he could help with last-minute preparations. By that time, though, the float was finished. Will's design of a blue crepe-paper wave rising behind the homecoming court had worked beautifully. I was one of the few students left in the shop, cleaning up stray scraps of paper on the floor. There was nothing for Sawyer to do.

"So let's go get a vegan dinner," he said, "on me. It has to be in downtown Tampa, though, where the vegans are."

I did a quick calculation in my head. The student council had spent some late nights on the float. My parents wouldn't expect me home until ten. I had time for sneaky vegan. "We need to go in separate cars, so they don't see mine abandoned here or catch me getting out of your truck."

"Okay."

"And I never want you to pay for mine. I get an allowance. You need your money."

"Don't worry about it." He grinned. "That night your family came to the Crab Lab, your dad tipped me a hundred bucks."

"You deserved every penny," I grumbled.

The restaurant he picked out had an Indian feel but an international menu. "I'm surprised at all the choices," I admitted. "I wanted to come with you, but I'd pictured eating carrots dipped in ketchup."

"I'm surprised too," he said, turning the page. "I'm glad we came. I never even thought about eating half this stuff."

"It would be great if you could shift your attention to what you *can* eat," I said. "Until now, it seems like you've been totally focused on what you can't have."

He reached across the table for my hand. "Yeah, I have been."

I tilted my head and frowned at him. "Is this worth it if it makes us both miserable?"

He didn't answer. He slowly rubbed each of my fingers with his, then circled his fingertips in my palm, shooting delicious fiery sensations up my arm.

That was my answer. As long as he made me feel so good, this was worth it.

And I remembered what Tia had told me at the movie Saturday night, which had made it sound like Sawyer had a deep vested interest in me. "Tia said you left your dad's house because of something he said about me."

Sawyer's eyes widened. He let go of my hand and put his own in his lap. "I don't want to talk about it."

"Sawyer," I scolded him. "You think you're being chivalrous, but *my* mother doesn't like *you*, either. She dislikes you for a totally different reason, but still. And *I'm* not moving out."

Sawyer took a deep breath and sighed. "I could almost forgive him for what he said. Prison's supposed to rehabilitate people. Of course it only turns them into monsters if they weren't already. And the races don't mix there."

"I know that."

"It's not what he said. It's that he was stone-cold sober, and he insulted the one person he'd found out I care about. A couple of weeks ago when you came to the Crab Lab with Aidan, my brother saw that I was upset and figured out you were why. He told my dad about it. My dad went out of his way to make a comment, not to insult you, but to hurt me. People who love each other don't do that."

"So you're not going to live with someone who doesn't love you," I said slowly. "Maybe that's too much to expect.

Maybe you move back in with him until May because you need a place to live and he's your father. As for the rest . . . maybe that comes with age."

He looked out the window onto the busy street, considering. Candlelight flickered across his face, glinting in the blond stubble on his chin. I wondered how old we would both grow before we got along with our parents and won the chance to date like everybody else.

"You need a roof over your head," I said, "and you need to eat. You can't do well at school or at work while you're worried about those basics. If you're determined to make a success of yourself, you need to start taking care of yourself first."

"That's exactly what Ms. Malone told me." He surprised me by standing, leaning across the table, and capturing my lips with his. As he sat back down, he promised me, "I'll think about it."

14

THE FOLLOWING AFTERNOON, JUST AS I WAS sitting my royal ass down on my crepe-paper throne in preparation for the parade, Sawyer came around the corner of the school dressed as the pelican. When he saw me, he jumped about two feet and threw up his wings in exaggerated surprise, then slapped his glove to his chest like he was having a heart attack.

I knew why. I'd changed my hair again.

The homecoming parade was a big deal in this town—because we didn't have that many big deals. So many people were in it that I was always surprised there was anyone left to watch it. And the school, which forced us to make up hurricane days, didn't mind letting half the student body out of last period to line up for marching band, suit up for dance

troupes, and gussie up for waving at the crowd from elabo-
rate constructions of wood and chicken wire.

That's why Chelsea, after she'd donned her majorette
leotard and pushed her tiara into place, had time to help me
pick out my hair. I was going full Afro.

"And the final touch." She slid my official homecoming queen tiara into my round hair, making a dent. She
squinted at me in the mirror. "Wow, I didn't know it would
be so . . . big."

"Me neither," I admitted. In fact, I was having second
thoughts about appearing in public like this, but there was
no time for a redo. "What am I saying with this?"

"Well, for one thing, you're giving Aidan a big 'up yours'
for making a comment about your hair a few weeks ago." She
shot the mirror the bird.

"True." I hadn't said anything to Aidan about calling the
cops on Sawyer. I had no proof, for one thing. And hardly
anyone in the school seemed to have heard about the inci-
dent. I wanted to keep it that way. No need to provoke him.

But if he hadn't liked my big hair before, huge hair certainly let him know how much I cared about his opinion.

"You're also telling the school how you feel about having
to struggle so hard just to hold a homecoming dance."

"I like it," I proclaimed, even though I didn't.

And so, a few minutes later when Sawyer fell on the ground and played dead in the sunshine, I knew why. I called, "Is it that bad?"

He leaped onto the float and took his head off—something he almost never did once he was in costume. Crepe paper crackled as he slid into place on the throne next to me. "I love it," he said, taking off a glove to slide his fingers into the back of my hair.

Of course he would love it. I felt myself glowing inside.

"It's fragile," I warned him, my voice trembling as he touched me. "It'll only stay this way for a short time."

"Like seaborgium," he suggested.

I laughed in an unregal way at this periodic table joke from nowhere. "It *does* look like a hairstyle that would have a radioactive half-life," I agreed. "It's for special occasions."

"This hair is a special occasion," he said. "It is its own holiday."

"With its own zip code," I agreed. "I'll disassemble it before tonight. It would never survive a back handspring."

"That's a shame." He moved toward me, his eyelids lowered sexily.

"Wait, lipstick, mmmm . . . ," I said as he kissed me.

I heard the familiar click of Harper's camera, and I broke the kiss in alarm.

"Sorry!" Harper called from the front of the float. She was wearing the cute clothes that had become her work uniform lately, cargo pants and a tight tank top, with the addition of her retro glasses. "I know I keep doing this to y'all, but I can't stand to miss a great shot. And your hair!"

"You won't put that in the yearbook, will you?" I pleaded. "You have to delete it. My mother can't see me kissing Sawyer."

"I'm not going to *delete* it!" she exclaimed, outraged. "But I'll put it in my 'Kaye's mom can't see this' file. Which is growing." Already spying another great shot, she wandered off without saying good-bye.

"Have you ever been felt up by a pelican?" Sawyer growled in my ear.

"I thought you said that's illegal in Florida."

"Hm," he said, leaning in to kiss me again. Technically this was grounds for suspension. School hours weren't officially over yet, and we were on campus. But the float had been dragged out of the shop building and parked behind the gym, at the very end of the floats and bands and horses and antique cars lined up for the parade. We were the pièce de résistance. Nobody was watching us steal this moment together.

Until Grace, who'd been elected homecoming senior

maid, climbed up onto her own throne and called, "Principal Chen! Sawyer and Kaye are having sex on the homecoming float."

"My God, can't we get any privacy in this parking lot?" Sawyer complained. He put his foam head back on but wrapped his wing around me, sitting back casually and propping one big bird foot up on the opposite knee like he was sitting around a bonfire at the beach with his girl.

Just after school let out, the parade began to crawl through town—out of the school parking lot, down the avenue shaded with live oaks—to make a very difficult ninety-degree turn-on-a-dime into the historic downtown. The entire route was lined four people deep. I gave them a Queen Elizabeth wave. Some of them pointed at my hair. Everyone smiled.

Everyone, that is, except my mother. I still hadn't told her or my father that I'd been elected homecoming queen. It was too much to ask that she wouldn't find out. She stood on a corner in front of headquarters for her bank, surrounded by her best employees, wearing shades so I couldn't see her eyes. I imagined her calculating how much money I was wasting if time was money and I could have been spending mine on Stephen Crane.

I kept having to remind myself to enjoy the moment. I'd

been elected *homecoming queen,* for God's sake. People might have voted for me for a variety of reasons, but one of them wasn't to get revenge on me because they didn't like me. I was popular, either because I got along with almost everybody or because I'd done a bang-up job on student council. Homecoming queen was an accomplishment few people could ever claim. Each time I came to this realization, I seized the moment like one of Harper's snapshots. Not many other students at my school would ever glimpse the beach from quite this angle, through the trees and six feet off the road, or look up and be able to touch the traffic lights framed with palm fronds overhead.

And the hour that the parade crept through town gave me time with Sawyer. Granted, we weren't really touching. We definitely weren't talking. He frequently jumped down from the float to high-five little kids, then pretended he was scrambling to catch up to us again with an exaggerated run. But there were also long interludes when he sat next to me on our throne, his feathery knees invading my personal space, his arm around me.

Even after I located my mother in the crowd, I wasn't self-conscious about touching Sawyer. I could say later that it was all part of his act. In truth, he gave me the warm fuzzies I'd always gotten when he treated me like his girlfriend

269

while he was in costume. Sawyer and I might argue or break up or even come to hate each other because my mother was tearing us apart, but the pelican would always love me.

When the parade was over, I drove home. Carefully I took off my prom gown and hung it up, then flopped onto my bed in my underwear, exhausted. I couldn't rest now, though. I needed to get up and start the long process of reconstructing my hair.

But as soon as I lay down, my mind raced. The student council's responsibilities in the parade had gone off without a hitch. Boxes checked: tick, tick, tick. Everything was set up for the dance tonight to go smoothly, too. Since I would be cheering during the game, I'd delegated all the last-minute preparations to parents and teachers. Tick, tick, tick. I was about to suffer the indignity of being kept away from my boyfriend at the dance I'd personally constructed, but at least I would get to see him.

My heart raced along with my mind. I took long, deep breaths through my nose, trying very hard to slow everything down. I was amazed at how fast my heart beat anyway, like it knew something I didn't.

I was really looking forward to consulting with Ms. Malone on Monday.

My mother breezed into my room. I didn't need to open

my eyes to know who was there. She was the parent who didn't knock. She paused at the foot of my bed. "Get your cheerleader uniform on," she sang like nothing was wrong. "You're not going to wear your hair like that to the game and the dance, are you? You've already squashed it. Let me help you."

Grudgingly I slipped on my top and skirt. I sat down in my bathroom while she worked my hair into twists, then pulled them out into curls of varying diameter, recreating how my hair had looked before. The feel of her hands in my hair was familiar, the motion of her arms in the mirror identical to a thousand repeats from my childhood. The difference was, we didn't speak.

A knock sounded on my bedroom door. "Come in," my mother called before I could. Dad peered at us, taking in the familiar act of sectioning and twisting hair, and our uneasy silence. Without a word, he left again.

Our football team had gotten so good that the games might have been boring with their guaranteed wins, except that we always seemed to get in trouble and come from behind at the last minute. And Brody always managed to get hurt. This time, in the second quarter, the opposing team's defense pushed through Noah and the other guard. Brody got sacked so hard that he flew several feet through the air before landing on his back with a two-hundred-pounder on top of him.

He did get up, very slowly. I glanced down the sideline and felt terrible for Harper with her camera around her neck and her hands slapped to her mouth in horror.

I had my own scare a few minutes later. I'd never paid much attention to the local cops who patrolled the sidelines, keeping spectators off the field, but Sawyer had noticed they were Sterns and Sorrow. He followed them around for a few minutes. He imitated Sorrow's walk. He tapped Sterns's shoulder and jumped to the other side when Sterns turned around. I was afraid the whole stadium was about to find out how the police frisked a pelican.

He was saved by halftime. He loped over to wait with me and the rest of the homecoming court for our cue. Finally the announcer called our names one by one, the crowd cheered, and we walked slowly onto the field while the band endlessly played the alma mater.

Sawyer never missed an opportunity to incorporate a staid institution into his act. I'd thought the weirdest thing that would happen during my reign as homecoming queen would be that I was escorted onto the field by a six-foot-tall bird. I was wrong. Sawyer stole my glittery sash that said KAYE GORDON HOMECOMING QUEEN and put it on over his own head, upside down. He stole my roses and stored them in his beak. They didn't quite fit. The stems hung out. He tried to steal my tiara. I slapped him. The tiara fell off anyway when he dipped me and pretended to kiss me.

The crowd roared louder than it had when Brody threw a touchdown. This town loved Sawyer.

And, I was realizing, so did I.

Along with the other cheerleaders, I showered in the girls' locker room, changed into my cute outfit, and hurried across the parking lot to the dance. The night was clear and perfect, with real stars behind the imitation ones blinking in the palm trees. The air was nippy for the first time since March.

It had gotten around school that my mother wouldn't let me date Sawyer. Several girls in the locker room had told me what a shame it was that Sawyer and I had been elected homecoming king and queen together but couldn't be each other's date for homecoming. Ellen told me she thought it was romantic. I supposed it was, in a *Romeo and Juliet* sort of way, if you liked your romantic nights to *suck*.

Strangely, I wasn't a trembling, teary basket case as I walked with the other cheerleaders toward the oasis of light and movement in the corner of the parking lot nearest the stadium. My pulse hummed. I'd delegated most of the work of running the dance to adults, but as Aidan was fond of reminding me, ultimately the responsibility of making it successful rested with me. It was a burden I wouldn't shake until the event was over. And two hours of cheering and dancing almost nonstop had left me a shell of myself, running on air.

That's when I spied Sawyer in his regular clothes, standing at the entrance to the cordoned-off area of asphalt that served as the dance floor, waiting for me. Any blood that had been left in my brain seemed to leave it, and I actually felt dizzy as he closed the space between us.

"We can't talk long with my parents around," I whispered. As I said this, I glimpsed Dad trying to coax my mother into some kind of 1980s dance, even though the music blasting over the speakers was dubstep.

"We're going to have a slow dance together at homecoming," Sawyer promised me. "Keep your eyes peeled for an opportunity."

The dance was already going full blast—and amazingly, almost everyone was *dancing* at the dance. There were a few outliers like Aidan, who stubbornly stood at the periphery, looking on, making snide comments to Angelica, and anchoring her there in his misery. But the majority of students, even the boys, were getting down. Probably this had to do with the fact that Will and Chelsea were in the middle of a dance-off rematch, and they were a positive influence.

Sawyer passed very close to me while I was in the middle of the Wobble with the rest of the cheerleaders. In fact, he smacked right into me, just like he always did on the football field, except this time there was no padding between us.

"I beg your pardon!" he shouted, catching me and holding me to keep me from falling over, which wasn't really necessary. While I was still in his arms, he whispered, "Are you looking for our chance?"

"I haven't seen an opening yet." My parents had been watching me closely. Didn't they ever pee?

"Tenacious boogers, aren't they?" Sawyer commented.

"Yes, my parents are tenacious boogers," I called as he let me go and disappeared back into the crowd. At least we could laugh about them while they made our lives miserable.

The next time I saw him, Will was trying to teach him to do the Dougie.

"I can't do it," Sawyer said.

With a glance at the edge of the crowd, I saw that my parents were talking to Ms. Chen. They would see us if they turned, but surely they didn't expect me to pretend Sawyer wasn't here at all. I said, "You do it in the pelican suit all the time."

"It's completely different in the suit," Sawyer said. "For you to do this without the suit"—he held his hands up slightly—"you'd have to do this in the suit." He held both hands straight up in the air. "Everything has to be exaggerated."

"That sounds a lot harder than I thought," Will said.

"It's exhausting." Sawyer *looked* exhausted, smiling with sleepy eyes. I wondered if he was skimming along his last wave of adrenaline, like me.

He turned to me. "Are they still watching?"

"Yes. Maybe later." I moved on before my parents got suspicious.

As I brushed past him, he touched my hand and whispered deliciously in my ear, "Later."

We had a few more encounters, but finally it was almost time for the dance to close down and we hadn't been alone together. I was grumbling about this to Harper as she snapped photos of the tired crowd. "Normally my parents would both be *all over* a catered buffet, but their daughter gets detained by the police just *one little time* and they're not hungry?"

Suddenly, from out of nowhere, Tia barreled into us. She swatted me with the end of one of her braids as she grabbed

Harper in a tight hug. "My dad is totally hitting on your mom. Sis!"

Harper peered over Tia's shoulder at their parents. "Or, she's just trying to get a good price from him on redoing the exterior of the B and B," she said, sounding strangled.

Tia let Harper go and held her at arm's length. "And you don't get only me in the bargain. You get Violet, and Sophia, and Izzy, and all their children and shitty boyfriends. Think what fun Christmas will be for you from now on!"

Harper looked decidedly uneasy. "They're probably just talking." Then her eyes widened. "Oooh, Kaye, don't look, but they're laughing with your parents. None of them are watching the dance floor. Now's your chance."

I clutched at Tia. "Will you alert Sawyer for me? Send him behind the stadium."

She saluted me. "Ten-four," she said, which I was pretty sure was not what people were supposed to say when saluting. She vanished back into the crowd. I headed for the buffet as if I needed a word with the caterer. I kept going, behind the DJ's equipment and the caterer's van, into the darkness.

Sawyer stepped from behind one of the concrete pillars that held up the stadium. "Finally," he said.

I melted into his arms just as a slow dance started, the last song of the night. He made no move to kiss me. I didn't ask. After a long night of watching my friends touch their dates without a second thought, all I wanted was to tuck my head underneath Sawyer's chin and feel his arms around me. We swayed just like that until the final lyric.

"That's it." The DJ's amplified voice bounced around underneath the stadium. "Thanks, everyone, and have a good night! Fight, Pelicans, fight!"

Languidly, like waking up from the best dream, I pulled away from Sawyer and looked up into his eyes. "Happy homecoming."

He stroked a stray curl away from my face. "Everyone had a great time tonight. Against the odds, you did amazing work on all of this."

"I wouldn't have been able to do it without you."

He kissed me for one long, perfect moment.

And then he let me go, already receding into the shadows. "I'll walk this way. You go that way. We've fooled them all. Ha!"

I looked back at him making his way around the dark side of the stadium. At the same time, he was looking back at me.

We would see each other at school on Monday.

But at that moment, it felt like our romance was over, and I would never see him again.

As I stepped back into the cordoned-off area of the parking lot, I heard my mother call, "Kaye!" Most of the school was already moving toward their cars elsewhere in the vast lot. The crowd I'd intended to get lost in was gone. My mother must have seen me come out from behind the stadium, and she'd guessed what I'd done.

I wasn't going to drag my feet toward punishment one more time. Standing firm in my strappy sandals, shivering a little in my light sweater against the cool night, I let *her* cross the dance floor to *me*.

She stood eye to eye with me, silently assessing me, before she said, "You have done an excellent job with homecoming."

"Thanks," I said without enthusiasm, trying to disguise my relief that she hadn't seen me with Sawyer.

"Ms. Chen and Ms. Yates both sought me out to tell me how proud they are of you, and what strong leadership skills you have."

"Ms. Yates?" I'd thought she hated me. It was amazing how people threw their support behind something after it had been a success and they hadn't lifted a finger.

My mother glanced over at Dad, who was still talking

with Tia's dad and Harper's mom. "Manuel says Tia's throwing an after-party at their house."

"She is," I said bitterly.

"Why didn't you ask me if you could go?"

"Because I'm grounded!" I hadn't even wanted to *think* about the party, much less tell *her* about it. All my best friends would go, and Sawyer would be there, while I stayed home. The pain was too much to bear.

My mother gazed at me like I was the biggest fool on this earth. Didn't I know I was only grounded when I displeased her? She told me, "You can go."

I walked away. I hoped she didn't expect me to say thank you.

But secretly, my heart was beating a fast pattern that sounded like *Sawyer*.

I *almost* turned around and asked, "You *do* know Sawyer will be there, right?" But I would have said that out of anger, ruining any chance I had of seeing him again.

As it was, surely she suspected he would be at Tia's party, as close friends as he and Tia were. It almost seemed as if my mother was giving me just enough rope to hang myself with.

A few hours later, I would find out how right I'd been.

*   *   *

I stayed later than anyone but Ms. Chen to make sure the DJ got packed up, the caterer was paid, and the chairs we'd set out were folded and carted back to storage inside the school. But I texted Sawyer that I was coming.

When I finally arrived at the 1910 mansion that Tia and her dad were bringing back to life, half the party seemed to be waiting specifically for me. Cheerleaders greeted me in the grand doorway and parted as I made my way inside. I caught a glimpse of Aidan leaning on the staircase railing, drunk, which bore investigating. But the crowd closed in, and I lost sight of him. Then I wanted to peer into the mermaid fountain in the foyer, which was Tia's current restoration project. Instead, she took my hand, ignored my protests, and dragged me straight into the kitchen to say hi to her dad and Harper's mom, who were sipping coffee.

After a polite chat with Other People's Parents about the marvelous dance I'd put on, Tia shoved me out the back of the kitchen and closed the swinging door behind me. Harper waited for me in the darkness.

"Walk straight through," Harper whispered. "Sawyer's out back. My mom's here, so he'll take you over there to the B and B, and you can be alone. We'll cover for you."

Alarmed, I said, "I can't ask you to lie. I mean, I could ask a lot of people to lie, but not you."

"We're not lying," she said. "My mom and Tia's dad just saw you here and can verify your whereabouts, see?" Then she put her hand on my arm. "It's okay, really. I'm willing to lie if I have to, because your mom is wrong about this. Go. All of us will say you were here with us."

15

SAWYER UNLOCKED THE HEAVY FRONT DOOR
of the B and B. "Take your shoes off, if you don't mind," he
whispered over his shoulder.

"We're sneaking?" I joked. "You're not supposed to have
girls in your room? There goes the neighborhood."

"No. Everybody in the B and B takes off their shoes late
at night so we don't wake each other up." He carefully closed
the towering door behind us, picked up his flip-flops and
took my sandals, and led the way up the ancient staircase.
Even in the darkness, his blond hair shone like a flashlight.

He closed and locked the door of his room behind us.
"Can I get you something to drink?" he asked. "I have water,
water, or water."

"I would love some water."

"Good choice." He disappeared into a bathroom.

My eyes wandered around the huge, high-ceilinged bedroom. Besides a massive four-poster bed, there was a carved dresser and a wardrobe with the door open a crack. Moving the door just a hair for minimal nosiness, I peered inside. Neatly pressed shirts hung there: his Crab Lab T-shirt, his Pelicans tee, a yellow polo, and the faded blue one. He was wearing the madras plaid, and that accounted for everything.

I snatched my hand away like I'd been burned as he walked back in with two plastic cups printed with the Crab Lab logo. "Something wrong?" he asked, handing me one.

"I guess I hadn't expected your room to be so neat."

"I cleaned up," he acknowledged.

"You knew I was coming over?"

"I hoped against hope that we would find a way." He sipped his water, looking uncomfortable. Now that I was here, he didn't know what to do with me. I suspected it was all the baggage we were carrying around with us now, floating behind me like I was towing it across the Gulf.

Trying to break the ice, I set my cup down on the table beside the bed. I hopped up on the high mattress and examined the blown glass figurines hanging in the window. Maybe they belonged to the room, but I thought I'd seen all Harper's mom's kooky art collections over the years. These belonged to Sawyer.

He slid onto the bed from the other side. "My dad learned to make those in prison. He used to send them to me on my birthday. This is my third birthday." He touched an orange fish. "This is my tenth." His finger swept around a red octopus, sending a shaft of red light swinging around the window casement. Mr. De Luca had definitely improved over the years.

"I don't keep them because of what he is to me now," Sawyer said. "I keep them because of how they made me feel when I was eight. Like there was somebody looking out for me."

"A guardian angel," I suggested.

"One in jail, yes. My mom always claimed she didn't have the money to take me to see him. Probably she didn't want to take a little kid into a state prison, which was an uncharacteristic stroke of brilliance on her part. I never met him until I moved here. Before that, it really was like he was dead." He didn't look at me as he sipped his water again.

I sat back on my heels, watching his pensive face brushed by faint light through the window. In the past few weeks Sawyer had seemed more like family to me than my own family. I wondered if he felt the same way about me. I almost asked.

I stopped with my lips barely parted. I must have expressed some tenderness like that to Aidan very early. I couldn't remember exactly, but I recognized the feeling of panic that washed over me when I was about to expose myself. I closed my mouth.

Sawyer turned to me, eyes hard, and deftly unbuttoned the first button of my blouse.

Something seemed missing here. The tenderness we'd shared last weekend at the beach had been beaten out of us by the police and my mother. But if I were to mention this, how did I expect him to respond? Wasn't this what I'd come here for? After his talk of us still being together next May, what we had in front of us was one night, like his many single nights with different girls. I'd known what I was getting into two Fridays ago when Tia convinced me to place his head in my lap.

I scooted down on the bed until I lay flat, and I reached up to unbuckle his belt.

An hour later, between soft kisses, he whispered, "Do you want to?"

"Yes."

He rolled out of bed. I clung to the sheets so they wouldn't slide off and expose me. He had no shame, though. He padded naked into the bathroom and came back with a condom, taking his time burrowing under the sheets and warming my body again. "Are you on something? In case this breaks, I don't want your dad to murder me."

"Oh, he won't murder you. My mother will have killed you already. But I have an IUD." In fact, my mother had suggested I get it when she saw that Aidan and I were growing more serious. I'd thought she was being silly at the time. Aidan and I hadn't done anything more than kiss. But the next summer, when he started to pressure me, I was very glad I had it.

As Sawyer opened the package and put the condom on, I tried to remember what I'd been thinking when I did this with Aidan. I couldn't believe I'd taken that step back then. I hadn't liked him nearly enough. I'd just *thought* I had, because I didn't have anyone to compare him with. And now that I did, sex with Aidan seemed like a real shame.

Sawyer looked over at me. "What's wrong? You seem sad, which is incorrect for this occasion. Maybe we should—"

I touched one finger to his lips to quiet him.

He nodded once, understanding. Then he rolled on top of me and settled his hips between mine, bracing himself above me on his forearms. His eyes roved across my face. "You look beautiful in nothing."

"So do you."

He smiled. "I never thought this day would come."

I didn't say "Me neither," because that would sound insulting. But I thought it. In the two years I'd known Sawyer, and watched him, and lobbed back the insults he served to me, I couldn't have predicted I would spend the darkest hours of homecoming night underneath him. Somewhere below me, past the foundation of this ancient building, under a layer of sandy soil and palm tree roots, past the ancient sea floor, deep within the earth's core, hell was freezing over.

A chill ran through me, starting on my bare arms and racing down my skin to my toes, despite the fact that we were draped with sheets and Sawyer's body covered mine.

He watched me, his blond hair tousled white across his forehead, his bright blue eyes just another tone of gray in the dusky room. He should ask me whether I was cold. But no, this was Sawyer, who knew exactly what made a girl shiver at a time like this. He should ask me if I was still sure I wanted to go through with this. But no, Sawyer wasn't one to ask again to be absolutely positive after he'd already gotten the answer he wanted—

"Oh," I heard myself exclaim as he moved into me. With a shuddering sigh, he set his forehead against mine and closed his eyes.

*   *   *

I didn't want to turn on the bathroom light, because that would break the spell. In the shadows of midnight I looked at myself in Sawyer's mirror and used my fingers to piece my curls back into place. The left side looked okay. The right was mangled, and there wasn't much I could do about it until I washed it and re-set it. And I couldn't see the back, but it felt flat. I'd have to tell my parents I'd driven around with my windows down. Not something I would have done a few weeks ago for fear of exactly this sort of hairtastrophe.

Something I definitely could see myself doing from now on.

Sawyer came in behind me and set his chin on top of my head. Normally I would have pushed him off me because this would cause more hair squashing, but his body felt too good behind mine.

"Do you have a second mirror, so I can see the back of my hair?" I asked.

"I seriously, *seriously* doubt I will ever be that sophisticated." He focused on my hair and fingered the curls. "Wow, you look like you just had sex."

"Do I?" I asked, heart sinking into my stomach.

"If it's any consolation, you look like you just had *excellent* sex."

Our eyes met in the mirror. His cocky grin faded, and we

were watching each other, dead serious. I was hyperaware of the warmth of his body behind me. Tingles raced across my chest, and the hair stood up on my arms.

I turned around to face him and caught a flash of his blond lashes as he bent down and his mouth took mine.

A few minutes later he finally broke the kiss to say "I love you." Hearing himself, he backed a few inches away and looked me in the eye.

"I love you, too." My voice cracked at the end.

"Will you marry me?"

This time his question wasn't as ridiculous as it had been every time before, so I wasn't as quick to say yes. I phrased my answer carefully and truthfully. "Ask me again when it's time."

He led me by the hand back to bed. I wanted to snag a T-shirt or a towel along the way to cover myself, but he wasn't entertaining ideas like that. Even when I tried to draw the sheets back over me, he tossed them away. I grabbed for them. He kicked them off the bed completely. I was exposed. The only cover was his hand smoothing across my skin.

"What's wrong?" he asked.

I took a deep breath, terrified to tell him. "If we get serious—"

"If!" he exclaimed, letting his head fall backward to the

pillow. "What just happened? Maybe we need to do that again."

"*As* we get serious," I corrected myself, "have you thought about what happens in May? What are you doing after graduation?"

"Oh, you think I'm not good enough to go to college?" After all we'd been through, sarcastic Sawyer was back.

I *did* assume he wasn't going to college, honestly, but I didn't have to admit it. "No, why?"

"Because if you'd thought I was going to college, you would have asked 'Where are you going to college?' instead of 'What are you doing after graduation?'"

"Okay. Where are you going to college?"

"You're nuts. I'm not good enough for college."

I grabbed my empty Crab Lab cup from the table and held it over him. "I'm going to hit you with this."

"I'm going to culinary school," he said quickly.

"You are?"

"Yes."

"Where?"

"New York."

"Have you gotten in?" I asked.

"I haven't applied. I'm waiting to make sure you get in to Columbia."

"Are you sure you want to do that?" I'd been worried about this. The idea that he would simply move to New York too lifted a weight from my shoulders. But it couldn't be that simple. "What if we break up? You'd be stuck there."

"I'm never stuck anywhere," he assured me. "If I get into trouble, I haul myself back out. But I wouldn't want you to feel obligated to stay with me if you met somebody smarter at Columbia. You'll meet guys in college who've been to Paris. Hell, guys who are *from* Paris. I'm just your high school boyfriend from back home. I don't want to be an albatross around your neck."

"Pelican."

"Right. If it makes you feel better, I've been incredibly jealous of you ever since I heard you wanted to go to college in New York. I've got to get out of here, and there's nowhere I'd rather go. New York is one of the world's best food cities."

He glanced sideways at me, seeming almost nervous. "If this seems stalkerish to you, I won't do it. I mean, New York is huge and we would never have to see each other. I started thinking about going because of you, but we don't have to date after high school. I don't want you to feel trapped." His words came out faster and faster. He was definitely nervous. *Sawyer De Luca was nervous.* "Oh God, what have I done? Say something."

I laughed, trying to put him at ease. "You just surprise me. Are you going to open your own restaurant?"

"I guess I'll have to, since I don't like people telling me what to do. This is when it's going to come in handy to have a finance major for a girlfriend. So I was wrong before. We can't break up."

"I don't know anymore about majoring in finance," I said slowly. "I'm rethinking everything." I squinted at him in the darkness. "This really surprises me. You've never talked about culinary school before." Maybe I just hadn't been listening, I thought guiltily.

"I can't afford it right now. I'll get a job in a high-end restaurant and learn all I can. When I've lived in New York long enough to qualify for in-state tuition, I'll find a community college where I can get a business degree. Eventually I'll open my own restaurant."

"Vegan?" I guessed.

"Yes. That can't work just anywhere, but New York has enough weirdos like me to support it."

"That sounds like a good plan."

"At least it's a plan. I don't know if it's good. Luckily, one thing that separates me from other people is that I don't need my life planned out and structured. If this doesn't work, I'll do something else."

"I would believe that, except you sound so defensive."

He watched me, careful not to reveal anything he didn't want me to see. His face was devoid of expression, this time not out of anger, but from fear.

"Sawyer," I whispered. "It's okay to be scared." I kissed his cheek.

"*You* scare me."

"You scare the hell out of me, but it's a pleasant kind of scary, right?"

"So far, so good."

I smiled. "I don't want to be the one to make you question your culinary school plan. I don't know anything about that stuff. I just wonder if you're selling yourself short. Right now, though, you're not feeling good about yourself. You wouldn't believe anybody who told you that you're better than what you're aiming for. Not even me. You may need a year to figure that out for yourself."

He shrugged, looking away, but I could tell he was listening.

"I agree you need to get out of here. You've been through too much with your family. If you could start over someplace else, I'll bet you would be a completely different person. And I'd really like to meet that guy."

He grinned, looking perplexed. "Thanks, I think."

"How are your grades?" I asked.

"They're good," he said. "I'm no valedictorian, but I have a three-point-seven right now, and I'm trying to bring it up."

"My God, Sawyer."

"What?" he asked.

I didn't want to say what I was thinking, which was *Holy shit, that is a high GPA, and all this time I thought you were a slacker.* I skipped over that part and asked, "How are your entrance exam scores?"

"High."

"How high?"

He chuckled. "Higher than yours."

"Now, wait a minute." I didn't want to insult him, but he had to be kidding, because I'd knocked my entrance exams out of the park. "How do you know what I got?"

"I don't," he said, "but Ms. Malone told me my scores are the second highest in the school, right behind Tia's. I actually got higher than Tia on the verbal."

I stared at him in disbelief.

"What?" he asked again.

I tried to make his crazy face with one eyebrow up and the other down. I couldn't do it, so I lifted and lowered my brows with my fingertips.

"Don't do that to your face," he said.

"Sawyer," I said, exasperated, "you have grades and scores that high and you want to go to *culinary school*? And you don't see anything wrong with this picture?"

"Of course not," he said. "It's never wrong to pursue something you love." He twisted one of my curls around his finger.

"But you *don't* love cooking," I pointed out. "You don't bum around the Crab Lab kitchen after hours, inventing new recipes, do you? You happen to be a vegan, but just because you have special dietary preferences doesn't obligate you to open that kind of restaurant. There may not be a huge population of vegans in the Tampa Bay area, but there are plenty in the world, and they're not all going to culinary school and opening vegan restaurants. I think you've only come up with this idea because you work as a waiter, you know restaurants, and you're scared you'll fail at something else."

"Like what?"

"College. Just apply for college. Apply to Columbia."

He laughed. For once it was an ugly sound. "I would never get in to Columbia."

"How do you know if you don't try? It sounds to me like you'd have a good chance. You might get a need-based scholarship. On the essay part of the application, tell them a sob story about your dad and your situation."

"My *situation*?" He gave me the raised-eyebrow look.

"Yes. And by 'sob story,' I guess I mean you should tell them the truth."

He shook his head. His hair made the softest sound against the pillow. "I don't have the money for college applications."

"If your scores are that high, Ms. Malone will find you some money."

He stared thoughtfully at my face. His eyes traveled down to my breast. He touched me softly.

I shuddered.

He slid his phone from the table on his side of the bed and peered at it, probably checking the time. "We'd better go before we are discovered," he said in a voice from a cheesy movie. Then he laid his phone aside and rolled so that I was underneath him again.

"Katherine." He kissed my lips. "Beale Gordon."

"Yes?"

"This has been the best night of my life."

"Mine too," I said. "Sawyer . . ."

"Salvatore De Luca," he prompted me.

"Salvatore?"

"No," he laughed. "I'm kidding. My middle name is Charles."

"Charles?"

"Yeah. That's why I don't tell people my middle name."

"It's not as bad as Salvatore. Anyway, this has been—"

His phone vibrated on the table. "Hold on." He slid over and glanced at it.

The next second he leaped up to standing and was fumbling on the floor for his clothes.

"What's the matter?" I exclaimed.

"Harper texted me." His voice bounced as he jerked his shorts on. "Somebody at the party heard where we'd gone and told Angelica. Angelica told Aidan. Aidan called your parents. He's drunk and he just admitted it to everybody."

"No, no, no," I chanted, like that was going to help. "Where are you going?"

"Stay here. I don't want you to see your dad beat the fuck out of me."

"Sawyer, wait!" But he was already gone, not bothering to keep his shoes off to avoid waking the rest of the B and B. His flip-flops clattered down the stairs, and the front door slammed.

As I pulled my own clothes on, I tried to picture what was happening, and feared the worst. Dad was mild mannered, but he was huge. Sawyer was not huge, but he had a temper. There was no best-case scenario to this.

It wasn't either of their voices I heard yelling as I ran out the back door of the B and B to the parking lot, though. It was my mother's. She was yelling at Sawyer.

A cloud of white dust was still settling over the gravel-and-shell driveway. As it cleared, I saw why. Both my mother's Mercedes *and* Dad's BMW were parked in the lot. Dad leaned against his car with his arms folded. Sawyer leaned against the Mercedes with his arms folded. They were like two captains of pirate ships in Tampa Bay, deciding whether to fire that first shot across the other's bow.

My mother was the one shooting from the hip, reciting to Sawyer a lot of his poor qualities that she'd listed for me in the past couple of weeks. "Hey," I said, which only drew some of the fire from him to me. I could see there was no way out of this now, though. I would never be able to go out with him again, if he even wanted to.

Help came from an unexpected place. Harper appeared from a trail through the trees, the same one Sawyer and I had followed to get here from Tia's house. "Hi, there!" she called as if my mother didn't sound murderous. "I beg your pardon. I'm so sorry. My mom's not here right now, but we have a rule at the B and B that we don't raise our voices because it might disturb the guests if they're sleeping." She nodded toward the second story of the Victorian towering over us. "Come on inside." She stepped away to unlock the front door of her own tiny house.

Nobody budged. Everyone glared at everyone else.

"Come on in," Harper repeated, daring to encircle my mother's waist with her arm and push her along toward the door. "Everyone's welcome inside, where you can continue to discipline your daughter and . . ." Harper was not the best at making small talk, which is why it had been a good idea for her to stop working at the B and B in the first place. ". . . castigate Sawyer," she finished.

Sawyer elbowed her.

"I said *castigate*," she told him.

"You see," my mother said straight to me as I followed Dad through the door, "this is what happens when you date trash. We all start acting like trash."

Sawyer dropped into one of the side chairs around the coffee table. He'd been ready to defend himself physically against Dad, but he was no match verbally for my mother.

"Gosh," Harper protested at the same time Dad started, "Sylvia—"

"No," I told my mother, "this is what happens when I finally stand up for something I want. You say you're training me to be a strong woman. But really, *you* want to be a strong woman with a weak daughter you can push around."

My mother stared at me in stunned silence.

"I refuse to be grounded anymore," I said. "I won't let you tell me who I can date. If you want to take away my car, fine.

Kick me out of the house and I'll get a job and a place of my own. I'll take the bus to Tampa and try out as a professional cheerleader."

Harper raised her hand. "I don't think those jobs pay very much—"

"Listen," Dad said to me. "Your mother came here to give you a piece of her mind. Which she did." He turned to my mother. "I *followed* you here to tell this young man that as far as I'm concerned, he can ask Kaye out if he wants. He should consider me an ally, and I will work on you." He held out his hand to her. "Come on, I'll take you out for a drink."

She looked at him. Her expression was somewhere between a glare and a smile.

He wiggled his fingers. "Come on, I'm loaded. I just sold another article."

She took his hand, but she refused to look at anybody as he led her toward the door.

Dad patted Harper on the head as he passed her. "Sorry, honey."

"That's okay, Mr. Gordon," she said. "Glad to be of service."

He touched the tip of my nose. "Be home by two. And don't go looking for an apartment just yet." He opened the door for my mother and closed it behind them.

I collapsed into Harper's arms. "I am so sorry!"

"No, don't be sorry! It's all worked out!" She called over my shoulder, "Sawyer, it's all worked out. Are you okay?"

Sawyer was silent.

Frightened, I walked over to stand directly in front of his chair. He glared up at me. He wasn't expressionless, as when he was furious. He had a look even madder than that. His anger showed in every line on his face. I'd never seen this expression before, but I knew it when I saw it.

"He's not okay." I reached down and cupped his cheek in my hand. "Baby, I don't blame you for feeling that way, but it doesn't matter now."

"It doesn't *matter?*" he exclaimed.

"Let's go back over to the party," Harper suggested brightly, "and forget all this."

"Let's do." I held out my hand to pull Sawyer up.

But I knew from the way he looked at me that it had not, in fact, all worked out.

16

HARPER WENT AHEAD, AND I HELD SAWYER'S hand, but the three of us didn't say much as we followed the path back to Tia's house. We were passing through several back-yards after midnight, and every adult in Florida owned a gun.

When we arrived, though, Brody and Noah were playing a very slow, sore game of hoops in the driveway. Brody took one look at Sawyer and said, "Oh God, what's wrong? Don't let him go in there." But Sawyer had already broken away from me and disappeared inside.

"Why not?" Harper asked Brody.

"Aidan is plastered, and Will is in rare form."

That made Harper and me speed up. As we hustled inside, I could hear Tia talking with Angelica right beside the door. "Aidan dated Kaye for three years, Angelica. You can't expect him to forget that overnight— Oh." She'd seen me, and she stepped into my path. "Sawyer just came in. He looks awful. What happened?"

I just shook my head, but Harper right behind me said, "Everything we thought, and worse."

From the next room, I heard Will's voice rising. Along with Harper and several other people, I peered into one of about six living rooms or dens or libraries on the bottom floor of the vast house.

The first thing I saw was Sawyer, with the same scary look on his face, standing in the opposite doorway.

Second I focused on Will, who was standing over Aidan, pointing down at him. Aidan was *definitely* drunk. There wasn't any alcohol officially at this party. My class's usual way around that was to go drink in someone's parked car, then come back.

I'd known Aidan to imbibe that way. But not like this. His eyelids were heavy, and he seemed to be having a hard time keeping his head high as Will shouted down at him in his Minnesota accent. "How could you do that? So she's your ex-girlfriend. *You* broke up with *her*. You're trying to ruin her life, along with Sawyer's, and you don't care if you take some of the rest of us down too. We're just collateral damage. What kind of student council president *are* you?"

"Like Minnesota is the moral center of the universe!" Aidan roared.

Sawyer was gazing at Aidan with pure hatred. And Sawyer had been known to swing a punch in the heat of the moment. Quickly I crossed the room and pushed Sawyer into the next one, which wasn't as crowded. I whispered, "Do you need to leave? I don't want you to get in a fight with Aidan."

"I'm not angry with Aidan," he said, slowly turning to focus his furious gaze on me. "I don't have any room left for that, because I'm so angry with you."

"With me?" I breathed.

He pulled a folded sheet of paper from his pocket. Before he'd even opened it all the way, I knew what it was. I saw Tia's drawing of me lying like a dog.

"I lost that," I said carefully. "Did you find it stuffed down in the chair at Harper's?"

He stared at me silently, then shook the note at me. "I was your *experiment*? I asked you something like that the other day, and you lied to me. You said no."

"You don't understand," I said quickly. Lowering my voice to a whisper, I said, "This is just between you and me, but the Superlatives elections got messed up. A lot of the titles are wrong, including yours, and mine. We're actually the Perfect Couple That Never Was." In a normal tone—which was shaking now, because no matter what I told him, he didn't look any less angry—I said, "That's why I've been curious about you for a while, not just because Aidan broke up with me."

Sawyer gaped at me. "So I *was* your experiment," he repeated. "You thought it would be hilarious to fuck around with me, knowing that I've had a crush on you since I moved here."

It was my turn to stare at him with my mouth open until I covered it with my hand. "No, I had no idea about that."

"Tia told you," he prompted me.

"No," I said, "she didn't." But if she'd known, that explained why she'd been so keen on throwing me together with Sawyer.

"Harper told you," he said next.

I shook my head. "Harper keeps secrets." I wished she didn't. I really could have used this information a couple of weeks before.

He nodded. "Everything makes sense now. When I talked about following you to New York, you looked at me like I had three heads."

"Because I never thought about it before, Sawyer!"

"I've thought about it for two years," he said acidly. "And what do I get for my trouble? I've made Aidan so jealous that he'll want to take you back. You're welcome."

"No—" I had no intention of dating Aidan again, ever.

"What are you going to do once you graduate from high school," Sawyer sneered, "and from college, and there's no pre-planned program for you to cycle through? There's no Most Likely to Succeed for the rest of your life to let you know you've succeeded. There's no office of student council vice president to let you know you're *almost* in charge, or head cheerleader to let you know you're the only popular girl anybody trusts to keep the rest of the cheerleaders out of trouble. How will you know how or when to be happy if nobody's telling you?"

Tears stung my eyes. "That's not fair."

He stepped very close to me. "You know what's not fair, Kaye? I risked everything for you. I could have been arrested. Your mother could still have me evicted and fired from the B and B." He pointed in the general direction of that awful argument. "She just called me trash, all for the sake of your experiment."

Now he pointed at me. "I have been playing you straight this whole time. When I told you I loved you, that's what I meant. I never intended to be your experiment, or your walk on the wild side, or your favorite mistake." He blinked, appearing for a moment like he had tears in his eyes. "I can't even look at you."

That hurt worse than anything else he'd said. He'd loved to look at me even when it seemed nobody else did.

He stomped back through the doorway, bullied right through Will's lecture to Aidan, and parted the crowd around the front door. I tried to push through, but by the time I'd run down the front steps, the taillights of his clunker truck were disappearing down the street.

I turned slowly toward the house. Tia stood in the doorway. Our note with her dog drawing was crumpled in her hand. Sawyer must have shoved it at her on his way out.

"He'll be back for work in the morning," Harper said. "I promise. He never misses work."

She and Tia and I sat on the low wall of the mermaid fountain with the water flowing between our toes before it cascaded over exquisite antique mosaics. The party was winding down, and so were they, with their elbows on their knees and their chins in their hands.

I was past wound down. I'd cried so hard in the past fifteen minutes that I felt half dead. At least DeMarcus had driven Aidan home to get him away from the alcohol supply secreted in someone's car, and from Will, and from me.

I wished so hard that Sawyer would reappear in Aidan's place. To give me a comforting hug, or to drag our awful argument out. Anything, just to have him here with me a little longer.

But I knew he wasn't coming back.

"Why didn't you tell me Sawyer's had a crush on me for two years?" I finally whispered.

"I've only known for a couple of weeks," Harper said. She glanced at Tia for help.

Seeing the look on my face, Tia held up her hands. "He told me a month ago and swore me to secrecy."

Two years, and a thousand times that he'd called me a name or tried to sit in my lap. All that time he hadn't been bugging me for a laugh. He'd been flirting, and hoping I'd flirt back, when I was dating Aidan. It must have been torture for Sawyer.

"If it's any consolation," Tia said, "he hates me too now. Harper and I never should have tried to push you two together. But he was completely smitten with you, and it was making him miserable. Once I started looking, it seemed to me that you had a crush on him, too, whether you admitted it to yourself or not."

"I did," I sniffled.

"You'll get back together," Harper said soothingly. "You just need some time."

"I don't know," Tia said. "Kaye's lost a boyfriend, but Sawyer's lost a lot more than a girlfriend. He's lost himself. The first time he ever felt worthwhile was when he won the mascot position. The second time was when you went to find him at the beach, Kaye. Not that I think you can really understand what low self-esteem feels like, when you've grown up with everybody calling you princess."

Harper kicked water on Tia's bare leg. "That was the wrong thing to say."

"She meant it," I said, "or she'd be apologizing."

"Well," Tia muttered. "I'm not saying you should get back together with Sawyer just because you feel sorry for him. He would hate you when he found out, you would resent him, and that would make everything worse in the long run. But if you really love him, you can't let each other go just because you're both stubborn."

"He doesn't want me back," I assured her. "You didn't see the way he was looking at me."

"We *have* seen the way he looks at you," Harper interjected. "That's our whole point."

I took my feet out of the cold water and lay balanced along the wall. I listened to the burbling fountain, Harper and Tia's hushed conversation, music blaring from a few rooms away, an argument between Quinn and Noah, and laughter. And I thought:

What if Angelica hadn't intercepted a note from me to Harper about my crush on Aidan in Ms. Yates's ninth-grade science class? He would never have guessed I liked him. I'd hidden it well. And the next week, I would have moved on to someone else. At that age, my crushes had *seemed* crushing, but they weren't so bad that I couldn't get over them when another boy caught my eye at the movies on the weekend.

Aidan wouldn't have asked me out. When Sawyer moved to town two years ago, I would have been available. He would have asked me out instead.

I would have said no.

He would have worked on me.

I would have said yes.

I would have lost my virginity with him instead of Aidan.

"Wait a minute," Tia protested. "Then who would *I* have lost *my* virginity with?"

I hadn't realized I was talking out loud.

"I'm confident you would have found someone," I said.

If I'd dated Sawyer for the last two years—well, there was no way that would have happened. We would have fought and broken up and gotten back together and broken up again. My last two years would have been less like training camp and more like high school. Less like an accounting course and more like a life.

I fell asleep with that wistful dream in my head. I was only vaguely aware that Brody carried me to Harper's car, and they drove me home.

17

I SLEPT UNTIL NOON. AFTER THAT I STAYED in bed for another hour, trying to go back to sleep just to avoid thinking about the night before. The bright sun wouldn't let me, and the deep blue sky flashed at me through the palm trees outside my window. If last night's cool front was any indication, today would be warm—not hot—and perfect for a jog. A jog would give me time to think, exactly what I couldn't stand. I rolled over for the millionth time.

A soft knock sounded at my door. I knew from the fact that the door opened without me giving permission that it was my mother. She sat on the edge of my bed and put her hand in my hair.

"Harper's mom called," she said. "We had a long talk. She's dating Tia's father!"

In answer I gave her a sigh.

"I guess I'm surprised enough for the two of us, then." She rubbed my shoulders vigorously, like trying to rub the life back into me. "Sit up and let's talk."

Slowly I dragged myself up against the pillows, because once she decided we were having a talk, she never went away until she was done.

"Oh, honey." She reached out to brush away the tears under my eyes. *Like you care,* I wanted to say, but that would just keep her here longer. I was all sassed out.

She smiled sympathetically at me. "Lynn actually called because she's worried about you. Harper told her what happened last night. Lynn wanted you—and me—to know that Sawyer moved out."

"Oh no!" I cried. "Where did he go?"

"Back to his father's house, though he'll still be working for Lynn in the mornings."

"Oh." I covered my mouth with my hand, relieved that he'd come back last night. And that he'd finally gone home.

My mother patted my leg under the covers. "You didn't tell me he's been having so much trouble."

"I didn't think that would help his case with you."

She nodded, gazing out my window at the blue sky. "Lynn loves him."

"A lot of people do."

"So does Harper's grandfather, which is saying a lot, because that man . . ." She didn't have to finish. Everybody knew Mr. Moreau was hard to get along with. If he loved Sawyer, Sawyer was special.

"Lynn says I've been too hard on him," my mother said, "and on you. After discussing it with your father, I think I was wrong to ground you, or to prevent you from dating him. But if you do have sex, you're using a condom in addition to your IUD every time, yes?"

"*Mom,*" I said with both hands splayed in front of me, "we broke up."

"Oh." My mother sounded sad.

I was so angry with her that I couldn't even feel anymore. I flopped backward on the bed and closed my eyes.

"Tell me what happened," came my mother's voice.

"He stuck by me through a lot," I said woodenly, "but you have been awful. There was just so much even he could stand, I guess."

She shifted up the bed and twisted a lock of my hair to make a tighter curl when she fingered it out. "I'm confident you can solve that problem," she said. "You are smarter, and stronger, and more of a woman than I've given you credit for. I'm sorry."

I opened one eye, and then the other, to stare at her in disbelief. She concentrated on pulling out the twist and placing the curl across my temple, framing my face. Finally she met my gaze. She said again, "I'm sorry."

My voice sounded throaty with crying as I said, "I have an appointment Monday to see a counselor at school about stress management."

My mother raised her eyebrows. "That's a positive step."

"I think so too. It was Sawyer's idea. He set it up for me."

She nodded slowly. "Why don't you invite him over to go out on the boat with you and your father tomorrow? He can stay for lunch."

"Because we are not spea-king," I enunciated. My mother didn't quite seem to get that Sawyer and I were broken up for good.

Then she said, "You need to eat breakfast, or lunch, or whatever you want to call it. I'll fix you anything you like. But right now, you need to hop downstairs, because Aidan is here."

"Oh. My. God." The last person on earth I wanted to deal with this afternoon. The thought of him made me feel like I weighed five hundred pounds and had sunk permanently into the bed. "I don't suppose you could tell him I'm asleep. Or dead?"

My mother shook her head, as I knew she would. She'd never in my life let me avoid a confrontation.

I rolled my eyes, put on a bra under my T-shirt, and slouched down the steps and onto the front porch. I never would have appeared like this in front of Aidan before, but I honestly didn't care what he thought of me anymore. My decision was reinforced when I saw he'd taken the swing with the comfortable cushion. I had to settle for the seat across from him. I didn't even bother to hold my head up, just collapsed across the wicker and waited for his bullshit.

"I came to apologize," he said.

Now I looked up at him, curious. This was one of those rare times he dropped his pompous tone and let me see the real boy he'd been hiding under all that bravado.

He really was sorry.

"I've been thinking hard about what I did to you last night," he said, "and what Will said to me afterward. I really regret it." He mumbled under his breath, "The hangover doesn't help."

I squinted my eyes to focus on him in the dappled shade. He *did* look a little green. I said, "I imagine not."

"The office of the president went to my head," Aidan said. "You've been telling me that, but I couldn't hear you. We've been drifting apart for a while. Probably ever since we started going out in the first place. I've been angry with you about that, which got rolled into my feelings about student council, and . . ." He heaved a sigh. "I hear you now."

"Good."

"The last time I was over here," he said, "I got that letter of recommendation from your mom. You were mad at me for waiting to break up with you until after. The truth is, I was thinking at that point that it would be cool if I got into Columbia and you didn't."

"Really." I swallowed. I'd understood he resented me. I hadn't realized how much.

"I should have known better than to ask you for a break rather than a breakup, and to try to hold on to you at the same time I was letting you go. I don't know where a lot of this negativity comes from. Maybe we just got together too young, and we were together too long."

I finally sat up. "It's not all your fault," I said. "Lately I've realized I was counting you as one of my accomplishments, something to put on college applications. You know, 'Dating the student council president, Most Likely to Succeed.' I thought that way in ninth grade. I guess I don't think that way anymore."

"Well, maybe we won't have to cross paths in college. I'm not sure I want to apply early admission to Columbia anymore. If we get in, we're locked in, and I'm not positive I want that to be my one and only choice."

"Me too," I said, seeing this for the first time. Flopping across the seat again, I asked, "Are you going to apologize to Angelica, too?"

He massaged his temple. "After last night, I think my relationship with Angelica is a lost cause. She's not a fan of drinking."

Or boyfriends who can't get over their old girlfriends, I thought. "Maybe there's still hope," I said cheerfully. "I overheard Tia talking with her. She was upset, which means she's into you. I've never seen Angelica express an emotion before, so that's huge."

He nodded slowly. "I heard you and Sawyer broke up. If I caused that, I'm sorry. If you actually wanted to be with him, I mean." He sounded doubtful.

"I did," I said.

A silence fell between us, long and dead, while Aidan squeaked back and forth on the swing.

"Well," I finally said, "we still have eight months of student council together. I'd like us to try to get along from now on. We've broken up, but that doesn't mean the last three years didn't happen."

"Right." He leaned forward in the swing, put his hand on

mine, and stroked his thumb over my palm. Maybe he was thinking about the fact that we'd been each other's first time.

As I gazed at him, I wished again that I'd waited. My attraction to him, and my dreams of spending the rest of my life with him, seemed to belong to another girl entirely. It was hard to believe I'd ever been young enough to love him.

I drew my hand away. "I'll see you at school Monday."

"Yeah." He stood, sending the swing into wild motion on its chains. "We need to start planning the student council haunted house."

"Oh boy. Maybe somebody else could head up the committee for this one. Will. Or Sawyer."

He coughed at my mention of Sawyer. But all he said was, "That will work. You deserve a break." He jogged down the steps, then turned around on the sidewalk. "By the way, Kaye, you did an awesome job on the elections, and the float, and especially the dance. I didn't want to admit it, but you were right and I was wrong."

"Thanks," I called.

I went back to bed.

But an hour later, I did get up and let my mother cook for me. I watched a little football with Dad. Then I spent a few hours doing something I rarely did at home: I blasted music in the backyard and worked out cheerleader choreography for a couple of new songs the marching band was playing.

My mother didn't say a word.

About four thirty, Harper surprised me by appearing in my driveway in my car. She had a key, but it was a real favor to bring my car over from Tia's without me asking. Brody was right behind her in her new (to her) car. He didn't get out to talk to me, though. He gave me a brief wave and disappeared into the back seat.

"What's up?" I asked Harper.

"Come with us to downtown Tampa, to the marching band's first competition of the year!" She announced this with the enthusiasm of a used-car salesman.

"Mmph. I don't feel like seeing anybody."

"I thought you hated being here with your mom nowadays."

I *had* complained to Harper about this in the last few weeks. But looking back at the house, I said, "I think we're over the worst of it."

"Well, you're the head cheerleader," she said. "You're the student council vice president. You have to support Will and Tia." She raised her eyebrows behind her glasses. "And I have things to give you, and things to tell you."

That did it for me. I'd almost forgotten that my time

with mischievous Harper and crazy Tia was drawing to a close. I needed to enjoy every second.

As soon as we'd set off in her car, she handed me a little satin pouch. "This is for me?" I asked.

"Yes. From Sawyer's dad."

"Sawyer's *dad*. What in God's name. Is it dangerous?" I dumped the contents of the pouch out onto my lap, then wished I'd been more careful. It was a little glass pelican, carefully handmade, colored like Sawyer's costume with white feathers and a yellow beak and feet. This one had a tiny red heart on his chest. A red ribbon was looped through the back of the figure to turn it into a necklace.

"Sawyer brought it over," Harper said. "His dad made it out of the blue and wanted to tell you he's sorry about what he said, and sorry you found out."

I wasn't sure how I felt about that, but I put the ribbon over my head and touched the cold pendant. "Sounds like he and Sawyer had a heart-to-heart."

"They did."

My stomach was beginning to twist. That was all I wanted to hear about Sawyer. I changed the subject. "So, your mom and Tia's dad are officially dating?"

"Yes! Well, they're going out on a date tonight."

I asked carefully, "Is that okay with you?"

"I've always liked Mr. Cruz," she said. "I do not want four sisters. Maybe they'll just date for a while. And speaking of dating . . ." She glanced in the rearview mirror at Brody, who stretched across the back seat with his earbuds in, snoring softly.

"Poor thing," she said. "He got sacked so hard last night. Did you hear it?"

I shook my head. "I saw it, though. He was airborne. It looked painful."

"I heard it from the sidelines. It made me ill." Then she grinned at me and whispered, "We did it last night!"

"You *did*?" I squeaked.

"Shhh! Yes. After we took you home, he started to feel really bad. My mom was still hanging out with Tia's dad, so Brody and I went over to my house. We thought he might start to feel better if he could lie down for a while. We decided we'd better go ahead and have sex in case he died."

"That's . . ." I didn't have a word for it.

"A really great excuse to do it," she finished for me. "He couldn't move, so I was in control. I think that's been my problem all along."

"You seem happy about it," I said. Then I laughed at the understatement. She was blushing and glowing.

"I *am* happy. He's so great." She looked into the mirror

again and smiled at the sleeping hulk of him. "For *not* being the perfect couple, I can't imagine it working out any more perfectly."

She must have suddenly remembered that Sawyer and I *were* the Perfect Couple That Never Was, in name only. She gave me a guilty look and put her eyes back on the road.

The parking lot at the stadium where the band contest was being held was littered with cars and buses. Harper cruised until she found our school buses, with our band hanging out the windows. She parked nearby.

While she was still helping Brody maneuver his damaged body out of her back seat, I popped out of the car and thought I recognized the car next to us. "Quinn and Noah are here," I mused, peering inside to see if it was really Quinn's. I was looking for the interchangeable components of his black leather Goth look. What I saw instead was Sawyer's madras button-down.

"Sawyer's here." Looking up, I recognized him before the words had escaped my mouth. In his mascot costume, he was bouncing along underneath the bus windows, high-fiving the marching band.

"Hey, pelican," I heard Tia call, "your girlfriend's looking for you."

Sawyer turned and saw me.

And least, I thought he did. I still wasn't sure which part of the bird head he saw from.

And then he was loping toward me with his wings open.

I crashed into him. His arms enveloped me. He squeezed me, picked me up, and twirled me in a circle. I never wanted to let him go. But the pelican was always kind to me. Sawyer was less likely to forgive.

When he finally put me down, I said, "Thank you for the necklace." I fingered it. "Or, thanks to your dad."

He nodded. Whereas this would have been a movement of an inch for anybody else, his beak moved up and down a foot.

"I'm sorry about last night."

He hugged me again.

"I don't want you to act like everything's okay between us in costume, when you're actually still mad."

He shrugged.

"Well, it matters to *me*," I said. "You have a hard time showing me how you feel when you're not in the costume. I have a hard time showing you how I feel at all. I'd really like us to try again. It took me a while, and a conversation with my dad, and another long while, to figure out that I love you with all my heart."

He put his hand over his own heart.

Then he reached up and tugged upward on his head. The thing was so big that it took a few seconds to pull off. Underneath, his hair was a riot of every shade of blond, and his eyes were bright blue. Looking deep into my eyes, he whispered, "Say that again, when I'm not in costume."

"I love you," I said, "with all my heart."

He put his free feathery glove into my hair and kissed me deeply.

"Wooooooo," the band on the bus moaned appreciatively, which made us break the kiss. Damn band.

Investigating, Ms. Nakamoto hung from the pole inside the bus and leaned down the staircase, out the doorway. "Mr. De Luca, Ms. Gordon, this is a school function."

"Yes, ma'am," I called.

"We'll get back to this later tonight," Sawyer told me knowingly. He put his head on.

Swinging hands, we waited for Brody to limp over, followed by Harper, Noah, and Quinn. As we walked toward the stadium in the orange light of late afternoon, I wondered if we'd be allowed into a band competition with Sawyer dressed as a six-foot bird.

We would find a way.

ACKNOWLEDGMENTS

Heartfelt thanks to my amazing new editor, Sara Sargent; my brilliant literary agent, Laura Bradford; and my critique partner, Victoria Dahl. 2gether 4ever.

Don't miss the first two books
in the Superlatives trilogy:
Biggest Flirts and *Perfect Couple*.
And here's a peek at

biggest flirts

"YOU MUST BE TIA CRUZ."

I glanced up at the guy who'd sat next to me and said this quietly in my ear, in an accent from elsewhere. We were on the crowded back porch with the lights off, but beyond the porch ceiling, the summer night sky was bright with a full moon and a glow from the neon signs at the tourist-trap beaches a few miles south.

The diffuse light made everybody look better: smoothed out acne, canceled a bad hair day. And I definitely had on my beer goggles. Boys grew more attractive when I was working on my second brew. This guy was the hottest thing I'd seen all summer. He was taller than me by quite a bit—which didn't happen too often—with dark hair long enough to cling to his T-shirt collar, a long straight nose, and lips that quirked sideways in a smile. But I wasn't fooled. In the sober light of day, he probably ranked right up there with the eighty-year-old men who wore Speedos to the beach.

What drew me in despite my misgivings was the diamond stud in his ear. Who knew what he was trying to say with this fashion statement. Unfortunately for me, I was a sucker for a bad boy, and his earring flashed moonlight at me like a homing beacon under a banner that said THIS WAY TO PIRATE.

I told him, "I *might* be Tia." What I meant was, *For you, I am Tia. I'll be anybody you're looking for.* "Who wants to know?"

"Will Matthews. I just moved here." We were sitting too close for a proper handshake, but he bent his arm, elbow close to his side, and held out his hand.

"Really!" I exclaimed as our hands touched. Our small town was stuck in the forgotten northwest corner of Pinellas County, on the very edge of the Tampa Bay metropolitan area. The guidebooks called us a hidden gem because of the artsy downtown, the harbor, and our unspoiled beaches, but the thing about a hidden gem was that it tended to stay hidden. Some tourists came through here. A few newcomers did move here. But most of them were, again, elderly men in banana hammocks. The families who serviced the snowbirds and tourists had lived here forever. My friend Sawyer had shown up only a couple of years before, but even his dad had grown up here. New kids at school were rare. Girls were going to be *all over* this guy: fresh meat.

Will pointed toward the house. "I introduced myself to your friends inside. They told me I would find you by the beer."

"My friends are a riot." My best friends, Harper and Kaye, didn't drink. That was cool with me. I did drink, which was not cool with them. Over the years, though, Harper's reasoned arguments and Kaye's hysterical pleas had mellowed into concerned monitoring and snarky jokes.

This time their witty line wasn't even correct. I was *not* by the beer. Along with six or seven other people from school, I was sitting on a bench built into the porch railing, and the cooler was underneath me. Technically I was *above* the beer. Drinking on Brody Larson's back porch was standard operating procedure. Most of the houses near downtown were lined up along a grid, backyards touching. When parents unexpectedly came home, interrupting a party, somebody would grab the cooler as we escaped through the palm trees to another daredevil's house to start over. If this was the first thing Will learned about our town, he was my kind of guy. I reached into the cooler, my braids brushing the porch floor. I fished out a can for myself and handed him the beer he'd come for.

"Oh." He took the can and looked at it for a moment. He was expecting, maybe, a better brand of free beer? Then, without opening it, he swiped it across his forehead. "Are you even sweating? Perspiring, I mean."

"Why do you want to know whether I'm perspiring, Mr. Matthews?" I made my voice sound sexy just to get a guffaw out of him.

"Because you look . . ." He glanced down my body, and I enjoyed that very much. ". . . cool," he finished. "It's hot as an ahffen out here."

I popped open my beer. "A what?"

"What," he repeated.

"You said 'ahffen.' What's an ahffen?"

"An ahh . . ." He waited for me to nod at this syllable. "Fen." Suddenly he lost patience with me. Before I could slide away—actually I would have had nowhere to slide, because Brody and his girlfriend Grace were making out right next to me—Will grabbed my wrist and brought my hand to his lips. "Let me sound it out for you. Ahhhffen." I felt his breath moving across my fingertips.

"Oh, an *oven*!" I giggled. "You're kidding, right? It's ten o'clock at night."

He let my hand go, which was not what I'd wanted at *all*. "I've been here one whole day, and I've already gotten my fill of people making fun of the way I talk, thanks." He sounded halfway serious.

"Poor baby! I wasn't making fun of you. I was just trying to figure out what an ahffen was." I elbowed him gently in the ribs.

He still didn't smile. That was okay. I liked brooding pirates. I asked him, "Who made fun of you?"

"Some jerk waiting tables at the grill where my family ate tonight. We can't cook at home yet. Most of the furniture showed up, but apparently the refrigerator got off-loaded in Ohio."

"Uh-oh. Was that all you lost, or did the moving company also misplace your microwave in Wisconsin and your coffeemaker in the Mississippi River?"

"Funny." Now he was grinning at me.

Warm fuzzies crept across my skin. I loved making people laugh. Making a hot guy laugh was my nirvana.

He went on, "I'm sure we'll find out what else we're missing when we need it. Anyway, the waiter at the restaurant seemed cool at first. I think both my little sisters fell in love with him. He told me I should come to this party and meet some people. Then he started in on my Minnesota accent and wouldn't let go." Will pronounced it "Minne*sooo*da," which cried out for imitation. Plenty of people around here talked like that, but they were retirees from Canada. I decided I'd better let it drop.

"Was this grill the Crab Lab downtown?" I pointed in the direction of the town square, which boasted said restaurant where I'd worked until yesterday, the antiques store where I still worked (or tried not to), the salon where my sister Izzy cut hair, and Harper's mom's bed and breakfast. The business district was rounded out by enough retro cafés and kitschy gift shops that visitors were fooled into thinking our town was like something out of a 1950s postcard—until they strolled by the gay burlesque club.

"Yeah," Will said. "We had misgivings about a place called the Crab Lab, like there would be formaldehyde involved. If there was, we couldn't taste it."

"The Crab Lab may sound unappetizing, but it's an unwritten rule that names of stores in a tourist town have to alliterate or rhyme. What else are you going to call a seafood joint? Lobster Mobster? Hey, that's actually pretty good." I doubled over, cracking up at my own joke. "The slogan would be, 'We'll break your legs.' Get it? Because you crack open lobster legs? No, wait, that's crab."

He watched me with a bemused smile, as if waiting for

me to pull a prescription bottle out of my purse and announce that I'd missed my meds.

I tried again. "Calamari . . . Cash and Carry? I set myself up badly there. Okay, so Crab Lab is a stupid name. I'm pretty attached to the place, though."

"Do you eat there a lot?"

"You could say that. I just quit serving there. Did this jerk who was making fun of you happen to have white-blond hair?"

"That's him."

"That's Sawyer," I said. "Don't take it personally. He would pick on a newborn baby if he could think of a good enough joke. You'll be seeing lots more of Sawyer when school starts."

"The way my summer's been going, that doesn't surprise me at all." Will stared at the beer can in his hand. He took a breath to say something else.

Just then the marching band drum major, DeMarcus, arrived to a chorus of "Heeeey!" from everybody on the porch. He'd spent the past month with his grandparents in New York. A few of us gave Angelica, the majorette DeMarcus was leading by the hand, a less enthusiastic "Hey." The lukewarm greeting probably wasn't fair. It's just that we remembered what a tattletale she'd been in ninth grade. She'd probably changed, but nobody gave her the benefit of the doubt. As she walked through, some people turned their heads away as if they thought she might jot down their names and report back to their parents.

I stood as DeMarcus spread his arms to hug me. He said, "Harper told me you were back here sitting on the beer. I'm like, 'Are you sure? Tia is *in charge* of something? That's a first.' But I guess since it's beer, it's fitting."

"Those New Yorkers really honed your sense of humor." I sat down to pull out a can for him. Obviously it hadn't occurred to him that, unless a miracle saved me, I was drum captain. Starting tomorrow, the first day of band camp, I would be in charge of one of the largest sections and (in our own opinion) the most important section of the band. I'd spent the whole summer pretending that my doomsday of responsibility wasn't going to happen. I had one night left to live in that fantasy world.

As I handed the beer up to DeMarcus, Angelica asked close to his shoulder, "Do you have to?"

"One," he promised her. "I just spent ten hours in the airport with my mother."

Will chuckled at that. I thought maybe I should introduce him to DeMarcus. But I doubted my edgy pirate wanted to meet my band geek friend. Will made no move to introduce himself.

As DeMarcus opened his beer and took a sip, I noticed old Angelica giving Will the eye. Oh, *no,* girlfriend. I lasered her with an exaggerated glare so scary that she actually startled and stepped backward when she saw me. I bit my lip to keep from laughing.

With a glance at Will, DeMarcus asked me, "Where's Sawyer?"

Damn it! Sawyer and I hung out a lot, but we weren't dating. I didn't want to give Will the impression that I was taken. "Sawyer's working," I told DeMarcus dismissively. "He's coming later."

"I'm sure I'll hear him when he gets here," DeMarcus said. True. Sawyer often brought the boisterous college drop-out waiters he'd already gotten drunk with on the back porch of the Crab Lab. Or firecrackers. Or both.

As DeMarcus moved along the bench to say hi to everybody else, with Angelica in tow, Will spoke in my ear. "Sounds like you know Sawyer pretty well. Is he your boyfriend?"

"Um." My relationship with Sawyer was more like the friendship you'd fall into when there was nobody more interesting in prison. Everybody at school knew he wasn't my boyfriend. We tended to stick together at parties because we were the first ones to get there and the last ones to leave.

I wasn't sure how to explain this to an outsider without sounding like a drunk floozy . . . because, to be honest, I was something of a drunk floozy. Not that this had bothered me until I pictured myself sharing that information with a handsome stranger.

I said carefully, "We've been out, but we're not together now." Changing the subject so fast that Will and I both risked neck injury, I asked, "What city are you from? Minneapolis?"

"No."

"St. Paul?"

"No, Duluth."

"Never heard of it."

"I know." He raised the unopened beer can to his forehead again. Perspiration was beading at his hairline and dripping toward his ear. I felt sorry for him. Wait until it got hot tomorrow.

"What's Duluth like?" I asked.

"Well, it's on Lake Superior."

"Uh-huh. Minnesota's the Land of a Thousand Lakes, isn't it?" I asked. Little had Mr. Tomlin known when he interrogated us on state trivia in third grade that I would later find it useful for picking up a Minnesotan.

"Ten Thousand Lakes," Will corrected me with a grin.

"Wow, that's a lot of lakes. You must have been completely surrounded. Did you swim to school?"

He shook his head no. "Too cold to swim."

I couldn't imagine this. Too cold to swim? Such a shame. "What did you do up there, then?" I ran my eyes over his muscular arms. Will didn't have the physique of a naturally strong and sinewy boy such as Sawyer, but of an athlete who actively worked out. I guessed, "Do you play football?"

His mouth cocked to one side. He was aware I'd paid him a compliment about his body. "Hockey," he said.

A hockey player! The bad boy of athletes who elbowed his opponent in the jaw just for spite and spent half the period in the penalty box. I loved it!

But my reverence for him in my mind didn't make it to my mouth. I had to turn it into a joke. "Ha!" I exclaimed. "Good luck with *that* around here. We're not exactly a hockey mecca."

"Tampa Bay has an NHL team," he reminded me.

"Yeah, but nobody *else* here plays. The NHL rinks are probably the only ones in the entire metropolitan area. A high school guy playing hockey in Tampa makes as much sense as the Jamaican bobsled team."

I'd meant it to be funny. But his mouth twitched to one side again, this time like I'd slapped him. Maybe he was considering for the first time that our central Florida high school might not have a varsity hockey team.

I sipped my beer, racking my brain for a way to salvage this conversation, which I'd really been digging. He held his beer in both hands like he was trying to get all the cold out of it without actually drinking it. His eyes roved the corners of the porch, and I wondered whether he was searching for Angelica as a way to escape from me if she and DeMarcus got tired of each other.

Before I could embarrass myself with another gem from my stand-up routine, the porch vibrated with deep whoops of "Sawyer!" The man himself sauntered up the wooden steps to the porch, waving with both hands like the president in his inauguration parade—but only if he'd bought the election. Nobody in their right mind would elect Sawyer to a position of responsibility. The only office he'd ever snagged was school mascot. He would be loping around the football field this year in a giant bird costume.

What didn't quite make sense about Sawyer De Luca was his platinum hair, darker at the roots and brighter at the sun-bleached tips like a swimmer who never had to come in from the ocean and go to school. The hair didn't go with his Italian name or his dark father and brother. He must have looked like his mom, but she lived in Georgia and nobody had ever met her. A couple of years ago, she sent him to live with his dad, who was getting out of prison, because she couldn't handle Sawyer anymore. At least, that's what Sawyer had told me, and it sounded about right.

After shaking a few hands and embracing DeMarcus, Sawyer sauntered over and stood in front of Will. Not in front of *me*. He didn't acknowledge me at all as he stepped into Will's personal space and said, looking down at him, "You're in my place."

"Oh Jesus, Sawyer!" I exclaimed. Why did he have to pick a fight while I was getting to know the new guy? He must have had a bad night. Working with his prick of an older brother, who ran the bar at the Crab Lab, tended to have that effect on him.

I opened my mouth to reassure Will that Sawyer meant no harm. Or, maybe he did, but I wouldn't let Sawyer get away with it.

Before I could say anything, Will rose. At his full height, he towered over Sawyer. He looked down on Sawyer exactly as Sawyer had looked down on *him* a moment before. He growled, "This is your place? I don't *think* so."

The other boys around us stopped their joking and said in warning voices, "Sawyer." Brody put a hand on Sawyer's chest. Brody really was a football player and could have held

Sawyer off Will single-handedly. Sawyer didn't care. He stared up at Will with murder in his eyes.

I stood too. "Come on, Sawyer. You were the one who told Will about this party in the first place."

"I didn't invite him *here*." Sawyer pointed at the bench where Will had been sitting.

I knew how Sawyer felt. When I'd looked forward to hooking up with him at a party, I was disappointed and even angry if he shared his night with another girl instead. But that was our long-standing agreement. We used each other when nobody more intriguing was available. Now wasn't the time to test our pact. I said, "You're some welcome committee."

The joke surprised Sawyer out of his dark mood. He relaxed his shoulders and took a half step backward. Brody and the other guys retreated the way they'd come. I wouldn't have put it past Sawyer to spring at Will now that everyone's guard was down, but he just poked Will—gently, I thought with relief—on the cursive *V* emblazoned on his T-shirt. "What's the *V* stand for? Virgin?"

"The Minnesota Vikings, moron," I said. Then I turned to Will. "You will quickly come to understand that Sawyer is full of sh—"

Will spoke over my head to Sawyer. "It stands for 'vilification.'"

"What? Vili . . . What does that mean?" Knitting his brow, Sawyer pulled out his phone and thumbed the keyboard. I had a large vocabulary, and his was even bigger, but we'd both found that playing dumb made life easier.

Will edged around me to peer over Sawyer's shoulder at the screen. At the same time, he slid his hand around my waist. I hadn't seen a move that smooth in a while. I liked the way Minnesota guys operated. He told Sawyer, "No, not two *L*'s. One *L*."

Sawyer gave Will another wild-eyed warning. His gaze dropped to Will's hand on my waist, then rose to my serious-as-a-heart-attack face. He told Will, "Okay, SAT. I'll take my vocabulary quiz over here." He retreated to the corner of the porch to talk with a cheerleader.

Relieved, I sat back down on the bench, holding Will's hand on my side so that he had to sit down with me or get his arm jerked out of its socket. He settled closer to me than before. With his free hand, he drummed his fingers on his knee to the beat of the music filtering onto the porch. The rhythm he tapped out was so complex that I wondered whether he'd been a drummer—not for marching band like me, but for some wild rock band that got into fistfights after the hockey game was over.

As we talked, he looked into my eyes as if I was the only

girl at the party, and he grinned at all my jokes. Now that my third beer was kicking in, I let go of some of my anxiety about saying exactly the right thing and just had fun. I asked him if he was part of our senior class. He was. It seemed obvious, but he *could* have been a freshman built like a running back. Then I explained who the other people at the party were according to the Senior Superlatives titles they were likely to get—Best Car, Most Athletic, that sort of thing.

My predictions were iffy. Each person could hold only one title, preventing a superstar like my friend Kaye from racking up all the honors and turning the high school year-book into her biography. She might get Most Popular *or* Most Likely to Succeed. She was head cheerleader, a born leader, and good at everything. Harper, the yearbook photographer, might get Most Artistic *or* Most Original, since she wore funky clothes and retro glasses and always thought outside the box.

"What about you?" Will asked, tugging playfully at one of my braids.

"Ha! Most Likely to Wake Up on Your Lawn."

He laughed. "Is that a real award?"

"No, we don't give awards that would make girls cry. I'll probably get Tallest." That wasn't a real one either.

He cocked his head at me. "Funniest?"

I rolled my eyes. "That's like getting voted Miss Congeniality in a beauty pageant. It's a consolation prize."

A line appeared between his brows. He rubbed his thumb gently across my lips. "Sexiest."

"You obviously haven't surveyed the whole senior class."

"I don't have to."

Staring into his eyes, which crinkled at the corners as he smiled, I knew he was handing me a line. And I *loved* this pirate pickup of his. I let my gaze fall to his lips, willing him to kiss me.

"Hi there, new guy!" Aidan said as he burst out the door. He crossed the porch in two steps and held out his hand for Will to shake. "Aidan O'Neill, student council president."

I made a noise. It went something like "blugh" and was loud enough for Aidan to hear. I knew this because he looked at me with the same expression he gave me when I made fun of his penny loafers. He was Kaye's boyfriend, so I tried to put up with him. But we'd been assigned as partners on a chemistry paper last year, and any semblance of friendship we might have had was ruined when he tried to correct me incorrectly during my part of the presentation. I'd told him to be right or sit down. The only thing that made Aidan madder than someone challenging him was someone challenging him in public.

"Blugh" wasn't a sufficient warning for Will not to talk

to him, apparently. Aidan sat down on Will's other side and launched into an overview of our school's wonders that Minnesota probably had never heard of, such as pep rallies and doughnut sales.

"Time for everybody to get lost," Brody called. "My mom will be home from the Rays game in a few minutes."

"Thanks for hosting," I told him.

"Always a pleasure. Looks like this time you may have more pleasure than you can handle, though." He nodded toward the stairs, where Sawyer was waving at me.

Sawyer held up his thumb and pointer together, which meant, *I have weed. Want to toke up?*

I shook my head in a small enough motion that Will didn't notice, I hoped. Translation: *No, I'm taking Will home if I can swing it.*

Sawyer raised one eyebrow and lowered the other, making a mad scientist face. It meant, *You'd rather go home with this guy than get high with me? You have finally lost your marbles.*

I raised both eyebrows: *We have an agreement. We stick together unless something better comes along. This is something better.*

He flared his nostrils—*Well, I never!*—and turned away. He might give me a hard time about it when I saw him next, but Sawyer and I never really got mad at each other, because why would you get mad at yourself?

I turned to rescue Will from Aidan and saw to my horror that Aidan was disappearing back into the house. Will stared right at me with a grim expression, as if he'd witnessed the entire silent conversation between Sawyer and me, understood it, and didn't like it. "Don't let me keep you," he said flatly.

Damn Sawyer! We would laugh about this later if I wasn't so hot for the boy sitting next to me. This was not funny.

Heart thumping, I tried to save my night with Will. There wasn't any time to waste. If word that Brody was closing down the party got inside to Kaye and Harper before I left, they would try to stop me from hooking up with the new guy. They might have sent him back to meet me, but they wouldn't want me leaving with him. They didn't approve of Sawyer, either, but at least they knew him. Will was a wild card. They would find this frightening. I found him perfect.

I slid my hand onto his knee and said, "I'd rather go with you. Could you walk me home?"

And then some.

ABOUT THE AUTHOR

Jennifer Echols has written many romantic novels for teens and adults. She grew up in a small town on a beautiful lake in Alabama, where her high school senior class voted her Most Academic and Most Likely to Succeed. Please visit her at www.jennifer-echols.com.